Praise for *The Girl in the Headlines*

"The action starts on the first page as readers are introduced to Andi's plight, and the pace does not let up until the final resolution."

—*Booklist*

"This is a propulsive...story rife with true-crime TV tropes and plenty of red herrings."

—*Kirkus Reviews*

Praise for *Truly, Madly, Deadly*

"A suspenseful whodunit with a cinematic climax."

—*Booklist*

Praise for *Copycat*

"Addie and Maya feel authentic; their charming interpersonal dynamic and the escalating pace of the plot result in a quick read."

—*Kirkus Reviews*

"A twisty roller coaster ride that mixes fiction with reality and truth with misconceptions...Lovers of mysteries will certainly enjoy this fast-paced page-turner."

—*Library Media Connection*

Praise for *The Escape*

"This mystery is marked by gripping psychological suspense, and the plot builds to a dramatic conclusion."

—*Booklist*

Praise for *The Dare*

"Brynna's guilt-induced psychosis makes for a page-turner in the spirit of Lois Duncan's classic *I Know What You Did Last Summer*; it will undoubtedly please the thriller-loving crowd."

—*Kirkus Reviews*

WHAT HAPPENED ON HICKS ROAD

WHAT HAPPENED ON HICKS ROAD

HANNAH JAYNE

sourcebooks
fire

Copyright © 2023 by Hannah Jayne
Cover and internal design © 2023 by Sourcebooks
Cover design by Katie Klimowicz and Trisha Previte
Cover image © Katarina Radovic/Stocksy
Internal design by Laura Boren/Sourcebooks

The characters and events portrayed in this book are fictitious or
are used fictitiously. Any similarity to real persons, living or dead,
is purely coincidental and not intended by the author.

Published by Sourcebooks Fire, an imprint of Sourcebooks
P.O. Box 4410, Naperville, Illinois 60567-4410
(630) 961-3900
sourcebooks.com

Cataloging-in-Publication data is on file with the Library of Congress.

Printed and bound in the United States of America.
VP 10 9 8 7 6 5 4 3 2 1

This is my love letter to the Pioneer High School class of 1994, but especially to Jennifer Fenton Spencer. From cheerleading to child-rearing, I am so lucky to still have you as my cocaptain after all these years. P-I-O, P-I-O-N-E-E-R!

ONE

"Take this next left!"

"No, Lennox, don't—that's Hicks Road! It's totally haunted!"

"A road can't be haunted. And besides, it's awesome. Left, right here." Allison Maren grabbed the steering wheel and gave it a sharp turn, the car lurching, tires squealing as the road went from smooth pavement to gravel.

"Allison!" Lennox Oliver said as she shoved the brunette half playfully. "Don't touch the wheel." The two passengers dissolved into giggles, and once her prickles of fear subsided, Lennox did too. It was nice to relax. She was new in town and had spent her first three weeks at Pioneer High trying her best to go unnoticed. It was halfway through the year, everyone had their friend groups already, and Lennox had no interest in being new-kid bully fodder. She was shy and thin with a head full of unruly brown curls and five different schools in her wake. While the scenery was great as she criss-crossed the country with her traveling ER nurse dad, the new schools—and new kids—were not.

"This is it?" Lennox peered out the window, waiting for her eyes to adjust to the tree-darkened street. She glanced at the clock: 9:47. She hoped that a streetlight or a swath of moonlight would cut through the trees and give her a better view of this supposedly haunted road. The headlights on her old Honda seemed weak, illuminating the yellow lines directly in front of the car and nothing else.

"Just looks like a normal road to me," Lennox said. "Trees, double yellow lines. Very road-like."

"It's not the road, exactly," said Allison, shifting in her seat. She pointed. "It's mainly the road and everything surrounding it."

Lennox squinted. The foliage wasn't particularly dark or menacing: big gnarled oaks interspersed with pine trees, an occasional cartoon-green splash of ferns.

"They say there is a cult of witches that practices around here," Eva Lorna said, her voice ominous from the back seat.

"So dumb!" Allison groaned. "And I heard it was druids."

"Like priests?" Lennox asked.

"Not even," Eva said with a definitive nod. "It's a sad story, actually."

"Sad why?"

Eva blew out a sigh. "Like, a million years ago or sometime in the eighties or something, there was this giant earthquake out here, and this family got trapped up on the top of Hicks. It was a mom and a dad and two little kids, a girl and a boy. Legend has it they waited for days for help—maybe even weeks. So long that the family started eating each other."

"What?" Lennox gulped.

"They ate the little girl first, and then I think the mom. The dad went crazy because, you know, eating his family. But the little boy..."

Lennox could feel the thrum of her nerves. "What happened to the little boy?"

"They say he developed a taste for human flesh. The police found him as he was finishing off his own dad. It had been months by that time. What they could see of his face was caked with blood. One of the cops swore the kid had grown fangs, like an animal. The cops tried to capture him, but he took off like a shot—on all fours."

Lennox snorted. "That's completely ridiculous. People don't just turn into animals!" She looked at her friends, who stared back at her, wide-eyed. "Come on, you don't really believe—"

Lennox felt herself tense up on the steering wheel, her eyes darting between the trees lining the road. With every inch of asphalt her car tires ate up, the trees seemed to lean in, choking out the sky, the pale flits of moonlight.

Lennox had been eating lunch alone those first few weeks, zipping through a grisly horror novel on her phone, when Allison had sat next to her and given her a wide grin. "You're new," she had said, half statement, half accusation. Lennox remembered the tightness in her chest, the wariness prickling behind her eyes. Another school, another mean girl.

"Uh-huh," Lennox had said with practiced calm.

"Where from?"

"Detroit." She'd thumbed a page.

"Cleveland. End of last year."

Lennox had dropped her phone in her lap. She hadn't wanted to seem eager or even the least bit excited, but a new kid finding another new kid in a sea of high schoolers who seemed to have known one another since birth was too good to pass up.

"Allison." The girl had put out her hand, and Lennox had shaken it awkwardly.

"Lennox. It's been about a month for me. Well, a month in town, but only three weeks in school. I was doing independent study."

Allison had nodded. "But then the pull of public school and all it has to offer was just too strong, huh?" she grinned.

"You guys!"

Another girl, this one with a white-blond pageboy haircut and cartoon-blue eyes had come bounding over to them. "You are never going to believe what I just heard."

Lennox snapped back to the present, to the ink-black road in front of her.

"If this road is indeed haunted, why am I driving on it?" Lennox asked.

"Because it's just a stupid legend!"

"It's not!" Eva pushed herself halfway into the front seat. "It's so not. My mom went to high school with this girl who was killed on this very road. And when they found her body, someone had eaten her heart."

Allison snorted and pushed Eva on the forehead. "Dude, you stink of vodka and Gatorade, and that never actually happened. It was a guy who got killed—they cut off his arms and legs. He was, like, the janitor's uncle or something. And then the janitor's hair turned white."

Eva fell back into her seat and exploded into giggles. "Those things have nothing to do with each other!" Allison rolled her eyes and Lennox shook her head.

"Besides, we can't be scared of what we can't see," Allison said with a sinister grin. "Let's turn these headlights off." She leaned into Lennox, her hand reaching across the wheel. "Turn 'em off!"

More laughter. Eva pounding on the back of Lennox's seat. "Turn them off, turn them off!"

"Don't touch—"

Lennox's eyes shot back to the road. A figure darted out from the left. Allison went for the wheel. Lennox stamped on the brake.

Those eyes. Wide. Ice blue. A swath of blond hair illuminated by Lennox's headlights. Then blackness.

Thump!

The car lurched. Tires squealed and spit up gravel.

"What the hell was that?"

"You guys—"

"We hit something."

"No, no, no we didn't." It was Allison. "No, we didn't."
Lennox's heart slammed against her rib cage. Her foot
was still on the brake, the pedal pushed all the way to the
floor of the car, her hands welded to the wheel.

"T-t-turn the lights back on." Eva's voice was a whisper
a hundred miles behind Lennox. Lennox's eyes were wide,
focused on the blackness, on the sea of nothingness in front of
them. But she saw her again and again in her mind's eye. The
girl, awash in her car's headlights for a split second. Wearing
a bright teal T-shirt. Her arms thrown up to protect herself.
Her eyes wide, her long blond hair fanning out. Darkness.

Thump.

TWO

"Turn on the lights."

This time Lennox's body complied. She put the car in park, turned on the headlights, and went for the door.

Eva grabbed Lennox's shoulder. "What are you doing?"

"I saw a person. I saw a girl." Lennox's lips felt numb. "We have to see—we have to help—"

"No." Allison shook her head again. "I didn't see anything."

"She had blond hair." Lennox brushed a hand over her own dark hair. "Blue eyes."

"I didn't see a girl," Allison protested.

"I heard—" Eva started, then stopped

Tears pricked at Lennox's eyes; her limbs went limp and heavy. "It was a girl, not a witch or a druid or whatever. And I think I—" A sob lodged in her chest.

"I definitely didn't see a girl. If you hit anything, it was probably a raccoon or even a deer." Allison sounded unconcerned.

"I saw her eyes." Lennox pushed open the car door, her body moving in molasses-slow motion, her mind thundering: *Call the police, call your dad, stay where you are, run like hell.*

Those eyes. Terrified, wide. And then...Lennox shuddered, a rush of cold air making goose bumps rise on her arms.

Eva and Allison looked like disembodied heads in the car's dome light. Lennox pushed her feet forward, her sneakers shuffling over gravel, fallen leaves. She scanned the side of the road, her eyes flitting from broken foliage to a slew of tiny rocks on the asphalt. She moved carefully and rounded the front of the car, the tremor in her outstretched hands illuminated in the waning reflection of her headlights. There was a slight dent in the grill of Lennox's car, puckering the light blue hood of the little Honda, and her fingers slid over it— expecting what, she didn't know. But all she felt was the hot metal, the pinch of chipped paint.

"Do you see anything?" Eva's voice floated on the darkness, and Lennox forced herself to continue to move, to push the dead weight of her tongue in her mouth.

"Hello?" Lennox called out. "Are you okay? I'm—sorry."

She was answered by the soundless night, by the *tick-tick-tick* of the engine cooling down, by her own breath ripping through her throat.

"I didn't see—I'm so sorry." Tears brimmed in her eyes and rolled down her cheeks. "I didn't mean..." Her voice was a raw whisper. "Hello?"

There was no body on the pavement.

No sound of someone groaning or footsteps jogging away. "Hello?"

She glanced back through the windshield, where Eva and Allison were huddled together. Allison kicked open the car door and leaned out. "If you hit anything at all, it was probably an animal. Maybe even a deer."

Lennox nodded. She wanted to believe her friend. She wanted to crawl back into the car and rewind twenty minutes and laugh about druids and witches and cannibals. She wanted to wipe the *thump* from her mind, to scrub away the memories of those eyes, those lips.

Parted in a scream.

She could still see the eyes, the lips, the hands splayed.

Lennox circled the car with new fervor, screaming now. "Hello? Please, are you hurt? We can help you!"

A light rain had started to fall, and Lennox jogged farther up the road, her eyes trying to adjust to the darkness as her headlights faded behind her. "Hello?"

"Lennox, come back!"

Eva stepped out of the car, and Lennox ran toward her, blinking in the bright light from her own phone. "Here," Eva said, handing it to Lennox. Eva turned her phone flashlight on as well, and the two girls poked around the car, looked around the road. Allison stepped out behind them, arms crossed in front of her chest.

"There's nothing here," Allison said.

"Didn't you see her?" Lennox snapped.

Eva and Allison exchanged a look, then studied Lennox, and suddenly she felt exposed, raw.

"Lennox," Eva said slowly, "I really didn't see anyone. Are you absolutely sure you did?"

Lennox gritted her teeth, her saliva going sour in her mouth. *I know what I saw!* she thought. And then, just as quickly, a voice from the back of her mind: *Do you?*

Suddenly Lennox was nine years old, bathed in the light of that old ranch house kitchen, and her mother was across from her, arms waving, lips moving as she talked animatedly to someone who wasn't there. A twinge of fear roiled through Lennox, a tiny lump forming in her chest, and she felt the mist of fresh tears at the backs of her eyes.

She shook her head slowly. "I—I don't know."

Eva patted Lennox's shoulder, and Allison threw her arms around her. "I'm so sorry. This was weird and scary. But we're all good, right?"

Eva nodded silently, but Lennox was staring into the fringed darkness, the blackness at the edge of the road. *She could have fallen down there... She could be injured.*

"I saw...something," Lennox whispered to herself.

She looked back at the car again, at the dent in the hood, and her knees went to putty. She dropped onto the street, feeling the rain soak into her jeans. Palms down, she crouched, craned her neck, looked under the car.

Her stomach clenched, and bile itched at the back of her throat.

Is that blood?

Something dark—just a spot, farther than an arm's length away.

"It was a deer." Allison was standing on the mountain side of the road, where Lennox had seen the girl run out. "You must have just clipped it. It happens all the time."

Lennox stood up, blood rushing to her head, making her vision wonky. She pressed her fingertips to her temples, steadying herself. "What makes you say that?"

Allison stepped aside, used her phone to illuminate the tromped-down foliage coming from the dark woods. "This is an animal path. See how it's all smashed over here? A deer was probably running through and you clipped it."

"But—"

"That's why the dent is tiny. If you'd really hit something, the dent would be, like, huge, you know?"

Eva stepped forward. "And this deer is…"

Allison strode in front of the car, pointed to the steep drop on the other side. "Probably kept running right on down there." She pointed her phone over the cliffside, the light illuminating two feet of broken baby pines before dissolving against ferns and the thick, shaggy trunks of redwoods.

"I'm sorry," Allison said, grabbing Lennox and pulling her into a hug.

Eva threw her arms around them and started to giggle, and then Allison was laughing too. "Or maybe it was one of the witches we hit."

That set off another round of giggles in Eva, and Lennox tried to believe it.

If the girl was real and she really had hit her, there would be a body.

If she had hit a body, there would be blood.

There would be *something*, right?

THREE

Lennox's dad was at work when she got home, and she was glad. She was certain the world could hear the beating of her heart as she walked through the dark house, resting her hand on the light switches but not turning them on. Normally Lennox hated the darkness, but tonight she feared the light.

She kept seeing those yellow streaks of headlights, the girl, her eyes, her face illuminated.

I didn't see anything. Nothing happened. There was no one there—we checked. Lennox kept repeating herself in her head, her words thundering through the vast emptiness but constantly swallowed by doubt.

You saw her, you did. You hit *her. You're guilty.*

Lennox tried to sleep, but each time she closed her eyes, her mind opened up, spitting images and questions and general chatter that made her eyes fly open and her heart thud. She looked around the room and tried to remember where she was, what state, which house, but they all blended together on nights like this when the din in her head was strong. Every rental house in every town looked exactly alike in the darkness: four walls, corner after corner, boxing her in. Finally, she clicked on the light and wriggled her fingers between her mattress and box spring, pulling out her sketchbook and the charcoal pencil pressed inside.

The sketchbook wasn't beautiful or professional; it was from a Walgreens somewhere, and it was smashed and wrinkled from living inside Lennox's bed and stained with Coke Zero and iced tea, but it was the closest thing to a memento Lennox had. She sketched page after page in every state: the cherry blossoms in D.C., the skewed view of rusted fire escapes from her bedroom window in Detroit, the girl in Bethesda who spent her entire lunch hour just staring at Lennox. Toward the back were the drawings Lennox kept folded over and tried her best not to look at, not to remember. The one of her mom's hands, fingers interlaced, railroad tracks of shaded veins and scars, her wedding ring slid up to the knuckle of her bony finger. Another of her mom in profile, the pencil lines traced and erased a half dozen times as Lennox had tried to remember when her mother had full, rosy cheeks, not the sunken slats that made her eyes look tiny and dark. There was one of her mother and father in shadow, drawn from a photograph clipped to her sketchbook. Their foreheads were touching as they looked down on a fat, half-naked baby Lennox, swaddled in a hospital blanket and screaming at the world.

Lennox flipped past these, the lump in her throat growing. She touched her pencil to the paper, and her body took over, arcs and lines populating the white paper, the sadness and anxiety melting from her body.

Drawing had always been her respite, her constant, and it was that way now as her hand moved, the sound of the lead soothing. She sketched until she felt weak, exhausted, and when she finally dropped the pencil, her eyes closed too, the notebook sliding from her lap and onto the floor. The trees along Hicks Road yawned in dark charcoal arcs, their branches like claws reaching out for the girl huddled in the middle of the street. The girl with wide-open, terrified eyes.

Lennox pushed around her milk-soaked Cocoa Puffs as she flipped through news article after news article on her iPad.

"Morning. Working on something for school, hon?"

Lennox's dad strolled into the kitchen, hair disheveled, robe hanging open, revealing his Whatsamatta U T-shirt and ancient plaid pajama pants. He worked ten-hour shifts in understaffed emergency rooms and had a wardrobe that consisted solely of pristine scrubs and dingy T-shirts he'd had for decades.

She glanced up, anxiety—and the two bites of Cocoa Puffs she had eaten—souring her stomach.

Should I tell him?

He swirled creamer into his coffee up, took a big, slurping sip, and smiled when the caffeine hit his system.

"Um, no. Maybe? Hey, you worked last night, yeah?"
Her dad nodded slowly.

"Did a girl come into the ER?"

He raised an eyebrow over the rim of his coffee mug.
"Any particular girl?"

"A teenager—probably my age? She would have been
blond, uh." Lennox tried to remember, tried to recall the
memory that had haunted her the whole night long, but her
mind worked to block it out, worked to blur the image, to
remind her of what the other girls had said: a raccoon, a deer.

"Is this blond teenager a friend of yours?" Her dad
was giving her one of his patented dad looks, the one that
gave off a "you can tell me anything but you're not off the
hook" vibe.

"Not exactly, I just heard she was in a car accident last
night. Maybe."

"So this not-exactly-friend of yours was in a car accident,
maybe. Was she at the party where you were? Was she perhaps drinking and then...because you know you can call any
day, anytime, no questions asked."

Lennox rolled her eyes. "Dad, this isn't a father-daughter
moment."

"Because if you and your friends are drinking, you can
tell—"

"I know, I know. I can call you at any time and you won't
get mad, blah, blah, blah."

He smiled, bobbed his head, and took another sip of

coffee. "At least that sank in. So, tell me about this girl. Are you worried that she was really badly hurt?"

Lennox blew out a sigh, ran her fingernail down a groove in the dining table that they had bought in Chattanooga, carried to D.C., and chipped on the way out of Detroit. It was railroaded with lines and minuscule cracks but looked great from afar...kind of like Lennox herself.

"Yeah."

"It was actually a pretty light night. I don't remember seeing any teen girls, but a four-year-old swallowed six Christmas lights, and there was a little girl with quite a head gash."

Fire shot down Lennox's spine. She thought of the small dent in the grill, the chip of paint standing upright.

"How little?"

"Five, six."

Lennox let out the breath she didn't know she was holding. "That wouldn't be her."

"I guess that's good, then." Her dad grinned and ruffled her hair like she was eight years old. "No one in the ER means whatever happened wasn't that bad. But you know we're not the only hospital in town."

Lennox wanted to revel in his effortless grin, but her mind was ticking.

It wasn't that bad, or the person she hit was dead.

The image haunted her again: Eva's laughter, Allison's hands on the wheel. Those eyes: wide, terrified. The flash of blond. Then darkness. Then *thud*.

Or, Lennox tried to reassure herself, *it was nothing. It was...* Lennox's heart did a double thump, and she sucked in a breath. "I am not my mother," she whispered under her breath.

Lennox's father reached out, covered her hand with his, and squeezed. "No, you're not. But where did that come from?"

She could feel heat blooming in her cheeks, burning its way to her scalp.

I'm not seeing things.

"I just meant..."

"It's okay to talk about her. In fact, Dr. Hartzong thinks it's a good idea."

Lennox nodded quickly. "Yeah, but I'm going to be late for school," she said, avoiding his gaze.

"Too late for a hug?"

She leaned over and hugged her dad, his familiar scent blanketing her in an immediate calm. They were a team, and he was her rock, two traveling buddies against the world. It had always seemed to Lennox that when they were together, nothing in the outside world could touch them.

"Love you, Dad."

Lennox loaded her backpack, silenced her phone when she saw Allison calling. She paused in the driveway, staring at the used Honda Civic that had been her pride and joy when she'd driven it off the lot a month ago, her consolation prize for yet another move, yet another school, yet another rental with off-white walls and someone else's welcome mat. Now the car sat like some ominous omen, a sinister reminder of the night before. In the daylight, the dent looked bigger, angrier, with jags she hadn't seen in last night's darkness. She rubbed her hand over them again, half expecting memories or insights to come roaring back, but there was nothing but dented metal cutting into the soft flesh of her palm.

You clipped something, and it ran off.

Why would a person be running along that road in the middle of the night anyway?

Lennox blew out a sigh. She was being ridiculous.

But I saw her.

Again, Lennox straightened. "I didn't *see* anything," she reminded herself. "There was no one there." She kicked the tire of her car, her stomach dropping when a pebble and a smatter of brick-red dirt popped out of the tire's tread.

"Dirt," she said before her mind had a chance to process, to scream, to make her drive back up that horrible winding road and see if she'd left someone to die. "It's just dirt."

"Lenn?"

She whirled, heart thundering against her rib cage. Her dad smiled from the porch. "You're jumpy."

"I just…" Lennox's fingers found the dent, and she pressed her backside against it. "Just surprised me is all. What's up?"

"Jacket." He held it out, and Lennox stared at it, unmoving.

"Oh."

"Come get it. You made me promise at our last place that I would never be seen outside in my leisure wear." He gestured to his battered pajamas, and Lennox rolled her eyes, setting her backpack over the dent. She sprinted to her dad, snatched up the jacket, and smiled.

"That was two places ago, and thank you for adhering to my regulations."

She busied herself getting into the car, taking her time, hoping he would get bored and go back inside. Instead, he sipped his coffee and blinked in the sunlight.

"Inside, Dad."

He stuck out his tongue at her but disappeared inside the house, shutting the door behind him. Lennox finally breathed, glancing at the dent. She could have just told him. She could have just pointed it out and said she'd hit something—an animal.

But then I'd be lying, she thought.

Lennox steeled herself and slammed the car door, sinking her key into the ignition. She drove the seven miles to school with the windows rolled down, the radio turned up, and a resolve to be more cool, more chill, like Allison and Eva. She didn't know the town well and didn't know Hicks Road at all. Eva and Allison would know if it was teeming with wildlife. They would know that people didn't walk down that road in the middle of the night. By the time Lennox pulled into the parking lot, she had almost convinced herself.

FOUR

Lennox made the left turn into the student lot, her car creeping along with the rest of the other students' cars. She almost felt normal, like one of the crowd. She had her parking pass affixed to the back window just like everyone else: an enraged blue mustang blowing smoke out of his nostrils with a red *P* hanging over him. Her pass was held on with Scotch tape for the inevitable eventual move to a new school, but no one could see that from the outside.

Lennox pulled into a space near the back of the lot, dodging kids slinging backpacks over their shoulders and zigzagging across the asphalt. She waited for her song to end before killing the engine: It was an old one, a Death to Sea Monkeys favorite of hers with a throbbing bass line and a refrain that always soothed her: *Nothing can get me / I'm numb and you're red / Nothing can haunt me / I'm better than dead.*

She turned the engine off and then jumped at the face outside her driver's-side window, the wide eyes and raised brows. Then, he put his hands up.

"Oh my God, I'm so, so sorry—I didn't mean to scare you."

Lennox clutched her heart and wrenched the car door open. "What the—"

The guy who was staring through her window smiled, a wide, relaxed grin, perfectly straight white teeth showing above his bottom lip. He was trying not to laugh.

"You're laughing at me?" Lennox was embarrassed.

The guy doubled over, hands on his knees, and Lennox could see that his shoulders were wide and well muscled, could see the licks of wavy brown hair poking out of his baseball cap. He looked like he was her age. "I'm sorry, I'm sorry," he said, straightening up, wiping a tear from his eye. "I didn't mean to scare you, but you should have seen your face."

Lennox felt her jaw tighten, her lips turn up. She crossed her arms in front of her chest, jutting out a hip. There was one in every school: some GQ-looking jock all the girls swooned over even though he was an asshole through and through.

"My name's Owen."

Lennox looked at his outstretched hand, feeling her lips turn into a snarl. "Yeah, I know." She slung her backpack over her shoulder and turned on her heel, heart clanging like a fire alarm, sweaty palms balled into fists. He was Mr. Popular at Pioneer High, but as far as she was concerned, he wasn't worth knowing.

"No, no, wait." Owen jogged up behind her, palms outstretched. "Let's start over. Hey, my name is Owen. I didn't mean to freak you out—"

"But you like to lurk outside people's car windows? Awesome. Nice to meet you, I'm late for class."

Owen sucked his teeth and grabbed his chest as though wounded. "Wow, who peed in your Cheerios?"

"Look, Owen, is it? I'm sure you're a really nice guy, but I've got a lot going on—"

Owen straightened up, fixed Lennox with his clear brown eyes. If this were a rom-com, she would have immediately gotten lost in them, some sappy song playing in the background, then tripped and smashed into his chest. But this was Lennox's life, and guys like this trolled every high school in search of fresh meat, and her car was dented, and she may have killed someone, and so—

"I honestly didn't mean to freak you out, I just took the spot in front of you and saw the dent in your car."

The heat that was making its way to Lennox's cheeks dissipated, replaced by a wave of ice water. Her chest tightened and her throat went Sahara-dry.

"The dent?"

Owen blinked, pushed a lock of hair back under his hat. He walked backward toward Lennox's car, tapped a thumb against the dent in the grill. "This. Not really a big deal, but if you don't get it fixed soon, it's going to rust and ruin your hood."

Lennox looked from Owen to the dent and back again. "What are you, some sort of weird insurance narc?"

Owen spat out a laugh. "You're funny. What did you say

your name was? Anyway, I just wanted to mention it because, you know, rust. What happened?"

Do something, say something, pretend to be normal. You hit a deer, a raccoon, the goddamn Statue of Liberty.

Lennox opened her mouth, but nothing came out.

Owen's eyes went wide, his lips turning down into a sweet frown. "Oh, gosh, I'm sorry—I didn't mean to pry. It doesn't look bad at all. Was it recent? You know what, you don't have to tell me, I was just trying to help. I know some guys who could fix it. So I thought—but never mind." He hiked up his backpack, and Lennox could see that his cheeks were red, that there was a touch of pink on the tips of his ears. She immediately felt bad.

"No, no—Owen, I didn't, I'm sorry." She blew out a long sigh, pinched the bridge of her nose. "My name is Lennox. I'm still kind of new here and I'm clearly just learning the language. The dent"—she gritted her teeth—"isn't serious. It just happened. Last night, actually. I, um." Her voice was low. "I think I hit a deer or something."

Owen grinned, and Lennox could see that his teeth weren't perfect after all, that the bottom front two were crooked. His nose had a sprinkle of freckles, and with that slight blush and silly smile, he was pretty cute.

"Nice to meet you, Lennox." The bell sounded, shrill and demanding. "Can I walk you to class?"

Lennox stifled a giggle. "People still do that?"

"What, walk? It's a thing here. Not too hard, one foot in

front of the other. Where did you say you were from, again? Some state that's clearly too advanced for walking?"

Lennox fell into step with Owen, cocking a brow. "You're a little obnoxious, you know that?"

Owen's eyebrows rose. "Just a little? Wow, I'm improving."

───

Lennox and Owen chatted the whole way to her first-period biology class. When he opened the door for her, Ms. Pierson pursed her lips as thirty-two heads swung to stare at Lennox. All the female ones seemed to soften when they noticed Owen, who smiled easily and waved as though he were a prince acknowledging his court.

"Seems like you know a few people here," Lennox whispered to him with a grin.

He winked, and it didn't even gross her out. "Hi, Ms. Pierson, just delivering your new student, Lennox. It's my fault she's late. I was telling her about all the great teachers and the fine curriculum at our fair school."

Lennox hustled to her seat, expecting Ms. Pierson to read Owen the riot act, but she just smiled and giggled like a schoolgirl. "Oh, Owen, you!" she said.

Eva leaned over to Lennox once she had settled. "That's Owen Rossum."

Lennox pulled out her notebook, feeling a little pleased, a little like royalty. "I know. Everyone knows." A zing went down her spine. At her previous schools, Lennox had been wallpaper when the cool kids walked the halls. Now here she was: new kid, new school, strolling into class with a senior celebrity on her arm.

"You have to tell me *every*thing."

Lennox wanted to lean over and tell Eva that Owen was kind of cute with his random banter and blush-stained cheeks, but something held her back, something tarnished the brilliant bliss of a cute guy walking her to class.

The dent.

He hadn't noticed *her*—he had noticed the dent in her grill.

Lennox's heart started to thud. Her breathing went shallow, her chest tight.

Nothing happened.

"Are you okay?" Eva whispered loudly.

Lennox blinked and maybe nodded.

Stop being such a freak.

"Uh, Ms. Pierson, can I walk Lennox to the nurse's office? She's clearly hyperventilating."

Every student in class was laser focused on Lennox. "I'm not," she said breathlessly.

"You do look a little peaked," Ms. Pierson said. "Do you want to go to the nurse?"

"Maybe can I just get a drink of water?"

Ms. Pierson nodded, and Eva jumped up, grabbing Lennox by the arm.

"Eva, I appreciate your willingness to help, but I think Lennox can make it five feet down the hall on her own."

Eva shook her head. "And if she can't? If she passes out and hits her head on the water fountain? Safety first, Ms. Pierson."

"Okay, okay, okay—"

Eva still had a tight grip on Lennox's arm as the girls clicked Ms. Pierson's door shut behind them. "Hey, where are you going?"

"Water fountain."

"Weird. But about Owen—tell me everything. And also, you do look a little pale. Maybe you should go to the nurse's office? Or out for sushi. We could go out for sushi."

Lennox leaned over the fountain. "It's nine a.m., and there's nothing to tell about Owen. He—he noticed the dent in my car out in the parking lot."

Eva frowned. "What dent?"

Lennox gaped. "Are we—from last night? Am I in the Twilight Zone or something? Last night on Hicks Road."

Eva was unfazed. "The deer left a dent?"

Lennox shook her head. "A small one." She considered telling Eva about the smear of blood that could have been dirt—but maybe she was being crazy. She didn't really *know* if the pebble in the tread was blood, and even if it was—and here, Lennox's stomach lurched, sloshing the water she had just drunk painfully in her belly—it could have been from an animal. It had to have been from an animal.

Right?

No person. No body. No one in the emergency room.

Lennox flashed back to Hicks Road, to the mottled moonlight on the pavement. There had been thick forest to her left, a steep, brush-covered drop-off to her right. No person would have been running in the woods at night. No person would have been able to edge down the embankment with any kind of speed.

She squeezed her eyes shut and shook her head. "I think I just need more sleep. Like, way more."

FIVE

Allison and Eva made a beeline for Lennox when the bell rang. "I hear you met our resident superstar," Alison said.

Lennox's eyebrows went up in mock surprise. "That being?"

"Ooh, look at her being all coy and aloof. Owen Rossum."

Lennox frowned. "You know about that? That was, like, fifty minutes ago."

"Yeah, so old news. I can't believe you didn't tell me and I had to hear it secondhand."

"From who?"

"Eva."

Lennox nodded. "Sorry, I didn't know it was such big news. He just—he noticed the dent in my car is all." She cut her eyes at Allison, hoping to see a shift of recognition, but Allison's face remained unchanged. "You know, the dent from last night?"

Allison and Eva looked blank, and Lennox groaned and dropped her voice. "From the party."

"Was Owen even there? I didn't see him," Allison said.

"I don't know—"

Eva grinned. "And you definitely would have noticed."

Allison shot Eva a murderous glance. "You wouldn't know who was there, Eva, since you were so busy sucking face with Kent Alexander all night."

Eva blushed and looked away. "Barf. We weren't sucking face. We were talking. Just very closely." She started to giggle, and Allison punched her in the arm. "Besides, I was doing reconnaissance, so you're welcome."

Lennox's eyebrows went up. "What reconnaissance?"

Eva popped an M&M in her mouth. "Kent goes to Lincoln. I was seeing if there was anything going on over there that we should know about. You know, parties, sleeper cells, the norm. Oh, crap, I have to get to my locker before the bell!" Eva took off across the quad, and Lennox frowned.

"I really need to catch up on what goes on around here. But wait." Lennox put a hand up. "So, there were kids from other schools at the party?"

Allison nodded. "Didn't it occur to you that, like, half the kids there were strangers?"

Lennox shrugged. "I've become kind of an expert at not noticing anything or anyone. When you move around so much, you learn not to get bogged down by facts. Everyone is kind of a stranger to me." She tried to smile, but it was weak, a twinge of pain creeping up the back of her neck. That was how Lennox lived her life: not close enough to touch. It made leaving much less painful, made moving on refreshing. But until that moment, shoulder to shoulder with Allison and Eva, actual *friends*, Lennox hadn't realized how much she'd missed connection.

She wanted to ask about the blond girl—or ask Eva to ask her make-out partner about her—but something stopped her. Lennox was happy where she was. She had friends, she had been invited to a party, she had even run into the most popular guy in school who was not horrible. If she became the girl stuck on a morbid scene that maybe never even happened, Allison and Eva would probably not want to hang out with her, because who wants to be friends with the crazy girl? Lennox shifted, a shiver running through her.

I'm not crazy, she told herself. But in an instant, her mind flashed back to some other state, some other day, some other school where Lennox was standing on the blacktop behind a chain-link fence and saw her: dark brown disheveled hair in a rat's nest around cheeks streaked with dirt. A coat that should have been elegant with its intricate stitching and fur collar but was torn, filthy, ill-fitting, and had pockets overflowing with crumpled plastic bags. Shoes that were too big, and that stare—brown-black eyes that looked right through Lennox when she ran closer, her fingers gripping the cold metal until they screamed in pain.

"Mom?" Lennox whispered.

The woman didn't blink, didn't flinch, didn't acknowledge that she had seen or heard Lennox at all, just gave that blank, hollow stare. She went back to rifling through the trash, and Lennox felt a hand grab her heart, squeezing it until she could barely breathe. The bell rang, and Lennox held tight to the image until her father picked her up from school, screwed up his eyebrows, and told her, "Lennox, you know that wasn't Mom. Mom is—"

"In a hospital, getting help. I know. But she was so—"

"Getting better is important to your mom, for us. For you."

"But—"

"I know how badly you want to see her, hon. Sometimes the mind plays tricks…"

Lennox fisted her hands until her nails dug half-moons into her flesh. The sting of the pain felt good, felt real. Her dad drove the short way around the school, sticking them in a line of parent pickup cars but avoiding the back lawn where the dumpsters— and the woman Lennox could have sworn was her mother— were. Two days later, Lennox and her father's bags were packed and sitting in the front hall, the table they took everywhere was carefully loaded into her dad's car, and they were gone.

Lennox looked at her new friend, the quad that was becoming familiar, and chewed her bottom lip. She liked what she had here. She wasn't going to ruin it with some phantom vision of a dark road.

"What do you have next?" Allison asked.

Lennox shrugged. "They're still trying to work out my schedule. Right now, I have to go to the office or I get the joy of having two Spanish classes back-to-back."

"*Dos clases de español! Muy mal.* And that, my friend, is the extent of my Spanish. Eva works in the office. Tell her to switch you into something fun like woodshop or aeronautics."

"They have that here?"

Lennox waved as Allison disappeared around a corner and then stepped into the administration office. It was like every other administration office she had ever walked into in the last five schools. The floors were nondescript industrial gray, flecked with a different gray that was supposed to obscure questionable stains into its questionable pattern. The chairs were covered in fabric that may have once been mauve and may have once been comfortable, and the walls featured the same posters with animated creatures or too-thrilled-looking students reading books with big smiles on their faces or sporting lab coats and holding steaming beakers. The only difference at Pioneer High School was a "wall of fame" featuring framed photos of their teacher of the year (a Mr. Yucca, who had a bald head and a jaunty thumbs-up) and members of the Associated Student Body. Lennox blinked at Owen, grinning out from his frame, looking relaxed and confident and so totally Owen: senior class president. He was wearing a baseball jersey in the picture, and Lennox smiled. All-American boy.

"Hey, Lennox."

Lennox whirled and grinned at Eva, who was behind the administration counter. She'd put on hot-pink cat-eye glasses and a librarian-looking sweater.

"What are you doing here? Tardy pass, excused absence,

want to apply for the 4H club?" She leaned in conspiratorially. "That one's closed, by the way. Apparently, all the good cows are taken."

Lennox nodded, trying to hide her smile. "I think I'm good with cows. I'm supposed to be here to talk with…"

"Oh, the counselor!" Eva said brightly.

Lennox's eyes widened, and heat itched her cheeks. "I thought that was supposed to be—"

"Oh, no." Eva patted at the air nonchalantly. "It's not serious, it's"—she cleared her throat—"obligatory. I know you're not crazy."

Again, Lennox shifted, wanting to tell Eva that there was nothing wrong with seeking mental health help, but there was still that hint of stigma, that need to prove she was "normal."

"Yeah, they just assigned me. It's not like I had an appointment or anything."

Eva shrugged and turned her back on Lennox, dragging out an enormous drawer full of file folders. "This one is you"—she pulled out a folder—"and Mr. Apex isn't in just yet, so…why don't you sit right there and wait?"

Lennox nodded, her eyes on the inch-thick file folder with her name on it. Eva had rested it on the counter in front of her, and Lennox wished it weren't sitting there. *What if Eva reads it? What if she tells Allison about my enormous list of previous schools and the reason I ultimately left? What if she finds out about my mom?*

She felt her heartbeat speed up, her eyes still focused on the folder. She cleared her throat. "So, is that, like, my personal file?"

Eva turned around, looking confused. "Huh?"

"That." She pointed, crossing the room. "Is there, like, juicy gossip in there about me?" She prayed that Eva wouldn't see through her paper-thin confidence.

Eva just shrugged again. "I don't know. Maybe if you consider your first-grade reading scores juicy." She cradled her chin in her hands and whispered, "They try not to let us peons get the good info about new students, but now I'm intrigued. Should I be worried about something? Is our mild-mannered Lennox Oliver really some psycho?" Eva frowned. "Nah, I can usually sniff out the kids who are going to cause problems. No offense, but you look pathetically normal."

Lennox frowned and Eva's eyebrows went up. "Oh! It's not a bad thing! You're just in San Jose, where everything is pathetically normal. So, congrats, you totally fit in." She grinned.

"I'm still not entirely sure this isn't you dragging me, but I guess I'll take it."

"Morning, Miss Eva."

Both girls turned to face Mr. Apex, the guidance counselor, as he walked through the glass double doors, grinning and swinging his briefcase. Lennox sighed. In his sweatervest and corduroy pants, Mr. Apex screamed "guidance counselor," and Lennox was suddenly well aware of what her friend meant by pathetically normal. Except for the combat boots, crusted with mud, that stuck out from under his pants.

"This is your new charge, Lennox Oliver," Eva said, handing Mr. Apex the file folder.

"I'm not that new," Lennox explained. "It's been a few weeks, but they can't seem to get my schedule right. Nice boots."

Mr. Apex glanced down at his feet and tapped his toe against the linoleum. Dried mud popped off. "Remnants of my other job. Guess I'm caught." He took Lennox's folder and smiled at her. "I'm Mr. Apex, and we will certainly get you sorted, okay?"

"Hey, Lennox—" Eva said just as Lennox was turning to follow Mr. Apex. She looked at Lennox, then pressed her lips into a smile. "Sorry, never mind. It was nothing."

Lennox made a mental note to circle back to Eva's "nothing" once she was done being grilled. She followed Mr. Apex down the hall before looking over her shoulder and offering Eva a small smile. Her heart was still thudding, spasms of fear reverberating through her stomach, as she wondered if Eva would read her file and tell everyone at school that Lennox was the daughter of a woman in a mental hospital. She tried to blink away the suspicion, tried to remember how nice Eva and Allison had been—were being—and chase out the thought.

"So, just out of curiosity," she started, "do the students in the office get to look at other students' files?"

Mr. Apex stopped in front of a door and put his key in the lock. "This?" He held up Lennox's file. "No. The students who work in the office have been vetted and know they aren't allowed to look into student files at all. Besides, there is always an administrator to oversee the office."

"There isn't today," Lennox said under her breath.

She didn't know why she was so unnerved. Eva was her friend and didn't seem the least bit interested in Lennox's file. *F-r-i-e-n-d*, Lennox spelled out in her head. *Someone who isn't out to attack you.* Lennox shrugged off her fears, and Mr. Apex gestured for her to sit across from him as he flipped through her file and opened up his laptop.

"Lots of schools," he said with a slow nod.

Lennox could have mouthed the words. She vaguely wondered if "lots of schools" was in the "what to say to transfer students" handbook, because she had heard it at least five times.

"My dad is a traveling ER nurse. We move around a lot, following his work."

"And how do you feel about that?"

Lennox blinked. "Is this, like, therapy?"

"Therapy?" Mr. Apex's eyebrows went up, and then he laughed too loudly. "No, no, just asking. Do you like moving around a lot?"

Lennox bit her thumbnail. "It's not the worst."

"So, are you happy here at Pioneer?"

She wanted to roll her eyes. She wanted to tell Mr. Apex

to fix her schedule and get it over with, because she'd had all the obligatory school counselor interviews she could take. She was used to the tiptoe questions—*do you like school, do you like this city*—*before* the real ones drifted in: *do you see people who aren't there?*

Lennox's stomach did that little churn that signaled anxiety, that little tap on her shoulder to remind her that when she was playing around with her new friends, she had hit someone with her car. She shifted, willing her body to stay neutral, willing her mind to flit off and imagine other things like song lyrics or the fifty states in alphabetical order. But there were those eyes again, those terrified eyes and the girl's palms that were no match for the hood of Lennox's Honda.

"I didn't hit—"

"Lennox?"

Mr. Apex was drilling her with a look, and she suddenly couldn't remember if her lips had been moving, if she'd been talking out loud. "I'm sorry, what?"

"Did you say something?"

Lennox cleared her throat, heat zipping up her spine. She pressed her lips together and shook her head.

"I asked if you liked this school."

"It's great," she said, with way more enthusiasm than she meant. "Really great. I'm really into the classes. My classes, except for the whole double Spanish thing. Am I supposed to see someone else about that?" Lennox turned in her chair as if that someone else would pop into the room and grant her schedule-changing wish.

Mr. Apex's smile was soft. "No, no, public-school funding. I am the official school counselor and the schedule coordinator. So, you have two Spanish classes and no other elective. Is there something you would like to do?"

Yes, run out of here! Lennox wanted to say. Instead, she pretended to think, then offered, "Art. Drawing. I love to draw and paint."

It almost pained her to say it out loud, to reveal her secret to this stranger, but drawing was the one thing that kept Lennox sane. She had notebooks filled with drawings of each new house, every new stop, the things that were supposed to be cool and awe-inspiring in the states they visited or moved to. She wanted the pictures to mean something, to be wonderful memories full of emotion, but they were mostly just places to her, places where she and her father had been and her mother had not. But deep in the backs of her notebooks, there were the sketches, fingernail-size and oozing with sadness, of the woman Lennox remembered as her mother, head thrown back laughing, or painting at her own easel with baby Lennox, fat and happy on the floor next to her.

"Art, huh?"

It was the only constant at the schools Lennox dropped into, even if some of the classes had been bare-bones or taught by off-season sports coaches.

Lennox nodded. "Yes, please, if it's possible. Or if there is still room." She smiled, trying her best to look friendly and agreeable.

"Sure, sure, sure," he said, bobbing his head with each word. "I'll see what I can do, but it might take a few days for everything to settle in. That okay?" Mr. Apex pressed his lips together in one of those patronizing guidance counselor smiles that Lennox was growing so used to. He paused for a beat.

"So, how is your social life?"

Lennox's eyebrows rose. "My social life?"

Mr. Apex leaned back in his chair. "Making friends, developing a social routine outside of school, that kind of thing?"

Lennox could feel heat at the back of her neck. "Outside of school?"

"Or dating? Are there any boys"—he seemed to catch himself—"or girls you're interested in?"

Lennox pulled her backpack up against her chest, feeling weirdly exposed. "Um, not really." Lennox's mind started reeling, tension heavy at the back of her throat. *Is he even allowed to ask me that? Is that even...legal? Should I mention the girls, our outings, just to get him off my back?*

No.

Maybe he is just trying to be nice. Maybe he is just trying to make conversation or mark off the part of my form that says I am adjusting and not in need of a straitjacket.

He looked at her expectantly, and the steadiness of his

gaze set Lennox's teeth on edge. *There is something about him*, she thought, something she couldn't quite pinpoint.

You're being silly, she admonished herself. *You're the one who's acting weird.*

The din of the bell sounded, and Lennox bounded to her feet. "Can we do this later? I have Spanish right now."

Mr. Apex was still watching her, and Lennox felt an overwhelming need to get out of the office, to put as much distance between herself and this man as possible. He nodded, and she was already pulling the door open, relief washing over her in a cool rush when she saw the hallway overrun with students. She dipped into the rush of kids and had never once been so pleased to blend right in.

Lennox slipped into the girls' room stall and slammed the flimsy metal door behind her, breathing hard. *Nothing about Mr. Apex was out of the ordinary or weird*, she said to herself. *Then why am I freaking out?*

Lennox stiffened when she heard the door open and squeak shut, her eyes tracing the two sets of sneakers that walked in.

"So, is she back yet?" the first girl asked.

Lennox scrunched one eye closed and peered through the one-inch gap in the door. There were two girls she didn't recognize facing the bathroom mirror, one fluffing shoulder-length brown hair, the other meticulously smearing eyeliner above her lashes.

The eyeliner girl snorted. "No, and my mom is totally losing her shit."

"You're not worried?" the other girl asked.

"No, it's only been a night."

The dark-haired girl frowned. "I'd be freaking out if my sister took off for a night."

Lennox stiffened, heat zipping up her spine.

"Well, your sister is six and adorable," the second girl started, "and mine is nineteen and most likely shacking up with her loser boyfriend again." The eyeliner girl brushed her blond hair over her shoulders, puckered her lips, and blew a kiss to the mirror. "Besides, if she doesn't come back by Friday, I'm selling her stuff."

There was a faint trail of giggles as the girls shuffled to the door.

Lennox's heart thudded. A girl was missing. A teenager. She grabbed the edges of the sink, the cool porcelain sliding under her damp palms.

"Get a grip," she said to her reflection.

The blond hair flashed in front of Lennox's eyes. The sickening thud reverberating in her head. Lennox gritted her teeth.

"There was no one there. I didn't see anything."

Lennox didn't hear the door open. She didn't hear the other girl step in, her eyes widening when she saw Lennox.

Lennox slapped her palm to her forehead. *And now I'm the girl who talks to herself.*

She flashed a small smile and walked into the hall.

SIX

"Do you think Mr. Apex is weird?" Lennox asked her friends that day at lunch.

"Yes," Allison said quickly.

"You think anyone over twenty-two is weird, though," Eva said.

Allison pointed a Cheeto at Eva. "You are not wrong."

"He just seems very...I don't know, stare-y?"

"Stare-y?" Eva bobbed her head. "I get it. I mean, you were the only person in his office, so him staring at someone else would be very—"

"Interesting. The guidance counselor who sees dead people!" Allison crunched her Cheeto and laughed, her lips electric orange.

"I would totally marathon that," Eva said.

Lennox smiled despite her unease. "You guys are weird. But he asked me about my social life."

Allison cocked an eyebrow. "Like what about it?"

"Did I have a boyfriend or girlfriend. Isn't that weird?"

Eva picked at her fingernails. "Depends. Was he asking you out?"

Lennox frowned. "I don't think so."

"I think he was just making conversation," Eva said with a shrug. "You know all those new teachers pretend they want to be friends. Besides, his other job is forest ranger or something, so he probably dug talking to you because you're not, like, a bear." She smiled, and Lennox couldn't help but relax, even if it was just a modicum.

"You are so strange. Oh, didn't you want to tell me something in the office?"

"Uh." Eva's eyes flashed. "Can't remember. Hey, guess who's up for Sportsman of the Year?"

"It's Sports*person*," Allison corrected. "And do I even need to guess? Owen Rossum. He's a shoo-in."

Lennox shifted her weight. "That guy is kind of everywhere, isn't he?"

"He's somewhat of a high school legend, yes," Allison said with a definitive nod. "But not one of those jerky legends. He's cool."

Lennox looked from Eva to Allison. "I've never gone to a school with so many legends. Druids, covens, super teenage boys."

"It's why housing prices are so high around here."

"So, you guys know Owen?"

Eva nodded. "Everyone knows Owen—sooner or later." Her voice seemed to take on a dark tone, but Allison scoffed.

"Eva just means that he's super friendly. You know, he hangs out with everyone. Really nice guy. But one of the ones who doesn't know he's super popular, so it doesn't go to his head."

"Like me," Eva said. "Except I know I'm popular and I definitely let it go to my head." She grinned.

"You're popular because you have direct access to hall passes, tardy slips, and get-out-of-jail-free cards."

"And don't you forget it."

"So Owen hangs out with the popular kids?" Lennox wanted to know.

Allison shook her head. "You know, we don't really have that kind of stereotypical social hierarchy here. Everyone is pretty cool and friendly; we all get along. Except for those weird gamer kids over there—no one talks to them—and the hoodies over there who worship Satan or Star Wars or something."

Lennox didn't want to smile but couldn't help it. "So, no real social hierarchy, but a real social hierarchy."

Allison looked mildly offended. "Hey, everyone likes the band geeks and the drama kids, so I say we're five by five."

There was a beat of awkward silence, and Lennox looked at her hands in her lap, trying to shake off the chill of unease that sat heavy in her gut.

Allison stretched her long tanned legs in front of her and kicked off her flip-flops.

"You know it's December, right?" Eva said, her hands disappearing in her sweater sleeves.

"December in California. Hey, Earth to Lennox."

Allison may have been snapping—or clapping, or tap-dancing for all Lennox knew—when she came out of her reverie. "Sorry. What'd I miss?"

"Eva thinks we live in the Arctic, Lennox. Now that I think of it, Lennox, that's a cool name."

Lennox shrugged. "Yeah, but there are no key chains with my name on them." She looked away, hoping to drop the subject.

"Where did it come from?"

Lennox shrugged, busied herself with staring into her schoolbag.

"You know, there is a singer named Annie Lennox."

Lennox didn't respond. She knew Annie Lennox. She knew every song that Annie Lennox had ever played, both solo and with the Eurythmics. She could hear her mother belting them out now, head thrown back as she pounded on the piano keys, Lennox on her lap, a fat, cheerful toddler gurgling along to "Sweet Dreams." Her parents had met at a Eurythmics concert and Lennox used to love the story— they were both pushing toward the front of the crowd in Croke Park. Dad always said that the sun was setting and the roar of the crowd sounded like the rushing of waves, that there were thousands of people there, standing shoulder to shoulder, but all he could see was Lennox's mother, her waist-length dark hair wild and waving as she danced, eyes closed, palms up. She wasn't sick then, and Lennox was desperate to know that woman, the woman her mother had once been, and so as child, she had listened to her mother's music and shrugged on her old band T-shirts, anything to hold on to the woman who wasn't sick, confused, paranoid, gone.

"Did your mom just like that name or something?"

Lennox desperately wanted to change the subject, but her tongue was heavy in her mouth. She wasn't ashamed of her mother, exactly—it's just wasn't the easiest thing to talk about. First, there was the fact that her mother was in a mental institution. Second, there was her schizophrenia diagnosis. And third, there was the looming, lurking fact that schizophrenia was hereditary, often showing its first signs in young adulthood.

Lennox could still hear the doctor's voice reverberating through her computer's speakers: *delusions, disordered thinking, an unnamed "they" out to get you.* She remembered those moments with her mother, the triple-locking of the door, the way her mother would peer out the window, pointing her finger at an imaginary "them," then pulling the curtains shut and starting her ritual of locking the door, unlocking it, locking it again.

But Lennox wasn't like that.

Lennox wasn't paranoid. Lennox didn't see—

Her eyes flashed to the girl, that night.

Nobody saw anything and neither did you.

"Allison, lay off. She clearly doesn't want to talk about her mom."

It was the first time Eva had ever countered Allison in

Lennox's presence, and she could feel the tension in the air. "Just leave her alone."

Allison stiffened. "Not everyone's families have skeletons in their closets. I was just making conversation. Maybe we can *all* share about the wonderful parents we have. You can start, Eva. What's your dad been up to?"

"Drop it, Allison." Eva pinned her with a glare, and Lennox's stomach continued to churn. From what she had heard, Allison's family was nice but overbearing; Eva's parents seemed idyllic with a slew of kids as bright and shiny as Eva. No secrets. No institutions, no wake of rental homes, new bosses, new schools.

Lennox cleared her throat. "So, there were two girls in the bathroom earlier. They were talking about a missing girl."

Eva and Allison looked up.

"Missing? Like, kidnapped?" Eva asked.

Lennox shrugged. "I don't know. The girl just hadn't come home, and I thought maybe...you know..."

Allison blinked. "Know what?"

Lennox dropped her voice. "Last night."

"Epic party!"

"No! The—" She dropped her voice. "The accident!"

Allison's mouth opened into a wide O. "Oh my God, you got in an accident? When? Are you okay? Did your dad freak?"

"What? No—on Hicks Road!"

Eva rolled her eyes.

"There was a girl on the road—I know there was. A blond. She had long hair and blue eyes, and I really think I hit her. I heard it. I felt it. And now there's a girl who didn't come home." Lennox's stomach was lead. "Do you think that could really be a coincidence?"

Allison crossed her legs. "Yeah, I do. I mean, come on! You saw a girl on the road, but neither of us did? I mean, at least I didn't. Eva?"

Eva looked up, paused for half a beat. "No. I felt something, but again, there wasn't anything in the road."

"But you said it might have been a deer." Lennox looked at Allison.

"I don't think it was a deer," Eva said, finger raised. "I think at most you hit a tree branch. Possibly a wayward raccoon with a death wish." She grinned.

"I'm glad neither of you thinks this is serious."

"You didn't hit a person, Lennox. We were both with you." Allison pointed to herself and then to Eva. "And neither of us saw anything. And there was no one on the road. And again, if you'd hit a real, actual, like, three-dimensional person—"

"I think I must have just clipped her—"

"And what? She was made of steel? News flash: cars are big. They're heavy. If you'd hit a girl, we would have all seen it. And heard it."

Lennox could feel her blood pressure rising, the *whoosh* thundering through her ears.

Allison put her hand on Lennox's shoulder. "Look, Lennox, I'm not trying to diminish what you think you saw, I'm just trying to point out some obvious facts. We stopped the car and looked around, right?" She paused, waiting for Lennox to respond.

Reluctantly, Lennox nodded.

"And there was no one there."

Again Lennox nodded. "But—"

"I know, the blond girl. Lennox, look around you."

Lennox glanced at the students clustered in groups, talking, laughing, picking at sandwiches, eating their lunches. "Yeah, so?"

"Half the student body here are girls with long blond hair."

"And that guy over there also has long blond hair," Eva said, pointing.

"So what are you saying? That all of them are here, so they weren't on Hicks Road last night?"

"No," Allison said, shaking her head. "What I'm saying is that you probably think you saw a blond girl. It was probably someone you saw at the party, and you were scared." She pressed her palm against her heart. "I'm sorry about that, by the way. What I'm saying is, you freaked out, closed your eyes, probably saw someone from school or from the party in, like, a flashback or whatever, and then there was the thump, and then—" She shrugged, lips pursed. "Nothing."

"So you think my mind created the girl because I saw a blond girl at the party?"

"Like a hallucination?" Eva asked.

Lennox stiffened, her fingers gripping her sandwich until it was a pulpy mess. Her mind flashed back to her mother all those years ago, sitting primly in a waiting room that was decorated to look comfortable and welcoming, like someone's living room. But beyond the couch and the nondescript wall art, there was a long hallway full of locked doors and orderlies in scrubs, and in a matter of moments, one of them was going to come and take her mother away. Lennox had heard them talking, had heard the words, even though their voices were hushed, their shoulders turned: *disordered thinking, delusions, hallucinations.* The next time she'd seen her mother, she wasn't smartly dressed or sitting primly; she was in a fuzzy sweater over a faded pajama set, her shoulders slumped, her eyes glassy. Someone had gone to the trouble of brushing her hair and putting lipstick on her, but Lennox knew her mother never parted her hair on that side and would never approve of the garish color smeared on her lips. She looked like a wax doll melting in the sun.

Lennox shuddered. "I guess it's possible," she said softly.

Lennox made it through the rest of the school day without thinking of the accident or the phantom girl, thanks to a pop quiz in history, a fire drill during Chemistry, and something called a math bowl in trig. She was almost giddy when Eva and Allison hugged her goodbye and they made plans to meet, almost carefree when Owen bumped her shoulder and gave her one of those totally-nonchalant-but-totally-loaded head bobs. He did the same thing to the guy next to him and to the school janitor, but Lennox still felt heat burning in her cheeks. Her heart did a little thump as she thrived in her seemingly normal-girl status: friends, plans, even the cute guy from school acknowledging her in his round of goodbyes.

It wasn't until she had her keys in her hand and was approaching her car in the parking lot that her stomach tightened.

A girl sat on the back bumper of Lennox's Honda Civic. Her head was bent, her facial features blanketed by a swath of white-blond hair.

Is she the girl? Is she looking for damages? Did I hit and run?

Lennox's mind was spinning, her throat tightening.

"Hey!" She willed her feet to move, to jog ahead and corner the girl, but she was rooted to the asphalt, her Dr. Martens a thousand pounds. "Hey!" she said again.

The blond girl looked up, squinted. She pushed her hair behind her ears and stood, slinging a bag over her shoulder. "Dude, sorry," the girl said, obviously annoyed. "I just had gum on my shoe." She started walking, and somehow Lennox pushed herself forward, vaulting after the girl and yanking her arm much harder than she meant to.

"What the hell? I just leaned on your car for a sec, okay? Sorry. Chill, I didn't do anything to it. Besides, it's not exactly a classic or something."

Up close, Lennox could see the anger in the girl's hooded brown eyes. Her lips were twisted into a frown, heavily made up with blue-black lipstick that matched the streaks of black in her hair.

"Sorry," Lennox said, pushing the words out of her mouth. "I'm sorry, I thought you were someone else. Didn't mean to…" Lennox trailed off, turning back to her car.

The girl obviously wasn't hurt. She wasn't limping or taking down Lennox's license plate number, so…*she isn't the girl from last night.*

Lennox would never forget those eyes: wide, terrified, the iciest blue she'd ever seen.

Because she *had seen* her. It didn't matter what Eva and Allison said. She'd seen a girl, she was sure of it.

Aren't I?

Lennox tried to blink away the unease, but it washed over her full force when she saw the slip of paper catching the breeze. It was held down by her windshield wiper. With shaking hands, she edged the paper out.

"Parking ticket?"

She frowned, walking around her car to examine which tire was over the white line or if she had missed the giant blue markings of a disability or no-parking sign, but there was nothing.

"Hey," Allison said, coming up behind her. "What's going on?"

Lennox waved the ticket. "Parking ticket, but I have no idea why."

Allison snatched it from her, then handed it back. "It says 'no parking pass.'"

"I have a parking pass. It's right—" She pointed to the back window, but there was nothing there. "Must be..." She squinted, peering through the back window: nothing. "Wait."

"It's supposed to be in the back, driver's side."

Lennox huffed. "It was."

But it wasn't.

Lennox opened her car door and climbed inside.

"It must have just fallen. I only had it on with tape." She crawled around the back seats, patting them and craning her neck to find the sticker, but it wasn't there. She couldn't even find the sticky remnants of Scotch tape where it should have been.

"I know I have a parking pass. I bought it and I stuck it right there," she said to herself as much to Allison.

Allison poked her head into the back seat. "I don't remember seeing it. Besides, they only check, like, once a month."

Lennox shook her head. "I know I bought it. I have the receipt." She leaned over and pulled the glove box open, rifling through a crushed Kleenex box, some candy she didn't remember stashing, and the Honda owner's manual that had come with the car. No receipt.

"What are you guys doing?" Eva asked, walking up and opening the passenger-side door.

"Lennox can't find her parking permit," Allison answered.

"Ew, sixteen-dollar fine," Eva said with pursed lips. "Total waste of two-point-five lattes."

"Ugh," Lennox groaned.

"Hey."

Eva and Allison straightened up. "Hey, Owen," they said in unison.

Lennox slid out of the back seat. *Did I buy a parking permit?* She tried to think back—she remembered handing cash to a woman in the front office and the woman handing her a sticker with a wildcat on it. But this was Pioneer, and the Wildcats were back in Detroit. She bit her lip, her mind flashing images that couldn't be right. She didn't have the Honda back in Detroit.

"Hey, Lennox." Owen said.

Lennox looked up, barely registering Owen standing in front of his car, backpack slung over his shoulder.

"Oh, hey," she said. "Sorry. I just—I thought—" She looked at Allison, Eva, and Owen all staring at her expectantly and forced a smile. "Sometimes my mind loops. Thought I bought a parking permit, but"—she shrugged, holding up the ticket—"I guess not."

"Hey, Owen, why don't you clear that up for Lennox? I mean, she's a new student; I feel like it would be nice of the student body to give her a freebie."

Owen grinned his golden-boy smile but shrugged. "Sorry, my jurisdiction ends at the parking lot."

Eva snatched the ticket. "Mine doesn't. Get me your receipt, and I can make this go away. Or I can get you an actual pass tomorrow."

Lennox wanted to nod and smile right along with them, to chalk the parking pass up to something she must have picked up at a past school, but she was certain she had seen the Pioneer pass in her car window. But try as she might, she couldn't remember actually purchasing it or taping it to the window.

Allison and Eva stopped at Lennox's car, and the slamming of Owen's car door snapped her back to reality. Lennox looked around, her eyes landing on the blond girl who'd been sitting on the back bumper. She was at the end of the lot, leaning against the chain-link fence, her phone out in front of her, but her eyes were focused hard on Lennox.

Lennox slipped into her car, turning up the radio to drown out the thud of her heart.

SEVEN

Lennox pulled her car to a stop in the driveway, leaving room for her dad to inch into the garage. She knew he wasn't home, knew how much space his car needed even though they'd been in the house only a short time. She knew because these rental houses were all the same: short, squat, square pastry boxes, all with sticky front locks and smart foyers that echoed when Lennox let herself in the door.

To Lennox, it had always been like this: a nondescript key looped on a lanyard that Beverly Feasgotten had made for her in the third grade, when Lennox and her parents had lived in a sprawling ranch house with a tree out front, a tire swing, and a lock that never stuck. They had been rooted there; there had been pictures on the walls and hash marks on Lennox's bedroom door, each one marking a half inch she'd grown, a quarter inch, two inches the summer she turned five. That house had always been alive with the sounds of her mother chatting on the phone, the radio playing, Beverly and Lennox dancing to a song they'd just made up. It felt like they had lived there forever, although the edges of the memory were starting to fray: Had that been her mother's voice or just the deejay on the radio? Had Beverly always been there, or was Lennox always at Beverly's? Had the tire swing that felt so normal and fun been at her house or at Beverly's? Either way, that was before, when Lennox and her mother and father had all lived in the same house in the same town and were three instead of two. It was in that other house in that other life that Lennox had come home from school and called down the empty halls to find her father on his knees in front the bedroom closet, doors thrown open, one side impeccably, impossibly empty.

Mom's clothes were gone. Her shoes, the high heels Lennox had shuffled around in, the boots with fur that had licked at her knees: all gone. Mom was gone.

Lennox relished the silence now. Noise was a distraction, a cover-up as time dragged slowly by. In the silence, there was solace...and secrets.

She dropped her backpack and helped herself to an apple, then made a beeline for her bedroom. It was nothing special, nothing uniquely Lennox: just four stark walls and a window without curtains. Her bed was pushed into the corner, the bed-in-a-bag they'd dragged from house to unassuming house. Straight lines, muted colors: anyone could live here. Her father urged her to settle in and decorate, to paint, make herself feel "at home," but it was the lack of anything specific that made Lennox feel at home, because home was always changing. Home was stark white walls and the invitation to make herself comfortable, tempered with the knowledge that it was only temporary, that everything—the house, the home, the city, the town—was only temporary.

They were modern-day nomads.

Lennox sat on her bed and popped open her laptop, sliding her headphones on to amplify the non-sound of the house.

She googled "car accident, San Jose." There were a mountain of those on the police blotters, along with a few terrifying things like a home invasion and the occasional "gunshots fired," but nothing about a hit-and-run, nothing about a blond girl gravely injured or possibly...dead. Lennox swallowed heavily.

Maybe her friends were right. They hadn't seen anything, and Allison had been sitting right next to her, Eva right behind. They would have noticed, they would have heard. Lennox gritted her teeth.

I saw her.

Did you?

A little voice, small but shrill, echoed in her head. *Did you see her? Like your mom saw people?*

Her heart started to thud, a live wire of heat crawling up her spine.

"Mom was sick," she whispered out loud into the silence. "My mother is sick."

It started with one little person. Then a voice. Then...

Lennox yanked off her headphones and snapped her

laptop closed, propping herself up against the cool white wall. She snatched her pillow and held it tight to her chest.

"I'm not like my mom."

But the memories were already crashing into Lennox's mind, splattering like raindrops on glass. When she'd come out of her bedroom to find Beverly standing in the kitchen, eyes wide, as Lennox's mother engaged in a full animated conversation with absolutely no one. The times her mother had looked at her, round eyes blank, unseeing, as if she had no idea Lennox was even there. Her mother, locked in the bathroom, screaming about faces morphing, screaming that Lennox's father was wearing the wrong face. The medications had worked for a while. But when Lennox had finally begun to breathe, had finally gotten comfortable in her house again, she'd seen her mother dumping the meds down the toilet, flushing and flushing, muttering about poison and mind control. She remembered the way it had looked when the toilet overflowed, a slow-motion shower of water and little pills spilling over the linoleum, licking the toes of Lennox's school shoes. And then one day, Mom wasn't there anymore. The closet was empty, and Dad handed Lennox a suitcase and a too-practiced smile and said they were going to "go on an adventure" while Mom was away getting better.

Maybe you're going crazy too...

Lennox shook her head, her mind in an endless spin. She had a therapist she met with online, someone her dad had hired who asked her inane and boring questions but wrote down everything she said. Her father said it was to make sure Lennox was calm and happy in the midst of all their moving, but she knew it was because he wanted to know the exact moment she cracked, the exact moment she started talking to people who weren't there like her mother had. Her therapist was tracking her like a wild animal, and while Lennox wanted to be mad at her dad for that, she also couldn't blame him. The look of sadness etched on his face when they had dropped her mother off at the mental health center was something that Lennox would never get over, was something that, even at just nine years old, she had sworn she would never let her father feel ever again.

Lennox pushed the laptop and headphones onto her nightstand and slid under the covers, her head like cement, weighing down her pillow.

"There was no one there," she whispered. "There was no one there." She pinched her eyes shut tightly against the late afternoon light, her jaw hurting from the way she ground her back teeth.

"Everything is going to be okay," she said, trying to comfort herself. "Everything is going to be just fine."

***

Lennox was awakened by her blaring phone. She sat bolt upright, blinking in the darkness of her bedroom. *Where am I?* Her mind raced, images of bedrooms and houses and cities crashing in her mind as she tried to get her bearings.

In bed.

In San Jose.

With her shoes on and her headphones smashed against her cheek.

"Hello?"

"Were you sleeping?" Allison asked.

Lennox clicked on the lamp on her bedside table and yawned. "Yes. What else would I be doing at 7:42 p.m.?"

"Didn't realize you had such an early bedtime. I was just calling to check on you. I wanted to make sure you're okay. I feel kind of responsible for what happened on Hicks, and I don't want you to blame me or worry..."

Lennox batted at the air. "Oh, I don't blame you at all. I was driving—"

"But I turned out the lights."

"You were just joking around."

"Okay, good."

Lennox stepped out of bed, clicking lights on as she padded down the hall. "No big deal."

"What are you doing now?"

She pulled open the door to the garage, strolling to the deep freeze. "About to cook dinner."

"Wow, you're super talented! I can't even cook cereal. There's so much I don't know about you, Lennox Oliver."

"I am something of a teenage enigma. And one day you can come over, and I will teach you, too, the secrets of microwaving a frozen pizza."

"You're a nerd. Glad you're okay."

"Thanks."

Lennox hung up the phone and was plunged into darkness as soon as the door to the house closed. She hit the light switch and nothing happened. "Don't freak out," she told herself. "You're not five."

She used the light on her phone to find her way to the fridge, to rifle through the freezer for a pepperoni pizza. When she shut the freezer door, her phone slid from her hand and clattered to the ground, the flashlight turning off in the process.

"Dammit!" she yelled, dropping to her knees and groping in the darkness. Lennox had only been down there a few seconds when her heartbeat started to speed up, pressure building behind her eyes. The darkness seemed to be closing in on her, pressing against her chest, making it hard to breathe.

"I'm fine, I'm fine, everything is fine," she told herself, hands and knees going numb on the freezing garage concrete. "Go to the house, get the flashlight."

But she was frozen. Lennox could feel the sweat beading at her hairline, a droplet running down the ridge of her spine. She clamped her eyes shut, and the girl was there, the girl from the road, her blue eyes wide, accusing, brows slanted down in anger. Her hands weren't splayed in front of her this time; they were fisted, a finger pointing at Lennox, her lips pulled into a grotesque snarl. *You killed me!* This phantom girl screamed, and Lennox shook her head, pressing her palms against her ears.

"No, no, you're not real! You're not real!" She sat back on her haunches. "I didn't do anything!"

Lennox's eyes were open wide, but the girl was still there, standing in her garage, and this time she was bloodied, battered, blond hair matted against a gashed forehead.

You left me to die!

"No, no! You are not real. None of this is real!"

"Lennox? Lennox?"

"I can't hear you. I'm not listening!"

Lennox was crying now, big wracking sobs that ached in her chest.

"Lennox!"

Lennox blinked in the darkness. The girl was gone. Her accusing, bloody grimace, gone. But the voice was still there.

Lennox found her phone, half buried under the refrigerator. She cleared her throat and whispered, "Hello?"

"Lennox, it's Allison. What's happening? Is there someone there with you? Should I call the police?"

"D-did you call me?"

Allison blew out a sigh. "No, you called me. Or your phone did. But when I picked up, you were talking to someone else. Are you okay? You sound—Lennox?"

Lennox couldn't stop the tremor that started low in her belly. It settled into each of her limbs next, a slow, thunderous laughter that made Lennox's eyes water.

"Are you laughing?"

Lennox wasn't sure if she was or not. Her body felt taken over; she felt unhinged but free.

"Dude, Lennox, you're scaring me."

Finally, Lennox snorted and took a breath. "I don't know what happened. I—I dropped my phone, and it must have called you, and I just—I'm sorry, I freaked out, just..." She sighed. "Got weirded out."

"That's what was so funny?" Allison sounded vaguely annoyed.

"I don't know. I'm sorry, sometimes my body takes over and weird stuff happens. Don't—don't say anything to Eva, okay? It's not a big deal."

Now Allison giggled, and the anxiety thrumming through Lennox's veins slowed. She didn't want her new friend to think she was losing her mind. "Are you one of those people who laughs at funerals? I read about it in psych: 'Nervous laughter is a defense mechanism against emotions that make us feel vulnerable.'"

Lennox breathed. "So you don't think I'm a freak?"

"Oh, I one hundred percent think you're a little left of center, but that's why I like you. Eat your pizza, okay?"

⸻

Lennox balanced her pizza on her lap while she flipped channels on the couch. Her laptop was open, and she glanced at it occasionally, rolling her eyes at the slew of pop-up ads on the screen and commercials on the TV.

At half past nine, Lennox's phone rang.

"Hey, Dad."

"Hey, daughter. What's up?"

"Wild house party, dancing girls, naked men...you know, the usual. Oh, and lots of drugs and booze."

"Sounds like you're making yourself right at home."

Lennox snorted. "Always. I'm watching TV and eating pizza. It's even something educational."

"That's my smart kid."

"How's work? Anything gnarly come in?"

Lennox could hear the beeps and muffled conversations on her father's end of the phone. "Kidney stone, broken toe. Nothing too major."

Lennox licked her lips. She wanted to ask again about the blond girl, if there was anyone who looked like her who could have been in a car accident, but her mind kept ticking, pulling her back. *You're normal, everything is normal. Don't worry your dad about something stupid.*

"Just wanted to check in and tell you I love you and to get to bed at a reasonable hour."

Lennox glanced at the clock. "I could tell you the same thing. What time are you off?"

"Right around three. Don't worry, I won't wake you. Love you, bug."

"Love you too, Dad."

Lennox hung up the phone, and even with the din of the TV and the hurricane of ads on her laptop screen, the silence was deafening. She wondered what it would be like if her dad were home and Mom were around, if there were siblings and bedtimes and fights for the bathroom. Usually, Lennox didn't have a problem staying home alone, especially in these newer houses with alarm systems and front-yard lights that flipped on every time a moth flew by, but tonight was different. Every time she closed her eyes, she saw the girl from the road, she heard the thump of her body. Every time she breathed, she heard a sinister voice rumbling in her head, reminding her that this was how mental illnesses like schizophrenia started, that her mother had once been fine and sane and purposeful until the voices had started calling to her.

Lennox went around the house, checking locks and flicking off lights. It was a routine she had learned from her dad.

No.

She lost her breath as a memory bubbled up. She had learned the routine from her mother.

Lennox had still been young, and Mom had still been there, humming the chorus to "Walking on Broken Glass."

Lock, touch, lock.

She could see her mother's fingers on the brass locks of that old house a thousand miles away, clutching Lennox's as her mom sang the routine like a nursery rhyme: Lock the door. Touch the lock, lock again.

Step away, double-check.

Lock, touch, lock.

Paranoid, anxious, fearful.

There were murderers, rapists, robbers outside.

Lennox remembered the muffled voices when she had gone to her room that night. Her father saying that her mother was scaring Lennox. That Lennox would grow up fearful and paranoid too. That there was no one out there—the demons were all in her head.

Lennox slid the lock closed, touched it, slid it open, locked it again.

Lock, touch, lock.

There was something serene and relaxing in the motions, in the routine. A closeness to her mother. When Lennox caught her reflection in the sliding glass door, she was jarred by another memory.

It had been in Detroit, or maybe D.C., before she had been able to see her therapists online. Another nondescript doctor's office where a therapist reassured her that there was nothing wrong with her and they were just bringing her in for a checkup.

"Like a tune-up for your car," the doctor said, her smile thin and well meaning but her tone setting Lennox on edge.

"I'm not a car," Lennox had whispered under her breath.

"So, tell me about your routines."

Lennox gritted her teeth. "I get up, brush my teeth, take a shower, eat breakfast."

This doctor cocked her head and pursed her lips, and Lennox was sure she wanted to sigh. "You know the routine I'm talking about, Lennox. Your dad mentioned—"

Lennox stiffened. Her dad was her ally, her partner, and he had betrayed her.

"The locks, Lennox."

"It's not a routine, it's a safety protocol."

"You know you only have to lock a door once."

The ugly mauve chair was uncomfortable.

"You don't need to double-check that it's locked."

Lennox swallowed.

Lock, touch, lock.

Her mother's doctors called them symptoms, disorders, hallucinations. But for Lennox, they were reality.

Lock, touch, lock.

What if I'm going crazy?

Lennox stepped back from the door, willing herself to cross the hardwood floor, to skip the two ground-floor windows, to not triple-check the front door. She didn't hallucinate. She wasn't schizophrenic.

This is how it started with Mom…

Lennox busied herself around the house, scrubbing the bowls stacked on the counter and dropping them into the dishwasher, folding the dish towels, gathering the mail and magazines scattered on the coffee table.

She paused at a catalog addressed to Wilomina Shaeffer DeLuth, smiling at the alter ego she had created on a desolate stretch of highway in Buffalo. She remembered signing the fake name in a motel's guest book, the way her father had raised his eyebrows and signed the name Bertram Howard

Shaeffer DeLuth III on the line underneath. Bertram and his daughter Wilomina sipped Cokes by the bleak pool until they shook those carefree personas off, picked up the keys to their new rental, and locked the door behind them.

Lock, touch, lock.

EIGHT

"You're coming over, right?" Eva asked the next day.

It wasn't so much a question as a command, and Lennox tried not to squirm in her seat. Eva's face was open and her brows were raised. If Lennox went to her house and hung out like normal girls did, what would that be like? She wanted to eat popcorn and talk about boys and maybe trade clothes— things she had seen in movies—but her jaded mind went to what she knew best: packing boxes, slamming the car door, driving away with another city in the rearview mirror. She had spent her life honing her disconnect skills, but there was something about the earnestness in Eva's face, the way she and Allison had embraced Lennox from day one, that made Lennox not just want but need to feel normal, connected, included. She would deal with the pain of driving away and never seeing her friends again later.

"Yeah," she said with a slow smile.

Lennox pulled her car to the curb and put it in park, glancing down at her phone one last time to check the address.

The looming house in front of her was Eva's: 1527 Lupin, a white two-story with carefully tended plants in complementary colors and an amoeba-shaped lawn that shone cartoon green in the fading light, giving no indication that California had been in the throes of a drought for the last forty years. The house was out of a sitcom where the family was perfect and the dog was shaggy and every issue was solved within thirty minutes and flanked by catchy theme music and a laugh track.

Lennox slung her backpack over her shoulder and carefully stuck to the gravel walkway, not wanting to get her single-parent/nomadic-teen vibes all over this happily-ever-after. Her heart thudded, and she tried to clear her throat, tried to remind herself that the majority of the country was like her: broken family, too-small sneakers, just barely getting by. This Norman Rockwell still life was the other.

Then why did she feel so off?

Eva was at the door before Lennox knocked, her smile enormous, the mauve streaks in her hair so fresh they looked neon.

"I love it," Lennox said, reaching out.

Eva twirled. "Thanks. Come in. Mom!" she howled over her shoulder. "Lennox's here."

A woman who could have been Eva's twin—right down to the too-bright mauve streaks in her hair—stepped out of the kitchen, wiping her hands on a towel. She smiled and held out a hand, touching Lennox softly on the arm.

"You must be the famous Lennox. I can't believe we haven't met yet. Eva can't stop talking about how cool you are."

Before Lennox could answer, this woman engulfed her in a hug that was surprisingly rough for how delicate her frame was. "I've heard so many great things about you. Welcome home. You can call me Tess, or you can call me Mom. Everyone does."

Eva rolled her eyes and groaned. "No one does, Tess. Can you just bring us some snacks?"

Tess cocked her head, and Eva rolled her eyes again.

"Please," Tess said with an eyebrow raised.

Eva turned to Lennox. "There she is. Momming again. Come on, let's go to my room. Allison is already up there, probably trying on everything I own."

Lennox took one last look around, drinking in the normalcy of the scene. Tess was already back in the kitchen, upending a bag of potato chips into a bowl and shaking her hips to whatever the smart speaker on the countertop was playing. There was an overflowing "family work board" pinned with permission slips and old photographs showing Eva and her sisters in that very kitchen, grinning while making pancakes or covered with chocolate ice cream. Someone had a soccer game at five, and there was 10 percent off a family meal at Pizza Guy. Every inch of the kitchen was rooted in togetherness and constancy; everything from the magnets on the fridge to the *Virginia Is For Lovers* mug on the counter said that this was what life was about, and the warmth and comfort left a hole in Lennox's heart. If she tried, she could vaguely remember a kitchen like this at a house she'd once lived in, with matching plates and a fridge full of food and photos and drawings taped to the cabinets. *That* house hadn't felt temporary. That house had painted walls and two cars in the garage.

"Are you coming, Lenn?"

It wasn't really a nickname, but it still made Lennox smile. She felt like she was part of something here.

A part that doesn't belong.

That voice niggled in the back of her head, the one that followed her from house to house and school to school, reminding her that she was a rolling stone and that being alone and unattached was the only way to avoid pain.

"Would you mind running these up?"

Tess was holding out the bowl of chips on a tray, a matching bowl of dip nestled in the center.

"No problem," Lennox said.

"There's the girl of the hour!" Allison was standing in Eva's enormous walk-in closet with a dress thrown over her head and another two in each arm. "I'm shopping. Ooh, chips! Don't you love Eva's mom?"

"Ugh, guys, she's so annoying. She's all 'please' and 'thank you' and 'what's the tea?' or whatever. She's, like, a thousand."

"Did I hear my lovely daughter calling me?" Tess was in Eva's doorway, that same sweet smile on her face. Lennox's eyes widened and she went red from head to foot.

"I brought you soda. Just remember to bring everything downstairs when you're done, okay? And I'll order pizza right after Ollie's soccer game. So, what are we talking about in here?"

Eva jutted out one hip. "We're talking about how I never get any privacy because you had to have thirty kids and be all up in my business because you lost your youth or whatever."

Tess's smile didn't falter "Isn't she a gem? Is it any wonder I took one look at her and decided to have three more kids?"

Allison laughed. "You've got it easy, Eva. Your mom is actually cool. My mom is all 'honor your commitment to school,' and my dad is all 'those are underwear, not shorts.'"

Lennox snort-laughed and slapped a hand over her mouth, causing the rest of the room to erupt in giggles.

"What about you, Lennox? I know your dad is all 'peace out, save the whales,'" Allison said.

"That's not my—" Lennox wrinkled her nose and thought about her dad's entire wardrobe, which consisted of scrubs and every free *Save the __* shirt he had ever encountered. "Oh yeah, that's pretty spot on."

"And your mom?" Tess asked.

Lennox gritted her teeth in a smile she hoped wasn't as repulsive as it felt. If she tried, really focused, she could remember a few good things about her mom—a picnic here, a push on a swing there—but it wasn't easy. Her dad was the fixture, and her mom had flitted in and out, either a lump in bed at

noon or a manic flurry of pink toys and cookie bakes that
lasted until dawn. Lennox could remember the sour-tinged
cut of her voice, the way she had snapped and apologized,
then just snapped and stopped apologizing. Lennox had been
her constant agony, and Lennox's dad hadn't been any better.
They had never been quiet enough when Mom had one of
her headaches, never appreciative enough when she'd woken
them up for a movie at three a.m. When Lennox was six, her
father explained that her mother was sick in her brain, that
her choices got a little wonky and messed up sometimes, but
that the medication would make it all better. And it had, for
a while. Lennox could remember her mother showing up at
recitals and school meetings, wearing clothes instead of pajamas, being funny and smart. She'd made healthy meals and
smiled a lot and done yoga and sung out loud until the one
day she hadn't. And Lennox couldn't really remember if her
mom had left the bed or if they had left the house after that,
and then suddenly it was just her and her dad and that round
dining table with the notches and their whispered family history, and her mother wasn't around anymore. At first, her
dad had talked about her and tried to make it normal. He
had brought gifts "from" Mom, but Lennox had seen them
on sale at the Rite Aid. Cards had come on her birthday,
and then around her birthday, and then not at all because
they were in a different state, a different time zone, and her
father had forgotten to talk about Mom. So Lennox learned
to forget too.

"She's…" Lennox shrugged, looking at her sneakers striking black against Eva's stark white carpet. "She's in Virginia." She cleared her throat. "She's at a medical facility."

"Oh, like a doctor?" Tess filled in.

"Ugh, Mom, you are so gross. Stop prying!"

Relief that Lennox hadn't known she was waiting for flooded over her. "Yes, exactly. She's a doctor at a big medical facility in Virginia."

"Is that how your parents met? Mom was a doc, Dad was a nurse?" Allison waggled her eyebrows. "That's super hot, all *Grey's Anatomy* or whatever."

Eva gagged. "Ugh, no offense. Old people dating just grosses me out."

"Now, now," Tess said, eyeing Lennox with a stare that said she wasn't wholly convinced.

Lennox looked away, doing her best to focus on Eva's bedroom, to find some way to steer the conversation to sneakers or homework or—

"What is that?"

Lennox's chest tightened and she felt the blood pounding in her temples. There was a heap of clothing on the floor of Eva's closet, discarded dresses, a single shoe, and a thick swath of long blond hair. Lennox started to blink, the walls closing in on her.

"Is that a person?"

She could hear the hysteria rising in her voice, could see Allison's and Eva's eyes widen. In molasses-slow motion, Eva picked her way through the room and grabbed a handful of the blond hair, holding up an enormous wig.

"This thing?" She pulled a face. "I don't even know how it got here."

"It's the wig from your sister's Supergirl costume, and it should have been put away for the year." Tess took the wig from Eva. "I don't suppose you need it for anything?"

"Gross, no. It looks less like a wig and more like a cocker spaniel. Take it out back and burn it."

Tess rolled her eyes and left the room.

Allison nearly pounced on Lennox. "Oh my gosh, snap out of it! You look like you've seen a ghost!"

Lennox's heart started to beat again. She licked her lips, shame burning her cheeks. "It's just a wig. I freaked out over a wig." She dropped her head into her hands. "I am losing it!"

Eva threw her arm around Lennox. "Luckily, we still love you."

"Okay," Allison said, standing, "I'm borrowing these three dresses and these shoes. And this purse. Cool?"

Eva shrugged, dropped a handful of chips into her mouth. "You know we're going to a baseball game, right? I am certainly not one to thumbs-down a glow up, but raw silk and metal bleachers are a no-go."

Allison cocked a hip. "Not for tonight. And it's not a game, it's an exhibition. Season is already over. This is where they show off their skills."

"We're going to a baseball game?" Lennox asked.

Allison pressed a hand against Lennox's forehead. "Are you feeling okay? Maybe the wig scared you out of your senses, but we already talked about this." She pursed her lips. "Today at lunch? I think it went something like, 'There's a game tonight,' followed by, 'Okay, let's go.'"

Lennox's mind raced. She had sat with the girls at lunch— hadn't she? In the dimming twilight, it seemed like she hadn't been to school in hours or days, but she nodded anyway, slapping a palm against her forehead and sighing, "I totally forgot!" with a smile she didn't really feel.

She laughed with Allison and Eva even as heat pricked the back of her neck, that tiny shadowy voice in her periphery whispering that forgetfulness was another warning sign.

"Here." Eva placed a rhinestoned PHS baseball cap her head, straightening her bangs in the mirror. "Do you like baseball?"

"Not even a little bit."

"Do you like Owen Rossum?"

Lennox felt a bloom of color in her cheeks, and Eva and Allison shrieked, both flopping on the bed in front of Lennox. "You totally like him!" Eva said, pointing.

"I don't even know him!"

"He walked you to class," Allison needled.

"We were both going to class and walking in the same direction."

"Together!" Eva yelled. "You're practically soul mates."

Lennox rolled her eyes.

Allison straightened, hands on hips. "So you don't want to go to the game, then?"

Lennox pinched her lips together, then grabbed the hat off Eva's head and fixed it on her own. "Oh, I'm going. Didn't I ever tell you how much I love baseball?"

"Excellent. But Lennox, you have to change. Step into my office." Eva yanked open her closet door again.

"Eva's so-called terrible mom is a total fashionista and buys Eva everything she wants. It's amazing."

Eva's eyes flashed as she looked over her packed closet, and Lennox was almost sure she saw something like sadness in them.

"Your mom is all right," Eva told Allison.

Allison rolled her eyes and snorted. "I'm like ninety percent sure that the entire reason my mother had me is so I could go to Stanford, become a doctor, and outshine my auntie Pearl's perfect twins. I'm not so much a child as a bet."

Lennox wasn't sure if she should laugh or offer her condolences, but Allison just pointed to the closet. "Go, find something. Be amazing."

"I—" Lennox opened her mouth and shut it again, looking into the closet. "I don't think anything in there would fit me. Besides, I'm kind of..." She gestured to herself, to her uniform of an oversized hoodie and jeans.

"Lies," Eva said, pushing her aside. "You just need to find the right thing. Like this." She pulled out a coral chiffon evening dress with a beaded belt.

"Totally," Allison said, mouth full of chips. "I can see you wearing that to coffee."

Allison and Eva exchanged looks and exploded into laughter. "No, this is perfect for cutting the lawn."

"Do you have anything that's not beaded or sequined?" Lennox said, laughing despite being draped in something that looked like the queen's curtains.

"See, Lennox? You fit right in!"

Lennox paused, knee-deep in Eva's closet and wearing half a beaded evening gown. There were chip crumbs all around them, and Eva began rolling Lennox's long hair into elaborate buns while Allison hobbled across the room in a pair of over-the-knee stiletto boots. The scene could have been out of a movie or a normal teenager's day.

And in that moment, Lennox wanted nothing more than to stay there in San Jose. She knew she would give anything, do anything to keep this feeling of inclusion and normalcy at any cost, because it was everything she had been missing going from house to house and school to school. Here, Lennox felt good. She felt accepted. She didn't even think about that night, about that girl, about the terror in her eyes, because here, she was part of something. And up until this moment, Lennox had no idea that was the one thing she'd always wanted.

NINE

Lennox blinked in the flood of stadium lights and made her way behind Allison and Eva as they beelined to a free bleacher.

"People actually go to these things? I thought that only happened with Texas football and stuff."

Allison looked over her shoulder. "It doesn't hurt that our boys' team is undefeated."

"And lots of their uniforms are too tight," Eva said with a salacious grin.

"I'm kind of loving this," Lennox said once they were seated with snacks and a fuzzy blanket over their knees. "So, what exactly is going on? And which one are we?"

Eva socked her in the shoulder. "Check your hat. We're the red, white, and blue; see the white uniforms? And I have absolutely no idea what's going on, except that guy is going to throw the ball to the guy with the bat and then he'll swing it, theoretically hitting said ball."

Lennox nodded and counted off on her fingers. "Guy, bat, ball. Got it."

"Let's go, Owen!" Allison yelled, cupping her hands around her mouth. "You've got this, Mustangs!"

"Sounds like someone is into this," Lennox said.

Allison didn't respond, and Eva bumped Lennox. "Yeah, Allison is weirdly sporty. Like, she actually knows all the players and their positions."

Allison groaned. "Baseball is our national pastime. And also, my dad was a major leaguer." She grinned and blew a pink bubble with her gum, then popped it. "I've been on the pitch since I was in utero."

Eva dropped her voice. "I don't know what any of those words mean. But my little brother is on the team too. Number twelve. First sophomore to make varsity. My mom isn't proud at all."

She pointed to the bottom bleacher, where Eva's mother was perched, wearing a number twelve jersey and waving a PHS pennant.

"So basic," she groaned.

Lennox shifted on the bleacher. Eva and Allison had talked to her into a pleated white miniskirt with red stitching and a royal blue tee that Eva insisted should be tied above Lennox's belly button. Lennox had refused that part but was mildly impressed by how she looked in something other than torn jeans and a hoodie. Eva and Allison had dressed up for the game too, and Lennox was glad. They looked like PHS superfans but cool, and even better for Lennox: they looked like everyone else at the game, like they belonged there.

She tipped a handful of popcorn into her mouth and looked around. The stadium lights were huge and bathed the whole field in daylight, but the school buildings were black and daunting behind her. Across the field, there was a chain-link fence and a swath of trees so choked, Lennox couldn't see anything else.

"What's back there?" she asked, gesturing with her chin.

"Percolation ponds. At least, I'm pretty sure they're still there. Are the perc ponds still back there, Allison?"

Allison's eyes were fixed on the game, and she didn't respond. Eva shrugged. "I don't know, it's just this weird stretch behind the school. Some ugly trees and these little ponds. I've heard people fished there, but the fish are radioactive or poisonous or something, and I'm pretty sure at least a couple of people have been murdered there or drowned there or kidnapped there or left there to die. Maybe someone lost control of their car or something?" She shrugged again. "Who knows? Chocolate?" She shook a box of Junior Mints.

Lennox frowned. "You guys seem to have a lot of spots where people drop dead or get hijacked by groups of people for nefarious purposes, don't you?"

Eva offered her toothy smile. "Yeah, and for homecoming, we decorate that whole back fence with streamers and posters. Come on! All of that is just rumors. Just something seniors tell the freshmen to freak them out and keep them in line year after year. It's a fun tradition. Besides, it's not like anything interesting ever happens here anyway. We have to keep the magic alive somehow."

"And teen murder certainly is magical."

Eva upturned the box of Junior Mints into her mouth. "Not always teens. Legend has it a cement worker in Sunnyvale was a serial killer and encased all his victims in blocks set into the sidewalk. Pretty certain they were all over eighteen."

"Well, that's refreshing. I'm going to go grab a Coke. You guys want anything?"

"One for me, please. And one more of these." Eva held up the Junior Mints box. "This one has a hole in it." She grinned, chocolate smearing her teeth.

Allison snorted. "You look like you're missing a tooth. Hey, isn't that your dad over there?"

Eva seemed to snap to attention, her eyes cutting toward the parking lot, where a dark figure leaned against one of the lampposts, arms crossed in front of his chest. He had a baseball cap pulled low over his eyes and red-and-blue windbreaker on.

"Guess your dad is pretty proud too," Lennox quipped, noticing both the jacket and hat had team logos.

Eva shook her head slightly. "He shouldn't be here," she murmured. She started to stand up, but Allison gripped her arm.

"Don't. You'll just make it worse. You can barely see him over there." Allison's voice was low, and Lennox couldn't tell if she was trying to hide what she was saying from Lennox or from everyone else in the bleachers.

Lennox wanted to ask what was going on. This guy didn't fit into Eva's perfectly curated house with the overcrowded calendar and pizza coupons.

Lennox looked at her friend, confused. "Is everything okay?" she asked, crouching down next to her. "Do you need me to do something?"

"No." Allison shook her head, smiling sweetly. "How about you just get Eva that Coke?" she said.

There was an awkward beat of silence before Eva nodded and whispered, "Yes. Thanks, Lennox."

"Sure." Lennox stood slowly, trying not to gape at the man in the darkness. A loud cheer came from the crowd, and everyone around them stood up, cheering—including a girl who caught Lennox's eye.

She was at the edge of the bleachers, hat pulled low on her head, blond hair tumbling down her back, and Lennox zoomed in on her, her heart clanging like a fire alarm.

It was her.

Her mannerisms. The way she spread out her arms, fingers splayed as she balanced, walking down the bleachers.

"Hey!" Lennox called, waving.

Allison turned to Lennox. "Do you know her?"

"That's her," Lennox breathed. "The girl from the other night."

The blond took a step down, and Lennox almost lost her in

a sea of red-and-blue baseball caps Lennox took the bleacher stairs two by two, not sure if Allison or Eva was behind her but not caring. She kept her eyes fixed on the blond ponytail, on the girl shimmying through the crowd.

"Wait," Lennox wailed, her voice immediately swallowed up by a cheer from the fans. "Excuse me, excuse me." She tried to push through the crowd, everyone on their feet and pressing together, shoulder to shoulder, squeezing Lennox out. "I need to get through!"

A couple in front of her turned and scowled but let her through just in time to see the blond step onto the dirt track and round a corner toward the snack shack.

"Hey, wait!" Lennox called, her sneakers crunching on the gravel at the bottom of the bleachers. "I just want to talk—"

She turned the corner, and three teens stared up at her, lips pulled down into frowns. An older couple blinked, and Lennox could feel the heat burn her cheeks.

"Did you see—a blond girl?"

Two of the girls in the threesome looked down at Lennox, and Lennox realized they were both blond—but not the girl she was following.

"Long hair. Wearing a baseball hat?"

"A baseball hat at a baseball game?" one of the girls trilled. "How very original."

Lennox's eyes caught on something then, a slash of bloodred lying in the grass. She snatched it up.

A baseball hat.

She stared at it, willing it to have some identifying information attached: a name, a phone number, a short note about how the owner had been on Hicks Road two nights ago.

"Lennox?"

She turned, eyeing Eva and Allison in front of her.

"Whose hat is that?"

Lennox wanted to say it belonged to the blond girl. It belonged to the blond girl who had disappeared, just like she had disappeared on the road that night. Lennox's heart started to thud, her tongue going heavy in her mouth. A fleeting image of her mother, disheveled, rambling, played in her mind like a warning—or a premonition. Lennox looked at her friends' concerned faces and back at the hat in her hand.

"I don't know," she said, ice water filling her veins.

Lennox looked around her. Her *friends* who had been there that night, her *friends* who wouldn't lie to her.

Lennox chewed the inside of her lip. *Great, I finally make some cool friends and then I immediately crack up. At a high school baseball game, no less.*

Her mind flashed back to her mother, to the lie Lennox had told, and she saw her mother in a white coat with an easy smile and a clipboard. A respectable, contributing member of society, like Lennox herself. And then the image dissolved into a dark gravelly road and the cackling voices of Lennox's so-called friends and the girl in the headlights.

Not real, Lennox thought.

Not real, she heard her mother say. Only her mother

wasn't a doctor now. Her white coat was a bathrobe, and she held no clipboard, just a single index finger pressed against her lips. "Don't talk to her," Lennox's mother said. "She's not real."

Lennox dropped the baseball hat on the edge of the snack shack counter and forced a smile. She wasn't going to crack up. Not now, not ever.

"We should go back to the game."

Allison took the lead, whistling as the crowd cheered, and Eva took Lennox's arm, the two falling back.

"Hey," she whispered. "About my dad? It's no big deal, but"—Eva locked eyes with Lennox—"thanks for being cool. Parental stuff can be so..."

Lennox felt her lips quirk up into a grin. "Weird? Hard? Frustrating? Embarrassing? Yeah, I don't know anything about that."

"You know something, Lennox Oliver? You're kind of cool."

TEN

Lennox had second period open since her schedule still wasn't finalized, so she slipped into the library when Eva and Allison went to class. She pushed open the heavy glass doors, shivering in the air conditioning that was obviously set to blizzard. Allison's words from the previous night still played in her head, and she was mad at herself for not being able to shrug the incident off, for not being able to be silly and carefree with her friends at the baseball game. But a feeling of dread had taken hold in her belly, an overwhelming sense that she was overlooking something, and try as she might, she couldn't shake it.

She made a beeline for contemporary fiction, fingers walking over the bright spines of books by her favorite authors. These were the kinds of books she'd read from state to state and house to house. They were about people facing insurmountable odds but always reaching their happy endings.

Not one of them had a dented car on the cover or a confused-looking heroine who realized 280 pages in that she had hit a log and her previous thirty-two chapters of stewing and imagining how she would look in prison garb were for naught. Lennox sighed, her mind wandering. When she turned, an entire table of kids was staring at her, mouths pursed, not one of them looking friendly or open. Each one looked more annoyed than the last, more accusing, and her mind raced: What had she done to disturb them? Had she groaned out loud, had her sneakers squeaked, was the roiling in her belly really that loud?

She blinked at them as another girl walked up, her long blond hair fuzzy and disheveled, her wide blue eyes empty orbs. She had a gash on her forehead that started at her part, red blood flecks like snowflakes on strands of gold. When she smiled, Lennox could see that her teeth were broken, and the lip that curled up was mottled purple and angry red. Her mouth and those broken teeth were covered in blood. It dripped down her chip in a thin rivulet, staining her button-up shirt and the shoulder of the guy she stood behind. Lennox's stomach lurched; her knees buckled, and she tried to scream. Nothing came out but a weak, strangled sound, and now everyone really was looking at her, including Owen, who poked his head out of the stacks. His eyes went wide when he saw Lennox, shoulder blades pressed against a rack of romance novels, knuckles white on the edges of the shelves.

"Are you okay?" he hiss-whispered.

Lennox couldn't blink, could feel the sheen of sweat on her forehead.

"She—she—"

But "she" wasn't there.

There was only a table with four students looking at her like she had grown a second head, and the one at the corner who had just had a dribble of blood on his shoulder a second ago was leaning down and whispering something to the brunette next to him.

No blond girl.

No gaping wounds, no rivers of blood.

"She was right there," Lennox said, her voice barely above a whisper.

"Lennox?" Owen asked again.

He came around the stack and pried her hand from the shelf; she leaned against him gratefully, her whole body under his control as she slumped.

"I'm sorry, I'm just—" *Seeing things.*

I'm seeing things.

But she was so real—

Lennox could see the girl's feet in her white Chuck Taylors, the toes filthy, covered in drops of bright red blood. *Did I actually see that?*

"When was the last time you ate? You look...don't take this the wrong way, but you look like death."

Lennox pressed her lips together and tried to smile, tried to force herself to act normal as she reminded herself where she was. Library. School. San Jose, California. Where dead people didn't just appear.

"No, I'm fine, I just…" She tried to sound nonchalant, but the words were churning in her head, and her mind refused to pick one.

She tried to take a step and fell headfirst into a display of yearbooks, cover after glossy cover of Mustang horses in various angry stances with steam shooting out of their nostrils tumbling on top of her. Lennox fell to the ground, two yearbooks cracked open in front of her, breaking her fall.

"Oh my God, Lennox!" Owen bent down and wrestled a bottle of water from his backpack, offering one strong arm to pull her up and pressing the open bottle to her lips.

"Take a sip, come on."

She didn't know if it was the chill of the water, the sharp edge of the yearbook in her back, or Owen's warm brown eyes, but Lennox snapped back to the here and now, to the incredible embarrassment of lying on a pile of yearbooks in the school library.

"Wow," she said, feeling heat singe her cheeks and the tops of her ears. "I feel…dumb."

"No, no." Owen crouched down next to her, slid aside a 1957 yearbook, and sat down. "This is totally normal. Lots of us fall headlong into book displays looking for a nice place to sit while we read about"—he snatched a book that was lying open, his eyes scanning—"what sophomores were concerned about in 1981." He dropped his voice into a gruff whisper and Lennox couldn't help but smile. "It was dating and the Cold War, bee tee dubs."

"Bee tee dubs?"

"By the way." He furrowed his brow and rested the back of his hand gently on Lennox's forehead. "You take one of those things to the head?"

Lennox wanted to say something smart, something that would erase the last twenty minutes, but all she could do was lean into Owen's hand and say, "That feels nice. Are you thinking of going to med school?"

"Yes, following in the footsteps of dear old Mom."

"She's a doctor?"

"No." Owen started closing the yearbooks scattered around Lennox. "She's the chief of police. But she can remove a splinter like no one's business. Did you want to check any of these out or stack them up to make a podium?"

Again, a blaze of heat slid down Lennox's spine. Owen was cute, cocky, and snapping yearbooks closed all around her, doing his best to make her feel less—

Lennox's saliva went sour.

The color photograph of the smiling girl in front of her could have been the girl from her vision.

From your imagination.

From that night.

She was grinning, her blond hair pulled over one shoulder and brushed until the light from the camera flash bounced off it.

"Wait—" She grabbed the book before Owen could close it. "This girl." She pointed. "Do you know her?"

Owen slid the book back from Lennox, studied the photo,

and nodded. "Yeah, that's Paula Barnes. Track and field star, president of Future Homemakers of America, delivered a nice heifer, apparently."

"What?" Lennox leaned over, recognizing Paula's butterfly collar, the clothes of the students surrounding her. "This is from the seventies."

"Seventy-seven, to be exact. Which means Paula's heifer is—"

"Hamburger."

Owen grinned. "I was going to say well digested." He pointed. "You're funny, Lennox. Now, tell me about"—he squinted—"Joe Iguazamo. Do you think he ever realized his dream of dancing on *Soul Train?*"

Lennox stood up, and Owen followed. "I can only hope so. So—"

"Shh!"

Lennox and Owen passed the table full of gawkers, and while Lennox went pale, Owen rolled his eyes, took Lennox by the elbow, and steered her outside. "Now we can talk without being shushed, and we can walk without fear of books attacking you." He grinned, and Lennox admired the easiness of his smile, the warmth in his gold-flecked eyes that made Lennox's stomach do a little double flutter. Somewhere in the back of her mind she wanted to talk about the accident, but somewhere even closer, she just wanted to hang on Owen's every word, to bat her eyelashes like a heroine in some swoony romance novel and find her happily-ever-after.

"I saw you at the baseball game the other night."

Owen's smile seemed bashful. "Yeah? You like baseball?"

"No. I mean, yes—I mean—"

"Owen! Good game last night, my man." A student clapped Owen on the back and grinned.

"Thanks, man."

When the other student moved on, Lennox asked, "So, do you know, like, everyone in this school?"

Owen shrugged. "I didn't know you." He pinned her with a stare. "I still don't really know you."

"What's to know? I run into things."

"With your body, with your car..."

Owen was still smiling that easy smile, but all the warmth that Lennox was feeling dissipated. "With my car?"

"That little dent. Sorry, did your parents give you grief?"

"No." Lennox shook her head, trying to shake off her angst, trying to force herself back to the normalcy of having a moment with a cute boy in the warm California winter sun. "No. It was just...tiny."

"Yeah, but, I mean, that's all I know about you. I'd love to learn more—"

The bell sounded, and doors opened all over the quad, students flooding out like a stampede of laughter and conversation.

"So, how about a date?"

Lennox felt herself swoon. Seven schools in five years, and all of them had cute boys with hot-chocolate eyes and easy smiles, but not one of those boys had ever asked her out.

"Yeah," she said with a nod that she hoped wouldn't betray her eagerness. "That sounds...cool."

Owen offered her one of those half smiles she had grown so fond of. "Cool."

ELEVEN

Lennox slipped into her desk in English class, leaning over to talk to Eva.

"I have a date," she whispered.

Eva looked over at her, her eyes widening. "Wait, what?"

"A date!"

"With an actual person?"

Lennox rolled her eyes and nodded. "Owen asked me out."

Eva's Coral Cutie lips dropped open into a surprised O. "Like, Owen Rossum?"

"Yes!"

"And you said yes?"

Lennox frowned. "Shouldn't I have?"

Eva turned to face her. "Absolutely you should have! Owen is, like...the cutest, hottest guy in the world. In our world. At school. He's all right, I guess, if you're into that relaxed-perfection kind of thing."

Lennox chewed her bottom lip, her joy deflating. "You

know his mom is the chief of police, right? That's a little...
nerve-wracking."

Eva nodded, her grin widening. "Not even! That's power,
baby. Maybe he'll take you out in a squad car."

"As much as I love being inconspicuous in a police car
with sirens and lights, I'm going to meet him there."

"You're driving?"

"I'm meeting him."

"Hello, feminist."

Lennox blew out a sigh. "Not being trapped in an enclosed
space with a guy I barely know is less about feminism, more
about intelligence."

"I'm all about being trapped with a guy I barely know in
an enclosed space. You watch too many true-crime shows."

"And I haven't been shoved in a trunk once."

Eva groaned. "You're missing out. But you have to tell
me everything."

Lennox was grinning even when Mrs. Harper shushed
them, her caterpillar brows rammed together in annoyance.
She had never had a friend to talk to, a boy to fawn over,
a date to prepare for. She had never felt as normal as she
did right now. She was part of the status quo; she was every
other teenager at every other high school who had friends
and maybe even a—she gulped, her stomach quivering
nervously—boyfriend.

As long as her dad didn't mess the whole thing up.

He was home when Lennox walked in from school,

wearing shorts and a T-shirt from the Greater Bethesda Fun Run that Lennox wasn't sure he'd ever run. He had on gardening gloves and was carrying a watering can.

"Where did that come from?" Lennox gestured to the can.

"Came with the house."

"The shorts too?" She smiled, and he cocked a brow.

"These are grade-A, one hundred percent new...circa ninety-nine. I could say the same about your sweatshirt."

"Neither this sweatshirt nor I was around in ninety-nine, but thanks for playing." She passed him and poured a bowl of Lucky Charms, then started picking out the marshmallows.

"I feel like I should say something fatherly about your choice of snack. So...just make sure you eat at least a few of the cereal parts to offset the marshmallows."

Lennox propped herself on the counter, resting her bare feet in the sink.

"Ew, ew, ew, Lennox Marie! Off the counter! I may not be the most nutritionally sound dad out there, but I'll be damned if I have to take my own daughter into work to patch a cracked skull or for sepsis in your gross feet. Here." He handed her the watering can. "Household chores are family chores. Come outside. The sunlight will be good for you."

Lennox rolled her eyes, wanting to slide into the easy rapport she had with her dad, but a little flick of anger burned there too. How long until they packed up and left this place as well? How long until the flowers they watered and tended became someone else's problem? She was tired of reliving this "happy family" diorama over and over again, pretending she loved the "new adventure" that came with each new house, each new school, pretending she didn't miss her mother and the life they'd had. Deep down, she wanted to know who her mother was now, because she couldn't just be that woman with the vacant eyes and the bathrobe knotted around her waist. She was once so vibrant and alive—*wasn't she?* It had been so long ago now since Lennox had seen her, and the good memories were starting to fray around the edges.

She cleared her throat as she followed her dad out to the front yard.

"Have you heard anything from Mom lately?"

"Hearing from her mother" generally meant the doctors' monthly check-ins, statements that were so clinical and cold that Lennox couldn't tell if they were talking about a person or a car.

Her father paused, and Lennox couldn't tell if he was considering what—or how much—to tell her, and that little tingle of annoyance flared up again. Her father seemed to treat her like an equal only when it was convenient for him.

He finished filling up the watering can and smiled at Lennox. "Nothing new, hon. Sorry."

Lennox kicked the ground. "Can we go see her some-time? It's been a really long—"

Lennox was surprised by the fierceness in her father's hug. "I am so, so sorry. I know this can't be easy for you."

Lennox stepped back and was surprised to find that she was crying and there were tears in her dad's eyes too.

"It's okay," she said.

"I'll see what I can do. Maybe we can arrange a trip over spring break or something."

Lennox wanted to believe him, but these trips never materialized. And the phone calls always seemed to come when Lennox was on her way home from school or had already gone to bed. Lennox's dad said it was because the hours at the facility were rigid and her mother's schedule was off, but Lennox often wondered if there was something else her father was keeping from her.

"Sure, Dad."

They worked in companionable silence until the sun started to set.

"Time to knock off. You have homework and I have to get ready for work."

"Hey, Dad," Lennox started.

He looked at her, eyebrows raised, one foot already on the steps.

She wanted to tell him about the date, about Owen, but she could tell he was already half at work, already calculating how long he had to shower and head out the door.

"Nothing," Lennox said finally. "I'll make you a sandwich to take."

Lennox waved to her dad as he disappeared into the garage, her heart starting to race. She closed the door behind him, took one step away, unlocked the door, then locked it again.

"I am not my mother," she whispered to herself, pressing her forehead against the closed door. But the second she closed her eyes, the girl from last night was there, a wry smile on her face as if she was teasing Lennox.

Am I real? the girl in her mind said. *Is this really happening?*

Lennox shook her head.

Did that night on Hicks really happen?

Lennox turned the lock and stepped through the garage door, pressing her fingers against the cold metal grill of her car. The puckered metal snagged her skin, a chip of blue paint flaking off in her palm. She wasn't sure if the damage—real and tangible—made her feel better or worse.

Inside, Lennox sat at her desk and rummaged through her drawer. When her hands settled on the black-and-white composition book she carried from state to state, she sighed. It was another "assignment" from her therapist: to write down bulleted lists whenever she felt overwhelmed. Supposedly, seeing a long list of "actions," "outcomes," and "next steps" would help guide her through whatever she was up against without triggering her anxiety while giving her an actionable plan.

She bit her bottom lip, picked up her pen, and wrote: *Action—I think I hit someone on Hicks Road.* Then: *Likely Outcome—Someone could be dead or injured (I'm responsible). I could go to jail (hit-and-run).* Finally: *Next Steps—*

Here, Lennox dropped her pen and rested her chin in her hands. What was she supposed to do? She groaned, picked up her pen, and turned to a fresh sheet of paper. Then she started again.

- *Action—I think I'm losing my mind. (Phantom blond girls, no one heard/saw anything on the road.)*
- *Likely Outcome—Everyone will find out / my dad will send me away / I can move into my mom's room at mental hospital.*
- *Next Steps—*

Lennox couldn't think of anything to write, but she knew what she had to do.

TWELVE

The last hint of twilight was being eaten by the inky black night when Lennox turned onto the road leading toward Hicks. Normally, she had trouble remembering much of anything, but it was as if her body was on autopilot, and even as the sweat beaded on her upper lip and her brain screamed at her to turn around, she kept her hands on the wheel, hugging the curves of the road as it edged the reservoir on one side, the tree-cluttered embankment on the other. There was something hanging from the tree just a few yards ahead, and Lennox felt her breath catch in her chest.

She slowed the car and flicked on her high beams, the swath of white-yellow light illuminating a mobile of tennis shoes strung over the power line. They were turning slowly, and Lennox's heart slammed against her chest, her mind calling up every horror movie where terrible people used the property of those they murdered as ominous warnings to others.

"Get a grip, Lennox! People have thrown shoes over power lines in every city you've ever lived in!"

She pushed the gas pedal as hard as she could until the shoes disappeared into the darkness behind her.

"Okay, okay," Lennox said to no one as she slowed her car, high beams still flooding the road. "I think this is right."

She leaned into a turn and rolled to a stop at a crossroads where the Hicks Road sign was bent on its pole.

This was the stop they had pulled up to when they'd left the party. She could hear the laughter of her friends, the light way they had talked and shoved each other, and every fiber of her being told Lennox to make a U-turn, head home, and sink into normalcy. She could forget that anything had happened that night. She could go about her life, a regular kid, and maybe she and her dad could even stay here in San Jose, where Lennox would have a regular group of friends and maybe a regular hangout spot. She wanted so badly to make it all go away.

Like you wanted to make your mom go away.

Lennox's saliva went bitter in her mouth.

I don't want her to go away, she thought, a sob tightening her throat. *I just don't want to* be *her.*

She rubbed her eyes, and the voice scoffed back, *You're on a desolate road in the middle of the night examining a crime that never happened. A girl that never existed.*

She heard her mom's singsong voice then, the riff of that

old Annie Lennox song, her mother drawing out the single word chorus: *Why...*

Lennox put her car in reverse and drove home, the Hicks Road sign lost in her rearview mirror.

"Where are we going?" Lennox asked when Eva linked arms with her after school the next day, directing her to Allison's parking spot.

"We're hazing you," Allison deadpanned. "Get in the car."

Lennox and Eva climbed in, and Allison pulled out of the student parking lot, making a right and merging into the clog of traffic in front of them. Lennox looked at her friends. "Should I be worried?"

"Yes," Allison said, overtaking the Prius in front of them.

"We're going to the mall!" Eva giggled.

"Traditional girl outing," Allison said, flicking on her blinker.

"This is hazing?"

Eva shuddered. "Shopping off the rack? Absolutely."

"What are we shopping for?" Lennox asked, clicking her seat belt on.

"The dance!" Eva groaned, like she couldn't believe it wasn't the first thing on Lennox's mind.

"Wait, there's a dance?" Lennox asked.

Allison and Eva linked arms with Lennox and pulled her to a dress shop. They pawed through racks of tulle and sequined evening gowns when Lennox sighed, found a chair, and sat.

"I'm trying these on!" Eva sang before locking herself in a dressing room.

"What's up, buttercup?" Allison wanted to know. "Sequins aren't your thing?"

"No," Lennox said, and then, after a long pause, "I just can't stop thinking about the girl in the road."

Allison groaned. "Lennox, you need to stop worrying. Nothing happened, and frankly, I'm getting tired of hearing you moan about it over and over."

Lennox opened her mouth and then closed it again.

"You got freaked out on a dark road. We all did." There was a hardness in Allison's eyes that Lennox hadn't seen before. "Drop it, okay?"

The was a beat of awkward silence before Eva crowed, "Stand back!" from the dressing room. She threw open the door wearing a floor-length ball gown that swallowed her tiny frame and looked like a wedding dress doubling as high-density housing. "You love?"

"It's a casual dance," Allison said, frowning.

"This is cashz'," Eva protested, hiking up her skirt and showing off her sneakers. "Casual footwear."

Lennox pressed her hand over her mouth, trying to suppress a smile. "I didn't even know there was a dance."

Allison frowned. "Wait, wait, wait. You are certain you hit a girl on a dark and twisty road in the middle of the night, but you aren't certain that there's a dance at our school in two weeks? Because there are posters everywhere, made by yours truly. Like, everywhere."

Lennox shrugged, feeling herself blush. "Sorry, I just didn't notice any posters."

Allison pointed. "Sorry doesn't cut it." She looked at Eva. "And neither does that dress. Go back."

"But wait, I missed something. What's going on?" Eva wanted to know.

Lennox rolled her eyes, and Allison took Lennox's long hair, coiled it into a bun, and plopped it on top of her head. "Lennox still thinks she ran someone over with her car, even though we were both there and saw nothing." She took a heavily rhinestoned pin and shoved it in the bun. "Voilà!"

Lennox's eyes went wide, her cheeks pinkening. There was a motherly looking woman in the store flipping through a rack of beaded shawls and two teenagers across the room who glanced up at Allison.

"Oh my God, Allison, shut up! I don't want the whole world knowing—"

"That nothing happened?"

Once Eva clicked herself back into the dressing room, Lennox leaned into Allison. "I know you think nothing happened, but I just can't shake this feeling." She shuddered, the overwhelming sense of unease settling back into her gut.

Allison's smile was soft. "Do you believe in ghosts, Lennox?"

Lennox took the rhinestone pin from her hair and put it

back on the display case. "No. Maybe? But don't try to tell me that you think I hit a ghost. I could buy a raccoon, but I felt something, Al. I know I did."

"And I'm not saying you're wrong. I'm just saying a lot of weird things happen on Hicks Road."

Lennox pursed her lips. "Druids? Witches?"

Eva poked her head over the dressing room door. "Look, I'm the only *real* local here, and I can tell you those are urban legends. Stupid stories from when our grandparents did stupid things on Hicks Road to when our parents did stupid things on Hicks and when we've done stupid things on Hicks. But..." She kicked open the dressing room door, an avalanche of peach tulle and sequins swallowing her frame. "Weird things happen on Hicks, and not *all* of them are legends." She held her palms up. "That's all I'm saying."

Lennox cocked an eyebrow. "So you're saying I didn't exactly hit a person or a ghost, but something weird happened, something weirder than me hitting an actual person who disappeared or who could have logically gone down the embankment where we couldn't find her because it was so dark? And who could have been injured, and who we just left for dead?"

Allison and Eva both nodded without missing a beat.

"I...don't think I buy that."

"Okay," Allison said, "how about this: if there was a girl who had gone missing, don't you think we would know about it? There would be a manhunt, or a...a girlhunt or whatever, and it would be all over the news. I mean, when that guy lost that dog that looked like the Star Wars guy, the whole town came together, and at least three stations aired the story."

Lennox nodded. "Even I know about Boba Fetch. But what about the girl in the bathroom who said her sister was missing?"

Allison shrugged. "Again, no flyers, no news, no nothing."

Eva slung a few more dresses over her shoulder. "You know what they say: the simplest explanation is usually the correct one." She held a dress in front of her and smiled. "This one has pockets!"

Lennox sighed. "I just don't think supernatural happenings are the simplest explanations."

Allison picked a crown from the display case and plopped it on her head, mugging for the mirror. "Suit yourself."

THIRTEEN

The sun was just starting to dip behind the trees when
Lennox pulled into her driveway, the T-shirt she'd bought
at the mall in a bag beside her. She hadn't found a dress—
Eva had found four—but she'd pretended not to care even
as she hoped that Owen would ask her to the dance. The
front door was unlocked, and Lennox's dad was barefoot,
stretched out on the couch, and watching the news through
barely open eyes.

"Hey, Dad."

He started, rubbing his eyes and clearing his throat. "Oh,
hey, honey. I was waiting for you to get home. Just watching—" He squinted at the television, where a coiffed reporter
in a windbreaker was talking about a rescue effort in the
"nearby town of Santa Cruz."

Lennox jutted her chin at the TV. "Where is Santa Cruz?"

Her father shrugged. "Apparently nearby. They are out
looking for a plane or a boat or a—"

Teenager?

Lennox shook off the thought. "Want spaghetti for dinner tonight?" she asked.

"I thought we could get some pizza. Maybe talk a little about your meeting, blow off some steam." He smiled, and Lennox stiffened.

"Meeting" was code for "therapy appointment," and "blowing off some steam" was her dad's nonchalant way of asking Lennox to tell him everything.

Deep down, she knew he just worried about her, but she could never avoid that little voice that whispered in the back of her head that he, just like her therapist, was waiting for the day the switch flipped. The day that Lennox went from looking like her mom to being her mom, cowering in corners, shouting at the top of her lungs, having conversations with people who weren't there.

Like the girl...

No. Lennox gritted her teeth. She wasn't seeing things. She didn't hallucinate.

"My meeting, right."

"Did you forget about it?"

She had, but she didn't want to let on. It was the fifteenth of the month, every month, and she usually started dreading the appointment three days before. But this time, she had forgotten.

Forgetfulness is one of the first symptoms, that little voice reminded her. Lennox flashed back to waiting at school while the cars in the parking lot filed out, the voices outside dying down when her mother forget to pick her up. She didn't know then—no one knew then—that it wasn't the mistake of an overburdened mother or traffic across town. It was the first sign of her mother's loosening grip on reality.

That's not happening to me.

Lennox was busy. She was having fun and hanging out with friends and getting to know Owen and her new school, and all of that was normal. Being a forgetful teenager was *normal.*

"No, uh, Dr. Hartzog had to cancel. That's why I went to the mall with my friends." She flashed a smile, knowing that her dad would find out soon enough that she was the one who didn't show. She imagined Dr. Hartzog making a tick in the "symptoms to watch out for" box on her chart. She would have to remember to call him first, make up some excuse that sounded normal.

"I'm just going to go change, okay?"

Once they were sitting on the couch, grease-stained paper plates in the trash, her dad leaned over, giving her a playful punch on the arm. "Come on, out with it. How is San Jose?"

"Less than terrible," Lennox said.

"It seems like you have friends to go places with."

"According to them, they were hazing me."

He put his arm around Lennox. "Just as long as you had fun."

She chewed her lip, then started.

"Hey, Dad, can I ask you something?"

Her dad turned around on the couch. "Anything, doll."

For some reason, Lennox needed to keep her distance. "It's...it's about Mom again."

She saw something flash in her father's eyes, a muscle twitch along his jawline as he swallowed. "You miss her, huh?"

Suddenly there was a lump in Lennox's throat, and she nodded, blinking quickly to bat back the tears. "Always. But...do you...when did Mom start to..." She busied herself playing with the fringe on a pillow. "See things?"

When Lennox looked up, her dad was right there in front of her, lips pressed in a thin line, his eyes soft.

"Are you worried about her?"

Lennox wanted to tell her dad that she was worried about herself. Even though she usually shared just about everything with her father, she couldn't get the words out. The idea that she might one day abandon him too, like her mom had, sat in her gut like a heavy black rock.

"Yeah."

"Your mom is a wonderful person. But she's sick. It happens, and it's no one's fault."

Lennox nodded. She knew this speech. She knew that her dad was going to take both of her hands in his and squeeze them gently. Then he was going to look into her eyes and tell her that it wasn't her fault, that her mother's illness had nothing to do with Lennox, and that even though Mom didn't say it anymore, she knew Lennox and loved her.

"She loves being your mom."

Lennox heard her father's voice crack, and a sob lodged in her throat too.

She loves being your mom because she knows you're sick too...

She tried to block out the voice, but it haunted her, always, in every state.

Lennox offered him a smile that was supposed to be reassuring, but behind it, all she could think about was her mother, when things had started to happen, when the focus in her bright blue eyes had dropped out and she looked right through Lennox, right through the ranch-style house and the overstuffed floral couch, and started to talk to people who weren't there.

When she was old enough, Lennox had taken her laptop under her covers and tapped out the words she had copied from the letter the hospital had sent her father: *acute schizophrenia.* The search engine popped out something like nine million results, but Lennox could remember the first one word for word: "Schizophrenia is a serious mental disease in which people interpret reality abnormally."

She saw the words now and gritted her teeth.

"I'm not like her," she mumbled out loud.

But the girl in the road...

Lennox pressed her eyes closed. "I saw her."

Did you?

Schizophrenia may result in some combination of

hallucinations, delusions, and extremely disordered think-
ing and behaviors that impair daily functioning and can be
disabling...

"When exactly did Mom...get sick?"

Lennox's father sucked in a breath, and Lennox waited, even though everything inside her told her to change the subject, offer ice cream, sing a song, do all the things she had done as a kid when her dad was sad, when he'd tried to hide the mist in his eyes, tried to smile against the frown.

"Not until about a year after you were born—not that your birth was a trigger or anything. She just... I mean, there were signs earlier, now that I look back. Little things, mostly. Then I just chalked them up to quirkiness." He smiled sadly. "I didn't know the signs back then. But it doesn't make your mother a bad person."

Lennox was gritting her teeth so hard her jaw began to ache. "No, she's not bad."

But you are, if you left a girl dead on the side of the road.

Lennox wanted to shake her head so hard the voices would fall out. She wanted to scream at them: *Am I seeing things, or am I a murderer, huh? Which is it?* But she knew that would only make things worse.

"Did these things start when she was..." She looked away, digging her thumbnail into the grooves of the old dining table, trying her best to seem nonchalant. "My age?"

Her dad blinked, and Lennox rushed on. "Just because I know that's often when it starts, in young adulthood. Or at least some of the signs." She studied the table again. "I mean, isn't that why I have the shrink brigade on Zoom?"

From the corner of her eye, Lennox could see her father staring at her as if considering what to say.

"Lennox, it's not a shrink brigade. I—we, remember? We both agreed that it would be a good idea for you to have someone consistent to talk to. Both about your questions about Mom and about our kind of different lifestyle." He smiled, but there was no mirth there. "I know it's not easy growing up without a mom—"

Lennox's eyes flashed, and she was surprised at the flame of anger that roared in her gut. "I have a mom."

"I know, I'm sorry. I meant not having a mom around for your day-to-day life. I definitely do the best I can, but we agreed that it would be nice to have that extra layer of—"

"Protection? Watchfulness?"

"Lennox, where is this coming from?"

Lennox sighed. "Nowhere. It's nothing. It's just that sometimes I wonder if these doctors are just waiting for me to...crack."

"Crack?"

"It's nothing, Dad."

"Lennox, they are not waiting for you to do anything. It's just an—"

Lennox shook her head. "I know, an extra ear to listen." She wanted to believe that was all her monthly shrink visits were, kind gestures from a father worried about his daughter and the nomadic lifestyle he impressed upon her. But sometimes Lennox couldn't shake the feeling that there was something more sinister going on, that she was some sort of live mine or ticking time bomb and everyone knew it. They were all just checking in, biding their time and comparing notes, waiting for that tick-tick-boom of schizophrenia.

The girl in the road flashed in front of her eyes, and Lennox blinked hard to get rid of her, the image burning into her mind.

Maybe she was already at *boom*.

"What age did it happen to Mom, Dad?"

Her father paused for a beat that seemed to take ages, and Lennox wondered if he was considering how to tell her that it had happened at exactly the age Lennox was now. That Lennox looked so much like her mom at that age, it was uncanny, and since she had her mother's eyes and her mother's talent for art, that it would only follow suit that she had inherited her mother's mental illness too.

"I don't remember, hon, honestly. Your mom and I were both so silly and weird in high school and college, who would have known?" He smiled, trying to lighten the mood, but it only made the rock in Lennox's gut feel heavier, more permanent.

"Okay," she said with a nod.

"Now, tell me the real reason why you need to know," her father said quickly.

Lennox locked eyes with her dad. "I just have this friend, and she thought she saw something."

"And?"

"And no one else saw it, so she was thinking that maybe...I don't know. It got me thinking that maybe she could have schizophrenia."

He smiled and rested his hand on Lennox's. "Well, my little armchair psychologist. There are a lot of reasons that someone might think they saw something they didn't."

"Like?"

"Trick of the eyes, trick of the light...ghosts." He grinned, and Lennox rolled her eyes.

"You are ever so helpful, Father."

"I do my best!"

Lennox was walking around campus in the too-bright sun, gripping her backpack as she tried to remember where her English class was. There was a hiss behind her, a *pit-pit-pit* coming from the window to her left. She tried to ignore it, tried to move toward Eva and Allison, who were waving at her from across the quad, but the *pit-pit-pit* was getting louder, more insistent, and Lennox's feet were leaden. Sweat beaded above her upper lip as Allison and Eva's waves grew more frantic and Lennox's body refused to react. She clawed at the cement, trying to move herself forward, but she was stuck.

Her own shriek woke her up, and she sat up, her sheets

twisted around her torso and sweat matting her hair to her forehead. Embarrassment flitted through her, and then she heard it again.

Pit-pit-pit, and then something that sounded like, "Hello?"

Lennox bolted to her bedroom window, and there she was—the girl from that night. Wide eyes, blond hair, her palms pressed against Lennox's window.

Lennox shook her head and reared back, tripping over her laundry and crashing to the ground. The girl in the window's eyes seemed to get bigger, rounded, and Lennox was sure she could see headlights behind her, a car about to mow the girl down.

"I'm dreaming, I'm dreaming, I must be dreaming."

Lennox looked around, her mouth opening and closing, and the girl stepped back from the window, her palms leaving slight marks in the condensation on the window.

"Wait!"

Lennox clawed her way to the window, but the girl had spun, was running away with her blond hair fanning behind her.

"Wait!" Lennox yelled again, picking her way out of her room and vaulting down the hall. She unlocked the front door and pulled it open hard, clearing the porch steps in one leap, her bare feet landing on the freezing concrete outside. The motion lights went on, flooding the entire front yard with harsh yellow light, and the girl was nowhere to be found.

"Hello?" Lennox asked, folding her arms in front of her chest to ward off the chill as she jogged to the side of the house. "Hello?"

She looked behind the bushes that surrounded her bedroom window, dropped to her knees, and crawled toward the garage. "Are you here?" she asked, unsure whether or not she wanted an answer. "Hello?"

Silence enveloped Lennox. The *pit-pit-pit* and the whisper were gone. The blond with the wide eyes, gone. Lennox rolled onto her bum.

She used her palms to push herself up, immediately snapping back when she felt the scatter of pebbles underneath her. She picked one up, rolled it in her palm. They were just pebbles from the flower beds in the yard, but these were scattered on the walkway.

Someone—something—was here.

Her stomach roiled and her hands shook as Lennox dropped to her knees and crawled toward the plate-glass picture window in the front room. She sucked in a shallow breath and raised herself up just enough to peek outside, certain she was going to come face-to-face with the blue-eyed girl scratching or pounding at the window, trying her best to get at Lennox.

Her heart thumped a thundering, powerful rhythm. The motion-sensor lights in the front yard were off, and the still bushes and lawn were bathed in dark blue shadows. No blond girl. No body, no person.

FOURTEEN

The sunlight beamed across Lennox and she squinted, her pounding head feeling like it was stuffed with cotton. The events of the night before came streaming back—the tapping on the window, the girl—and Lennox did her best to shake them off, to tell herself that she had to have been dreaming.

She dressed quickly and slid on her headphones, pushing the dial as far as it would go until the screaming of her favorite band drowned out the screaming in her head. By the time she was in the driveway, she had convinced herself that she was half in her head, half on the receiving end of a stupid prank. She sat in her car and locked the doors, giving herself a half second to breathe and recalibrate. She scanned the yard, her breathing normal until she saw the scattered pebbles by her bedroom window.

Pit-pit-pit.

She unlocked her door and kicked it open, ready to investigate, ready to tell herself there had been a mole, a squirrel, some other rock-throwing animal in front of her window, when the tiny piece of yellow paper floated down on her as if from the sky. She looked around, squinting at her driver's-side window, which was open a crack, then unfurled the paper, convinced she would see *HA HA* scrawled on it—a stupid sick joke from Allison or Eva. But the words scrawled on the paper weren't a joke. They were much, much worse. Written in tall, thick letters were the words *FIND ME.*

The girl.

She *saw* her.

"I know I did," Lennox said out loud.

The note was proof.

There was a girl, but there were no news reports, no missing teen posters, no vigils. *But maybe...* That voice started again. *Maybe no one misses her.* The thought set Lennox's teeth on edge. If she were to disappear after her father left for a shift, how long would be it before someone missed her? She thought of the days when her father clocked in at some ungodly hour while Lennox was still asleep, when she woke up to an empty house and come back to one, her dad either still at work or back in his room, black-out curtains drawn, dead to the world. Even when she'd been home, especially toward the end, Lennox's mother had barely left her room, so Lennox couldn't be missed. What if this girl's life was the same? What if she had parents who were there but not there?

Before she even thought about it, Lennox had her keys in her hand.

Lennox drove to Hicks Road with the radio a low murmur,

her heart hammering. Each time she turned, she envisioned someone following her: a Honda, a blue Toyota, a Prius with the emblem missing. They all seemed to be watching her, accusing her, knowing she was going back to the scene of the crime to find—*what?*

A body?

Her stomach lurched at the very idea, and the sweat on her palms stuck her hands to the wheel. Lennox had no idea how many people traveled Hicks Road. How long did it take to find a body, anyway? *Depends if anyone is looking for it.*

Lennox's stomach lurched, bile itching at the back of her throat.

I'm going to throw up, I'm going to throw up, I'm going to throw up.

She pulled into a gas station parking lot and kicked her door open, plunging her head between her knees and doing her best to breathe deeply, hoping she wouldn't barf. Sweat beaded across her cheeks, and when she sat up and glanced at herself in the mirror, she was shocked to see the tears rolling down her cheeks.

She didn't even know she was crying.

Lennox wiped her tears with the backs of her hands and pressed her fingertips to her cheeks. "Everything is fine," she said to her reflection in the rearview mirror.

Lennox tried to smile, but it came out like a grimace.

Remember not to smile like that in your mug shot.

Hicks Road looked far less sinister in the daylight. The

sunshine dappled the asphalt, and the trees lining the road were a lush and cheery green, giving way to wide-open spaces and jigs in the road that made Lennox feel like she was in a car commercial. She focused hard on the road and drove slowly, hoping an animal would dart out in front of her, proving that Hicks Road really was a wildlife crossing of some sort so that it would become undeniably apparent that what she had seen— and what she had hit—was an animal. That wouldn't be great, as Lennox would never want to hurt an animal, but it wouldn't be vehicular manslaughter either.

The sun was high in the sky by the time Lennox approached the hook in the road where she had felt the thud. She expected to be overcome with panic or dread or a sense of knowing, but she just kept edging her car along at a snail's pace, wait- ing for the telltale break in the road, for the giant flaming arrow that said *LENNOX HIT SOMEONE HERE AND THEN DROVE AWAY.* But there was nothing save for the glowing white sunshine filtering through ancient redwoods, the roadside rocks and ferns, a picture out of a *WISH YOU WERE HERE!* postcard.

Is it possible I was wrong?

There was something like giddiness flowing through Lennox even as her eyes stayed fixed on the road, sweeping the expanse of black asphalt, looking for anything that would tell her what had happened that night. There was nothing. At least, nothing she could see from her vantage point in the driver's seat. The legends, the "weird things" she had been told had happened here, faded into the reality of a bright road winding through the woods.

This isn't so bad, Lennox thought, slowing down her car. *I've been freaking out over nothing. It's true, it was late. And dark. And I had just been to my first party ever, and I'd had one drink, and we were all giddy and laughing, and so many girls here are blond, and...*

Finally, Lennox pulled over to the shoulder and stepped out, the pavement under her sneakers uneven and rough before it broke into mostly dirt.

I think this is it, she said to herself, standing in the middle of the road and turning around. *Right?* But for a few feet ahead and behind, everything looked the same: trees, rocks, ferns; trees, rocks, ferns. She walked a few feet, trying her best to discern blood or hair or chipped paint in the road, and nearly collapsed on weak, relieved knees. Her friends were right—there was nothing there. She was just a panicky chick who had listened to one too many true-crime podcasts and had an overactive imagination—

There.

To her left, a bank of trees.

The ferns were tamped down.

A hum, like the whirring buzz of bees, started in her head. The ferns were tamped down, and dirt and gravel were smashed into this part of the road.

Like someone kicked them forward. Like someone came out of the forest...

No.

She followed the dirt across the street and onto the soft shoulder on the other side. There was a heap of pine needles and leaves and dirt and detritus, and it had clearly been disturbed.

No.

It looked like someone had dragged something through it—or been dragged—and on the other side, a young bush was folded over itself, tender stems snapped in half.

"It could have been anything," Lennox said, trying to console herself, trying to make her words clean up the mess, clean up that night, clean up her memory of anything happening. Then, without thinking, Lennox was stepping forward, placing one foot in front of the other on the soft ground. It was obvious something had slid across the dirt here. She couldn't tell if it had been on two feet or four, lying on its side or rushing off. But there had been something. Lennox could feel the tension rising in her chest.

"Okay, Lennox, get ahold of yourself. No body, no blood. Tamped-down bushes don't prove anything."

She was finally able to breathe. "It could have been a deer." She shrugged, slapping at the bush with the snapped branches. "Or an elk." Lennox had no idea whether elk were common on this side of the country or on a roadside in a major California city. She decided she would find out after she went home, took a shower, and apologized to Allison and Eva for thinking she was a murderer and they were her joking accomplices. She was considering making the girls cards when the sleeve of her sweat-shirt caught on one of the broken branches to her right.

A delicate gold chain was glinting in the sunlight, stretched from branch to branch like a decoration on a Christmas tree. Lennox reached for it with shaking hands.

The chain was broken, snapped at an awkward angle, and in the soft dirt and dried pine needles was a tiny golden heart, pressed into the soil, caked with mud.

Lennox's heart started to thud.

If someone came through here wearing this chain...

She pushed herself to standing on trembling legs, eyeing the road, the edge of the embankment.

If someone fell headfirst...

The tracks and disturbance made a little more sense now. It could have been a person. Lennox started to shake, her fingers numb as she dug into the dirt and pulled out the heart. She slipped the necklace into her pocket and sleep-walked back to the car, her body on autopilot.

Someone had been there.

Lennox blinked and pushed the car door open, looking around her and half wondering how she had made it to Java Script, the bookstore café that had been her first refuge in San Jose. Funny that she had never noticed the entrance to Hicks Road right across the street.

No one looked at her as she got out of her car; the broken

necklace in her pocket wasn't some weird beacon signaling to the world that something had transpired that night, something bad enough to snap a delicate gold chain right off the neck of a wide-eyed blond girl.

I don't know that. Lennox gritted her teeth against the bombardment of accusations in her own mind, tried to make way for logic and intellect. People hiked near Hicks Road. The necklace could have been from anytime, anyone. It could have been tossed out of a car or—or—

"Hey, Lennox, right?"

Lennox snapped to attention, her skin suddenly feeling too tight. She focused on the man behind her, the man with the sandy blond hair holding the door. He was smiling a friendly smile, dressed in a wrinkled denim button down and khaki pants, and Lennox knew she had seen him before. Her mind thundered—*this school, that school, my dad's job*—

"Mr. Apex," she finally said, her muddled mind putting the image and name together. "Sorry, I didn't expect to see you here."

His laugh was easy, but it did nothing to calm Lennox's frayed nerves. "I guess it's always a little weird to see a faculty member out in the wild." He made air quotes, and Lennox bit her lip.

In the wild?

Had he been there—on Hicks Road, in the wilds of the forest? Is he following me? Does he know something?

Lennox's saliva soured, and her whole body went leaden

even as her mind commanded her to run. Mr. Apex cocked his head.

"Lennox, are you okay?"

"I have a date." She didn't know where it came from, but she blurted it out while Mr. Apex was looking at her, the edges of his lips half quirked while Lennox burned with heat. "I don't know why I said that."

"Well, that is great. I was just going to get some coffee."

Walk! Lennox commanded herself. *Walk into the café and be normal.*

"Yes." She pushed the word past her teeth. "It is good. It's good that...you're here." She walked into the café, burning red up to her hairline.

"So, what's the best drink to order?"

Why won't he leave me alone?

Lennox's hand went into the pocket of her jeans, fingers wrapping around the gold chain. There was a weird comfort there, a weird connection that she didn't expect to feel, and for the first time since she had found the thing, Lennox felt like she could breathe.

"Double chocolate mocha," she said definitively. "With a caramel drizzle."

Mr. Apex nodded, his eyebrows going up. "Well, that sounds like a diabetic's nightmare."

Lennox ordered her drink and waited for it on the other side of the café, still feeling vaguely awkward about Mr. Apex invading her space. When he got his drink, she was happy to see that he raised it to her with a nod, then slipped out the front door and into his car. Lennox stared at it, uneasiness racing through her. Had she seen that car before? Her mind spun, brain wracking. The car seemed familiar, but from where? Hicks Road? Something cold ran through her, and just as easily, it stopped. Mr. Apex was an administrator who parked in the faculty parking lot. If Lennox had seen his car before, that must have been where.

Lennox sat and finished her mocha, letting the hot chocolate linger on her tongue while she thought about the necklace and everything she knew. When she laid it out, she realized it was nothing. Five days ago, she had *thought* she'd hit a girl with her car. Today she had found a broken necklace in the same spot. There was definitely some broken foliage, but there was nothing else: no body, no shattered glass or evidence of a major accident, and of course the necklace could be from anywhere, from any time. She pulled the golden heart from her pocket and wiped it clean on a napkin, rubbing until any trace of dirt was gone and the bauble gleamed in the harsh fluorescent lights of the coffeehouse. A gold heart, nothing special. It didn't open, and there was no telltale engraving, no tag indicating who the necklace belonged to. There wasn't even any way to knowing when the necklace landed there, when it was forgotten in the dirt. There had been cigarette cartons, crumpled beer cans, and all manner of ancient detritus on the side of the road.

Yeah, Lennox thought. *But the necklace is different.*

Even from a distance, Lennox could see that the cans and cartons were covered with a thin sheen of dirt, that the bright colors of the labels had been faded by time in the elements. But the necklace was relatively new, still shiny. It hadn't been in the woods for months. Maybe just...days?

But it proves nothing.

No missing-girl posters, no news reports on the airwaves, no parents begging for a teen's safe return.

"Of course," Lennox muttered to herself. "Because nothing happened."

FIFTEEN

Lennox stepped out of the shower to the ringing of her phone.

"Hello?" she panted.

"Is Owen already there? Why are you out of breath?" Allison giggled.

"Owen, right." It seemed like weeks since they had spoken, years since she had been on Hicks Road. "You know about that?"

"Yeah. How come you didn't tell me? You told Eva but not me?"

Lennox frowned. "I'm sorry, I didn't realize—"

"And now I'll hate you forever. Open the door! Nice couch, by the way."

"What are you talking about?" Lennox padded out to the living room and rolled up on her toes, peeking at Allison and Eva waving wildly from the front porch.

"What are you guys doing here?" she asked, pulling open the front door. "How did you even know where I lived?"

"Oh, she's clearly never had best friends before,"

Allison said, walking straight in and dropping her bag on the couch.

"We're helping you get ready for your date." Eva held up a duffel bag and a makeup case that looked like she was spending a month on the Orient Express.

"We're just going to a movie," Lennox said.

"And what are you planning on wearing to this movie of which you speak?"

Lennox shrugged, and Allison narrowed her eyes. "Exactly! Eva, we came just in time. Show Lennox what we have for her."

Eva unzipped her bag and an entire clothing store popped out. Sequined dresses, tops with spaghetti straps, jeans that Lennox wouldn't fit into if her life depended on it, and an entire collection of strappy sandals with varying degrees of sparkle and heel.

"Don't you think this is a little much?" Lennox held up a velvet minidress with lines of sequins down the sides. "Again, movie. Popcorn, hot dog."

"Never eat a hot dog on the first date."

Eva shook her head like this was the most normal dating advice in the world.

"I don't even want to know why or how you figured that out. How about my own jeans and this top?" She pulled something deep purple and otherwise unassuming out of Eva's clothing pile.

"Ew, no. I don't even know why I have that in there."

Allison was carefully picking through the pile now, discarding piece after piece on Lennox's coffee table until she came upon a long-sleeved black shirt with a plunging neckline. "How about this and your jeans? I'll go get them."

She made a beeline for Lennox's room before Lennox could protest, certain the U-shaped neck would graze her belly button. She didn't have the full C-cup breasts that Eva had, but to her surprise, the shirt fit well, the sleeves hitting right at her thumbs.

"Oh, this is soft."

"Better for petting," Eva said with a grin.

Lennox immediately though of Owen's hands, how strong and big they were as he clutched her arms and stared deeply into her eyes at the library. Her heart started to thud.

"Here you go." Allison tossed Lennox her jeans, and she caught them in one hand, but not before the chain and the heart tumbled out, landing on the pile of discards.

"What's this?" Allison picked up both pieces, examining them in her palm. "It's broken."

Lennox's breath caught, and her first instinct was to lie, to make up some story about how the necklace was her mom's or something, anything to make it sound like she was a regular girl with regular friends going on a regular date and not some rootless transplant who was hunting a phantom in the woods.

"It's a necklace," was all she said.

Allison carefully slid the heart onto the chain and held the

necklace to her collarbone, the little bauble glittering beauti-
fully against her skin, and something in Lennox sharpened.
It wasn't Allison's necklace. It didn't belong around her neck.
It was Lennox's.

"It's mine," Lennox said, reaching for it.

"It's pretty. Where did you get it?" Eva asked.

Lennox looked at her friends. *Actual friends.*

"I know this is crazy, but I went back up to Hicks Road
just to see if there was anything there. Like, just to make my
mind stop being all"—Lennox shook her head—"crazy."

"And there wasn't, so you bought yourself a necklace?"
Eva said hopefully.

"This was caught on one of the bushes on the side of the
road."

Allison flopped onto the couch and used the pile of
clothes as a footrest. "And a broken necklace tells you what,
exactly?"

Lennox slipped into her jeans and took the necklace from
Allison, sliding it back into her pocket. "Nothing, I know
that. I mean, it could have been from anyone, anytime, right?"

"It looked pretty shiny and new."

Lennox pulled the bauble out again and examined it. "I
may have cleaned it off."

She didn't want to look up, to see the horrified expressions on her friends' faces. Even she knew she was starting
to fall into morbid territory, but she couldn't let go of what
she'd seen that night. And now that she had the necklace...

She tried to remember, tried to call up the image of the girl to see if somewhere in her memory she saw the necklace, to see if somehow, she could make a connection. But all she saw were those terrified eyes.

"So, do you guys recognize this at all?" Lennox tried to sound nonchalant, holding up the necklace.

"I think I saw it on Amazon," Eva said with a frown.

"No, do you recognize it from someone? Do you remember anyone wearing a necklace like this?"

"Yes. Approximately twenty thousand people," Allison said, holding up her phone. She was on the Amazon web page.

"You typed in 'gold heart necklace.'"

"Sure did." Allison seemed annoyingly smug, but Lennox tried to keep her composure.

"But those aren't this necklace."

"Does it matter? Clearly gold heart necklaces are popular. Anyone at any time could have been wearing that."

"Could have even been pioneer people," Eva said.

"That's what I'm saying. Do you remember anyone from school wearing this necklace?"

"I don't mean Pioneer High School people, I mean people from the pioneer days. They had jewelry, right?"

"Not Amazon jewelry."

Lennox gritted her teeth. "It's not from Amazon. Or at least that's not the part that's important."

Allison rolled her eyes. "So you found a necklace on the side of the road. Big deal. If you had found a gum wrapper, would you have been this bent? 'Oh no, there must have been someone out there because forest animals don't chew gum!'"

"I once saw a bear at a circus blow a bubble. It was very confusing," Eva said wistfully.

"You guys, I'm serious!"

"We are too, Lennox, but you're making something out of nothing. If this"—Allison snatched the necklace from Lennox's fingers—"were something that someone really cared about, they would have come looking for it or put up a sign or offered some sort of reward. Look." She tapped a few buttons on her phone and turned it toward Lennox. "I put in 'lost necklace San Jose' and got six million results. Mostly jewelers, ads, a few articles about some smash-and-grabs. No forlorn girl seeking her precious bauble. It was probably just some people hiking around—"

"Or doing it in the woods," Eva snickered.

"—and the thing popped off. Don't try to make it more than it is."

"Well, if it's not that big of a deal, I can just post a found ad on social media, right? Maybe someone is looking for it, but they don't know where they lost it."

Allison handed Lennox her laptop. "And if it is from someone you hit—which I'm not saying you did—then you've just implicated yourself in a hit-and-run, and also you were driving after curfew with people under eighteen in the car." She pointed to herself and Eva, and Eva's eyes widened.

"Oh, that's right."

"Wait, what? I just drove you guys home, that's not illegal."

Allison looked pained. "I'm so sorry, Lennox, but it's the law. You can't drive with anyone under eighteen in your car after ten o'clock at night."

"That's not a law."

Eva nodded. "It is around here. It's kind of new."

"You guys both knew this, and you let me drive you around anyway?" Lennox gaped.

"No, no, no." Allison put her hands up. "It wasn't like that."

Eva shook her head. "I didn't even think about it. We had planned on only staying at the party for a little bit. But when we left—"

Lennox cradled her arms in front of her chest. "It was definitely after ten. We were definitely breaking the law."

There was a beat of silence, and then Eva stood up. "Why are we even talking about this? Nothing happened. That's a gross broken necklace that could be from a dog for all we know, and you have a date. Can we not be all doom and gloom in this very special moment?"

Allison grinned. "Right? Can we stop talking about this?" She tossed the necklace on the coffee table, and while Allison was lining up shoes for Lennox to try on, Lennox slipped the necklace in her pocket.

SIXTEEN

Fingers of purple-blue darkness were starting to cut across the sky when Eva opened the front door, Allison behind her.

"Okay, so have the *greatest* time," Eva said with a wide grin. "And be sure to tell us everything."

Lennox nodded. She was decked out in half her clothes, half Eva's and had been primed on what to say and what not to say on a date, which she had pretended to listen to carefully. Allison had done her eye makeup, and Eva had raided the pantry, thrilled that Lennox's dad gave her free rein on snacks she didn't have to share with siblings. By the time Eva had started shoving her loaner wardrobe into her bag, all thoughts of anything except Owen and her date had evaporated, and butterflies were starting to flap in Lennox's stomach. She tried not to chew the lip that Allison had just swept with lip gloss and looked at both of her friends.

"Thank you guys so much for doing this."

Allison and Eva exchanged bemused looks, and Allison narrowed her eyes. "This isn't your first date, is it?"

Lennox blinked, the mascara on her lashes suddenly feeling heavy. "No, why would you say that?"

Allison put her hands on her hips, but her smile was soft. "It is, isn't it?"

Lennox sighed. "Does it show that much?"

Eva batted at the air. "It doesn't even matter. I have technically never been on a date either. Not like a one-boy-one-girl thing."

"You? But you're so pretty! I'm surprised."

"Never be surprised by my beauty, darling," Eva said, brushing her hair behind her ear. "No, my parents won't let me date because they don't think my younger siblings are birth control enough. That being said, don't do anything I wouldn't do. Or wouldn't be allowed to do."

Lennox laughed.

Allison held out her hand, palm-up. "Give me the necklace."

"What?" Lennox asked. "No. Why?"

Allison crossed her arms over her chest, her long hair swinging. "Because you're carrying around gross discarded jewelry on your first date. That's weird, and also, I don't want you to think 'I may have run over someone, even though I definitely didn't, and here's a broken necklace as proof' is a great conversation starter."

Lennox should have been annoyed at Allison's insistence, at the way she cocked an eyebrow and pinned her with a glare, but she couldn't fault her friend. She had spent the last five days wrapped up in a self-made mystery that was driving her a little batty. She took the necklace out of her pocket, but instead of giving it to Allison, she looped it around the key rack hanging by the front door.

"How about I leave it here?"

Neither Allison nor Eva moved, and Lennox groaned.

"How about I leave it here and swear six ways to Sunday that I will only talk about things guys like, like cars and jock itch?"

Eva exploded into giggles, and Allison nodded sharply. "That's all I ask."

Eva stepped forward and engulfed Lennox in a tight surprise hug. "Be super-duper careful, okay?" she whispered against Lennox's cheek.

Lennox was taken aback but hugged her friend and chuckled. "I will be."

Once the girls were gone, Lennox made a beeline for the full-length mirror in her dad's room and examined herself. She was tall with broad shoulders and a boyish body, but the jeans and Eva's black shirt looked good on her. She liked the ensemble, slid into her old black Converse, grabbed her keys, and headed to the garage.

The garage was dark and empty, and without the usual heap of just-moved-in or about-to-move-out boxes, the place looked cavernous and eerie. There was a door that led to the side yard with a window on the top; the yellow from the streetlight filtered into the garage, giving everything an eerie glow. In the darkness, something moved, and Lennox jumped, slapping her palm against the garage door opener so the room was swept with automatic light.

There was nothing there, but Lennox was still panting, blood thundering in her ears.

"Get a grip," she mumbled to herself, heading through the garage to her car. "The girls were right." She thought of Allison and Eva, her friends, grinning and happy and acting like *normal* people.

She could be normal too.

Lennox pulled the car door shut and sank her key into the ignition, turning over the engine and turning the radio up to maximum volume. She cranked down all the windows and flicked on the headlights.

The girl.

She flashed in front of Lennox's windshield—no, just an image of her, the sound of the thud, and Lennox's heart jumped to her throat. She attempted to put her hand on the gearshift, but she was shaking, her eyes darting from the windshield to the rearview mirror and back again.

"Put the car in drive, Lennox," she told herself.

It's so dark. What if I hit someone again?

What if—

Tears, hot and pitiful, rimmed her eyes and raced down her cheeks. Her head was throbbing, the mascara Allison had so expertly applied running in ugly black streams across her skin.

"I can't do this."

She flicked on the dome light and looked around the car, her car that she had loved and felt so safe in and now it was terrifying to her, smothering, menacing.

I'm going completely crazy.

She scratched at the car door until her fingernails grabbed the handle and she was able to push out; she fell on her knees on the driveway, feeling the cold of the asphalt through her jeans as she breathed in huge gulps of air. Her heart slammed against her rib cage, her blood pressure rising so sharply she could feel it in her skull. Lennox pressed her forehead against the ground, then rolled onto her back, spread-eagle, briefly considering that any neighbor watching would probably call the police on the teenage girl sprawled out in the driveway, but she didn't care.

Lennox didn't know how much time passed before she rolled over onto her belly and dialed Owen.

"Hey, I was just about to call you. Is everything okay?"

Lennox looked miserably at her car, at the keys she had tossed on the grass. "I—uh, my car isn't working."

She tossed the lie off carefully, expecting Owen to reschedule or groan. Instead, without missing a beat, he said, "Text me your address, I'll be there in five."

"You don't even know where I live. How can you be here in five?"

"You don't even know how I drive. I'll be there in five."

Once again, she wanted to revel in the sweet banter, in the

kind words of this normal guy, but she was still spread-eagle
on the ground, and now she had grass in her hair and stains
on her knees.

"See you then."

SEVENTEEN

Lennox did her best to fix her makeup and brush the dirt from her knees and was waiting on the sidewalk when Owen pulled up. Something flittered through her stomach when she saw him behind the wheel, grinning, his eyes focused directly on her. She smiled and waved, waiting to hear the voice in her head screaming at her, telling her she was too eager or forward or crazy or weird, but nothing came, and she pulled open the car door and slid in next to Owen.

He smelled of soap and hair gel and didn't stop smiling. "Was that five minutes?"

Lennox pretended to look at her nonexistent watch. "Five minutes, thirty-three seconds, but I'll allow it."

He shrugged as they pulled away from the curb. "You should see how fast I can get to LA."

"Is that where we're going?"

Owen cocked his head. "Sort of."

Lennox chewed her bottom lip. "I do have a curfew..."

"You know LA is six hours from here, right?"

She felt heat in her cheeks. "Oh, right. But also, I didn't know that."

Owen nodded. "Because you're new around here. I almost forgot. Where are you from again?"

Lennox's stomach sank. She didn't want to have that conversation again, the one about how her mother got sick and her dad followed his work and she was the carry-on luggage that got stuffed in the overhead compartment each time a new assignment came up. She wasn't ready to remember all the past schools and kids who had never acknowledged her except to exclude or make fun of her. She wasn't ready to be the sad girl.

"All over," she said simply, then smiled, hoping that was enough.

"Military brat?" Owen asked.

Lennox pulled her shoulders to her ears. "Something like that. So, are we going to a movie? If not LA…"

"The next best thing!" Owen clicked on her blinker and took a hard turn, smashing Lennox against him. "You're forward."

"Your seat belts suck." They grinned at each other and locked eyes, and Lennox felt like she was in a movie where the two main characters had instant chemistry and would probably end up making out after the musical montage.

She sat back in her seat as Owen thumped down a driveway that should have been paved and wound into a wide lot dotted with cars.

"Drive-in movie?"

Lennox hadn't been to a drive-in movie since she was five and her parents still spoke.

"Is this okay? I thought since we ended up in one car, it might be kind of fun. Besides, my glove box can hold eight boxes of Mike and Ikes." Owen grinned.

Lennox nodded enthusiastically, though ice water seeped through her veins. She wasn't well versed in the dating world, but she was hoping to be somewhere away from cars, away from the lanes of blacktop stretching out.

Be normal, she told herself. *You're on a date, not in the woods.*

When Owen pulled into a spot, Lennox looked around, gripping her knees.

"Are you okay? You seem a little nervous."

"Me? No! Just, you know, scary movies." She pretended to shudder.

"*Finding Nemo* is a terrifying one." Owen said, gesturing toward the cartoon water filling the screen. "Popcorn, candy, hot dog, Coke?"

"Yes, please," she said meekly.

She watched Owen hit the concession stand and studied all the people around him.

Owen pulled on the door handle, and Lennox jumped. He cocked his head and smiled. "I feel like I'm always freaking you out."

"Maybe you shouldn't sneak up on people."

"Next time I need to get in my own car, I'll be sure to hit the panic button to warn you."

Lennox smiled. "Sorry. It's just...this town and all its weird legends. Apparently, you never know if you're going to run into a banshee or a druid."

Owen sat in the driver's seat and handed Lennox a treasure trove of snacks. He pointed at her with a kernel of popcorn held between two fingers. "First of all, they are just legends. Second of all, it's cannibals and druids. A banshee would just be silly. And also, they all pretty much stick to Hicks Road. They'd never come down here. Word on the street is that they hate Pixar movies."

"So, you know."

Owen nodded. "I know all. You don't grow up around here without learning about your neighbors. And who hangs out on deserted roads." He popped a few kernels into his mouth.

"So, Hicks is really deserted, huh?"

"Except for the occasional party, there's nothing happening up there."

"No houses or anything?"

"There is an abandoned insane asylum, but that's way at the top."

Lennox's eyes widened. "There is?"

"Legend has it, and history and Google Maps have proven that it's one hundred percent not true."

Lennox swatted Owen but smiled, feeling her tied-in-knots stomach beginning to ease.

"Have you been up there?"

Lennox nodded but stuffed her mouth with popcorn, hoping Owen would drop the subject.

She tried to focus on the movie she had seen a dozen times, but her mind kept wandering. Finally, Owen leaned over.

"Okay, maybe *Finding Nemo* isn't the greatest of Disney movies—that award would go to *Snow White and the Seven Dwarfs*, clearly—but something is definitely on your mind. Is it me? Do I smell?" He picked at his shirt and gave it a mock sniff. "Is it Nemo's dad? Because he's a better swimmer than I am?"

Lennox smiled despite the unease in her belly. "Though I am definitely attracted to the good-swimmer, full-of-gills type, it's definitely not you. And you don't smell either. I mean, you don't smell bad."

"Great, I'll tell my mom."

Lennox rolled her eyes. "I'm sorry I'm distracted. It's just…" She sighed. "This is really silly. Not silly, I guess, but…have you ever done something and then wondered if you actually did it?"

Owen slowly bobbed his head. "Yes. My sophomore year."

Lennox slugged his shoulder. "Seriously!"

"Okay, I'm serious."

Lennox chewed her bottom lip, wondering how much to tell Owen. From the corner of her eye, she spotted a couple walking, the guy with a backward baseball hat, the girl with stick-straight blond hair that brushed her shoulders. They were holding hands, and Lennox sucked in a sharp breath.

"I think I may have hit someone with my car."

Owen blinked. "Okay, that's…serious. Did—did—did you—"

"Kill them?" Lennox couldn't believe she had used those words, and now they were out in the car, knives in the dimly lit cab as Nemo swam around on the huge screen out front. "I don't know."

"How do you not know? I mean—"

Lennox let out a long, slow breath. Her heartbeat was a weird, slow, steady rhythm, and her mouth was bone dry. "Are you going to turn me in?"

There was a beat of silence as Owen's eyes locked on Lennox's. "Did you kill someone?"

Lennox broke their gaze and stared at her hands in her lap. "I don't know."

"How do you not—"

"It was dark and I thought—think—I saw someone, but there was no one there when we stopped—"

"We?" Owen's brows rose. "There were other people in the car?"

Lennox nodded. "Eva and Allison. It was last weekend, after the party."

Owen's eyes widened, his cheeks going pink. "Everyone was drinking at the party."

Lennox shook her head fiercely. "Not me. I mean, I had

one drink, but that's it, I swear. I wasn't drunk, I was just Allison and Eva were playing. We were being stupid, just joking around. It was dark."

"Hicks has no lights, and it's not an easy road anyway because of the—"

"Banshees?"

"It's druids, but I was going to say curves." Owen reached out and took Lennox's hand. His were remarkably soft and warm against her ice-cold fingers. "It's going to be okay, Lennox. Just tell me what happened."

"We were driving down the road. It was super dark, like I said, and…my headlights…went off." Lennox's eyes flashed; she didn't want to involve Allison any more than she already had. It never left her mind that she was talking to Owen with the soft eyes and encouraging smile or that his mother was the chief of police. "Right before, I saw someone. A girl."

Owen sucked in a breath as he squeezed her hand. "Go on."

"I saw her, and then the lights went out, and I heard a thud. I know I hit her—or something. The girls are sure it was just a deer or something, but Owen, it didn't sound like that. It sounded like I hit someone. I slammed on the brakes and turned the lights back on, but there was no one there."

"But there was that dent."

"Right, the dent. And I got out of the car and looked all around, but I couldn't find anyone. I called out and there was no answer."

"So, you think what happened is that you hit this person

and...killed them." Owen didn't let go of her hand, but Lennox began to wish he would as hers started to sweat.

"That's what I thought. But then last night, someone came to my house. The girl—she came to my house and was knocking on my window, and there was blood and—and I sound totally crazy, don't I?"

"Did you talk to the girl?"

"No, it was late and—"

"And maybe it was a dream?"

Lennox shook her head. "I thought so too, but then there was a note. In my car. It said 'FIND ME.'"

Owen blinked. "Lennox, listen carefully to me."

Her eyes widened, and she tried to swallow, but her mouth was full of sand.

"The probability that you actually hurt someone is small. Infinitesimal, even." A smile played at the corners of his mouth. "The dent would have been bigger, the body would have been sprawled on the road, it would have been obvious. And"—he held up a hand—"if the person wanted you to find her, why would she go to your house and not let herself be...found?"

Lennox frowned.

"Is it possible you dreamed about the girl and the note was something else? Maybe from a friend or something?"

Lennox began to protest, but then the events of the past few days came crushing over her. She couldn't remember if she'd bought a parking pass. She had forgotten about her therapy appointment.

"I don't think I would have forgotten about someone dropping me a note—"

Allison flashed into her mind, and Lennox could almost feel her cool palm pressing against Lennox's forehead. She had completely forgotten about the decision to go to the baseball game too.

"You've been under a lot of stress, haven't you?"

Lennox wanted to smile at Owen. She wanted to feel his relief, his certainty that everything was okay. But something still weighed on her.

"I saw her, Owen. Blond hair, blue eyes. She was about our age."

Owen bobbed his head knowingly. "It's possible you saw someone, but the idea that you hit them is nearly impossible. It doesn't happen that way."

Lennox snatched her hand back with more angst than she meant to. "How do you know?"

"I've hit several people with my car."

Lennox frowned. Owen laughed.

"You're making fun of me."

"I'm not, I'm not, I'm sorry! That must have been really traumatic for you, and I totally get that. But if there was no body, no blood, no nothing, then frankly, nothing bad happened."

Lennox let out a long breath. She knew Owen was right, and the more she told the story out loud, the more ridiculous it sounded.

"Look, I am sorry, it must have been really freaky. But have you been torturing yourself about this all week?"

Lennox barely shook her head. "A little."

Owen scooched toward Lennox and threw his arm around her shoulders, pulling her as close as the center console would allow. She instinctively tucked her head under his chin, the thrill of being *this close* to Owen wiping out all the energy of that night. "You're a really good person. But you're beating yourself up over nothing. If there was an accident and someone got hurt—even if it was just a little bit—my mom would know about it. And I have a police scanner, so I would know too. And I can honestly tell you that it's been pretty slow the last week. I mean, there was a guy doing doughnuts in the Dunkin' Donuts parking lot, which was kind of ironic, but that's pretty much it." He offered a reassuring smile, and Lennox melted into it.

"Thanks for that. But I just feel like...like I should remember more than I do."

"What do you mean by that?"

Lennox sat up straighter. "I remember everything from that night: what I wore, what we were doing—"

"That I was checking you out in the corner?"

Lennox's stomach fluttered. She wanted to stay focused, but it was Owen with his hot-cocoa eyes, and the way he cocked his head made Lennox want to throw everything *else* about that night out the window. "You were? I didn't even notice you."

He looked away, his nod almost imperceptible. "Wow, harsh."

"I didn't mean—" Lennox put her hand over her mouth, stifling a nervous giggle. "No, if I had seen you, I would have been all, 'hey,' but probably not because I'm ridiculously awkward. Did you know there was a nacho cheese fountain in the kitchen?"

"Thrown over for nacho cheese. I guess I can see that."

"A nacho cheese *fountain*."

There was a beat of silence. Lennox wanted to sink into it and keep up her banter with Owen, but that night still gnawed at her, wouldn't stay in the back of her mind.

"I remember the cheese fountain—"

"Well, it's a fountain of cheese, so who wouldn't?"

"And I remember getting in the car, but those few seconds—seeing the girl, the lights going off, stopping—I feel like I'm missing something smack in the middle, you know? Like, I'm seventeen, I shouldn't be having lapses in memory."

Owen shoved a few pieces of popcorn into his mouth and chewed, considering. "I don't think it's officially a lapse in memory. I think things happened really fast and you had a normal reaction to something scary happening."

"I guess…"

"Tell you what. How about we drive to Hicks right now? It's about the same time of day, and you can see that the road is kind of tricky, so it would be crazy for someone to be out there taking a midnight stroll. I mean, the road is steep."

A chill ran up Lennox's spine. "Thanks, but no. I just—it feels way too creepy to be there at night."

Owen cocked a brow. "You don't think I can keep you safe?"

Lennox's eyes went wide and she batted her lashes. "I don't doubt your absolute strength and prowess, but I've heard there are druids up there."

Owen's lips quirked into a half smile. "And someone recently told me there were banshees. So, you know, if you *did* actually hit something, you likely did the whole of San Jose a favor. I believe the residents would be very grateful."

It was impossible for Lennox to feel anything but a tickling warmth in her belly when she looked at Owen and his half-closed eyes, when she noticed the softness of his lips as he leaned into her. All memory of everything except that very moment were gone to Lennox when Owen kissed her.

EIGHTEEN

Lennox practically floated into the house when Owen dropped her off. She was so far gone in Owen-land that she didn't realize the kitchen lights were on, didn't even notice her father standing at the stove, scrambling an egg.

"Hey there, stranger."

Lennox stared at her dad, scraping his egg onto a plate and grinning.

"I thought you were working tonight," Lennox said.

"And it's nice to see you too."

"Oh, sorry." She hung up her purse and hugged her father, then cracked an egg into the frying pan for herself. "Hi, Dad. Nice to see you. I thought you were working tonight."

He father took the pan and handed Lennox the full plate, motioning for her to sit down as he made a show of attempting to flip the runny egg in the pan. It didn't move, and Lennox stabbed her egg, chewing absently.

"I got in at midnight. Speaking of midnight, you're home late."

Lennox stopped midchew. It wasn't that her dad was strict or even paid that much attention to Lennox's social life. But occasionally he slid into these moments of father-knows-bestdom where he decided it was time to impart some esoteric wisdom, and Lennox was not ready for one of those conversations after her thrilling night with Owen. She shrugged, keeping her eyes on her plate. "Was just out for a movie with the girls."

"Ah, Alicia and...the other one."

A flash of annoyance set Lennox's teeth on edge. "Allison and Eva. Neat of you to take an interest."

Her father blew out a sigh, and he pinched the bridge of his nose. "I'm sorry, Lennox. You know I try to keep up with all your friends—"

"I do have so, so many," she deadpanned.

Lennox's dad squeezed her shoulder. "It's not that bad, is it, hon? I'm doing the best I can, you know."

Lennox tried to keep the anger up, but she did feel sorry for her father, and he did try—mostly. He had kept them in decent houses, and Lennox wanted for nothing, and now she had Owen. Sweet, comforting Owen with his arm around her shoulders and his clean soap smell and his absolute certainty that nothing had happened that night on Hicks Road. The idea—even a hint of the idea—that Lennox could have a nice normal life as a teenager with a boyfriend and two best friends and maybe even stay in this same school long enough to graduate made her feel buoyant and ready to forgive her father for anything. So rather than grouse, she got up and kissed her dad on the top of his head.

He smiled and squeezed her hand. "I've got a good kid."

"That you do. I'll see you late."

⸱⸱⸱⸺⸺⸺⸺⸱⸱⸱

Allison and Eva were standing in the parking lot when Lennox pulled into her spot Monday morning.

"I can't believe it has been this long and we're still waiting for an update," Allison said when Lennox opened her car door.

"Update?"

Eva groaned. "Your date! We called you approximately three hundred and fifty thousand times, and you *never* answered. I mean, was the date really that great?" Eva raised her eyebrows. "Are you *that* kind of girl?"

Allison's nostrils flared, and she swatted Eva. "Eva, don't be gross. But seriously, Lennox, tell us everything."

"Okay, but wait. There's something I didn't tell you. The night before, I saw—"

Owen's voice, sweet like spun sugar, came back to her. *"...just a dream..."*

Allison held up a single finger. "If you're going to tell me you saw a blond girl, I'm going to have you committed."

Lennox's eyes flashed, and Eva's went wide.

"I'm kidding, but for the love of all that's Prada, tell us about the date!"

"Lennox!"

All three heads swung toward the male voice. It was Mr. Apex, dressed like every guidance counselor Lennox had ever seen in teen movies, and Lennox briefly wondered if there was a store for that, or a guidance counselor website where every suit was basic and every tie came in colors like "calming blue" or "do-you-want-to-talk-about-it green."

"Hi, Mr. Apex."

He was grinning way too brightly and carrying a plastic cup with the Java Script logo on the side. He held it aloft like it was some kind of secret he and Lennox shared, and Lennox wanted to melt into her shoes right then and there.

"Thanks for the rec. This place is the bomb. Can you drop in and see me before class?"

Allison and Eva leaned in so close, their foreheads bumped, and Lennox had to laugh. "Did he just say 'the bomb'?" Eva hiss-whispered.

"I can't tell if he's stupidly harmless or a serial killer," Allison said under her breath.

"You guys are so mean!"

Allison gave Lennox a once-over, and her lips quirked into a smile. "Were you about to tell us that after your date with Owen, you stole away and roasted Mr. Apex's coffee beans at Java Script?"

Eva exploded into laughter, and Lennox's neck burned.

"No, oh my God, ew, he's, like, thirty!"

"And a snappy dresser!" Eva snorted.

"You guys, he just asked me where to get coffee, and then he obviously went and got it." *Multiple times.*

Lennox's mind vaulted back to the coffeehouse, to Mr. Apex showing up behind her. *Was he waiting for me?*

She glanced over the girls' heads to Mr. Apex slipping his key in his office door. He was a guidance counselor. He liked coffee. She'd gone to Java Script three times herself the weekend she'd discovered it.

FIND ME.

You have bigger things to worry about.

"You guys—"

"Lennox, now, please?" Mr. Apex was staring at her, standing in his doorway, his jovial familiarity gone.

"I'll see you in a little bit," Lennox whispered, slamming her locker shut and sliding her backpack over her shoulder.

"Tell us everything," Eva reminded her. "Unless it's about Apex, then gross, don't tell us a single thing."

Lennox was standing in the middle of the hallway with students swirling all around her, but she felt like she was walking to her doom. There was something about the way Mr. Apex's expression had changed, the way his voice seemed to fall into a clipped cadence that set her teeth on edge, that made her hope he wouldn't shut the office door and she could keep a foot in the safety of the hallway.

"You wanted to see me?" Lennox asked.

"Yes, hello." Now his smile was more relaxed, his tone of voice friendly, even, but as he closed the distance between them, shutting the door behind Lennox, she flinched. He blinked.

"I'm sorry, I guess I'm just a little jumpy today."

He dropped his keys on the desk, a compass attached to the ring, its jaunty little bubble pointing north. Mr. Apex noticed Lennox studying it and slid it into his drawer. "Compass. I hike a lot."

Lennox remembered his muddy boots. Had Mr. Apex been in the woods that night? The thought arrived out of nowhere, a completely baseless theory spawned from boots and a compass, and she shook her head.

"Everything okay?" He pressed his lips together in a bloodless smile, and Lennox needed to look anywhere else. She couldn't focus on Mr. Apex's eyes, on the odd set of that smile, so she glanced over his shoulder, just enough so it didn't look off, and when she did, she saw the scratches on his neck, red and angry-looking, just peeking out from the collar of his button-down.

"Are you okay?" It was out of her mouth before she could think about it, and she silently reprimanded herself for always blurting things out.

"What's that? Oh." Mr. Apex pressed his palm against his neck. "This? No, that's nothing. I got a new cat and...it's having a little bit of a time adjusting to my apartment."

Lennox's heart thudded. There was something too familiar, too plain about Mr. Apex's apartment and his cat. Again, it felt off to Lennox, and she found herself fisting her hands, digging crescent moons into her palms. "So, you wanted to see me?"

"Oh, yes, have a seat."

Lennox sat daintily at the very edge of the chair, glancing at the sea of students silently filing by the window in Mr. Apex's office door. She saw Owen in profile and wanted to leap at the window, wanted to yank the door open and disappear into his arms and into the crowd of students.

You're acting crazy, Lennox told herself as she looked across the desk to where Mr. Apex was staring intently at his laptop screen, waiting for it to boot up. *This is a guidance counselor in a school office during the school day. He's not going to kill me. Why do I think everything is out to get me?*

FIND ME.

The words seared into Lennox's brain.

"So, Lennox, I wanted to talk to you today about a few things." His left hand was resting on Lennox's file—her thick file—while his right tapped away at his computer, and Lennox swallowed, certain she was about to get the school counselor version of "Do you feel like you're about to snap?"

At this point, Lennox had no idea how she would answer.

"We need to get your schedule sorted out. Sorry," Mr. Apex said, gesturing to his computer. "It'll just be a minute before this campus info loads. I work on four other campuses, so it takes some time." He flashed a smile.

Something prickled along Lennox's skin. "So you go to other schools in town?"

"The two other public high schools and two charter schools." He straightened his tie. "Not enough of us to go around, so I have to, heh, go around."

Lennox forced a smile at his bad joke. "You must work with a lot of teenagers, then, huh?"

He nodded without looking up from his screen. "That I do."

"And you probably know all the gossip."

Apex's eyebrows went up. He looked at her over his screen and smiled. "I suppose that's true. Why, do you know any good gossip?"

"I'm only here at the one school."

"So you're saying there is no good gossip at this school."

Lennox cleared her throat. "I mean, nothing, like, *news-worthy* around here that I know of. But I did hear that there was a hit-and-run at one of the other schools."

"A hit-and-run? Really?"

Lennox pushed her hair over her shoulder, gathering momentum. "I mean, it was, there was just a rumor that this girl was the victim of a hit-and-run."

Mr. Apex set his lips in that hard, thin line again. "Well, Lennox, I wouldn't call that gossip. I mean, if a student was hit and the person just left, that's a crime."

Lennox nodded. "Oh, yeah, of course it is. It would be terrible. But did you hear anything about that? About a girl who got hit? Or a student who just didn't show up for school?" She felt like she was babbling, and Mr. Apex looked like he was getting more and more confused.

"Are you saying that you know a young woman who was hit by a car?"

"Uh…"

"Are you—were you maybe in this car that hit a young woman?"

Lennox's head was spinning. She felt like she was being interrogated even though she was the one who had started the conversation. Suddenly, she couldn't remember that night. She had been driving, hadn't she? The girl was in the car— no, at the party. No, in front of the car. Lennox was sitting next to Allison, and Allison was driving with Eva. A thick band of pressure formed along Lennox's forehead, and she pressed her fingertips against her temples, rubbing in small circles. The light in the office was too bright, and everywhere she looked, she saw flashes, phantoms, halos of diffused light around the bookcase, Mr. Apex's laptop, Mr. Apex.

"I'm sorry, my head just…" It was aching, like claws against her skull.

Mr. Apex rummaged through his bag, then slid a half-size bottle of water across the desk toward Lennox. "You can tell me if you have something to say. This is a safe space."

Lennox took the top off the bottle and drank gratefully. She was out of breath, panting, by the time the ache in her head started to subside. "I'm sorry, I think I was just…" *What? Going crazy?*

"What were you saying?"

Mr. Apex leaned forward in his chair, his voice going

low and soft. "Is there something you want to confide in me, Lennox? I do have to tell you that I'm a mandated reporter if you think you are going to hurt yourself or others."

Lennox capped her water and looked around. "I'm not going to—I'm not hurting anyone. I didn't hurt anyone." *That I know of.*

Mr. Apex didn't say anything, and Lennox felt the need to fill the silence. "I didn't. I was just—it was just a rumor I heard about someone maybe hitting someone or something." Her voice sounded high-pitched and tinny, strange to her own ears. Even as she backpedaled her story, she was getting confused. "I just—why did you want to see me again?"

Mr. Apex steepled his hands in front of his face. "Before we move on, I want you to know my door is always open. If you want to talk, to hash anything out, you know, just friend to friend, I'm here."

Lennox looked up and shivered. She couldn't tell if "friend to friend" was straight out of the *How to Talk to Odd Students* handbook or if it was some creepy I-won't-tell-if-you-don't kind of stuff. Either way, Lennox wanted to put as much distance between Mr. Apex and herself as possible.

"I need to get to class." She gathered her backpack and stood, but Mr. Apex waved her back to sitting.

"I'll write you a note. The last time you were here with me, we were talking about your elective."

"My elective?"

"You were hoping to get into AP Spanish and take drawing as your elective."

For the life of her, Lennox couldn't remember the conversation. But she was having trouble remembering anything these days.

"Okay. I mean, yes."

"Well, I'm happy to say you've been admitted to both. Ms. Kincaid is the art teacher here. And she's looking forward to having you in her class. She said the art portfolio you submitted was quite advanced and beautiful."

Lennox nodded dumbly. Her father had given her a black leather folio for her drawings and paintings ages ago. She took it from school to school, sliding in drawings of students she'd never see again, of landscapes that all seemed to blend together. She knew the portfolio was hers, but had she brought it to *this* school?

"I admit I took a look before submitting it, and you really are quite talented."

"Thanks," Lennox mumbled.

Art was the one constant in all the times and places she had moved. She was always either catching up or waiting for the class to catch up to her in all her other subjects, but art was the one place she could just *be*.

"It looks like that class is after lunch."

Lennox took the papers Mr. Apex printed and handed to her and may have smiled or waved or told him goodbye; she was on autopilot by the time she stepped into the empty

hallway and looked around, feeling exposed and uncomfortable. There wasn't a single person around, so why did she feel
like she was being watched? Lennox stuffed the printouts in
her backpack and hurried to her biology class.

NINETEEN

By the time Lennox made her way to the art wing, her mind was consumed with sequined dresses and the sandwich she hadn't finished eating. Even with all the schools she had attended, she had never been to a school dance, had never had reason to, and now she was not only going to the dance; she was going in a sequined minidress. Lennox's closet was a solid mass of blue denim and hoodies, and the only dress she owned was a black knit one with long sleeves that she trotted out when whatever hospital her dad was working at had a holiday party. It went past her knees and was delightfully shapeless so Lennox could do what she did best: fade into the background. But now, sequins?

"You must be Lennox."

Ms. Kincaid was tall and lithe with a short blond bob and a paint-stained apron. She smiled and reached out a hand, and Lennox wasn't sure whether to shake it or kiss it.

"Yeah, that's me. I guess I'm in the right place?"

There was an arc of easels set up, and Allison was waving wildly from one. "Lennox! Over here!"

Ms. Kincaid gestured for Lennox to sit. "I guess you already know Allison."

Lennox nodded and beelined for her friend. "I didn't know you were in this class."

Allison nodded. "Yeah, and Ms. Kincaid is awesome. She let me make all the dance posters here as one of my projects. I didn't know you liked art."

Lennox shrugged, and Ms. Kincaid slid Lennox's portfolio onto the easel. "You're very talented, Lennox. I'm very excited to have you here. I think you'll be a great asset to our group."

Lennox warmed. She had never been part of a group. She had never been to a dance. Half of her wanted to cower and beg her dad to move on, but the rest of her flickered with anger. She had never been part of a group or gone to a dance because her mother had left her and her dad dragged her from state to state looking for—*what?*

FIND ME.

Not everyone is searching for something, Lennox tried to tell herself. *Not everything is some big dangerous mystery.* Lennox's mind immediately went to a sketch in her book of a big, floppy flower arrangement full of hydrangeas and lilies. She could remember sitting on her knees on a wingback chair, sketching furiously while her mother flipped through a magazine on the couch across from her. Her father was talking to someone, and from the sketch, from the flower arrangement, it looked like a nice, simple scene of a family in the living room enjoying their time together, because Lennox hadn't bothered to sketch the orderlies walking down the hall to the left of her mother. She hadn't found a way to represent the too-clean smell of peroxide and bleach into the sketch, hadn't wanted to draw the plain-looking woman sitting behind an enormous stack of medical files, methodically stamping each one as she balanced a phone receiver on her shoulder and read off visiting hours and what time lunch was served. It wasn't a big dangerous mystery. It wasn't a family having a nice Sunday. It was a drawing of the last time Lennox saw her mother before the orderlies escorted her away, before the lady behind the desk tried to tell Lennox and her parents that the view from her mother's room was exquisite. It was a few bushes and a length of grass. Lennox could see that even as her eyes filled with tears. She clearly remembered the click of the door as they walked away.

For a while, Lennox's mind had played tricks on her. She saw her mother everywhere, on sidewalks and streets in Bethesda and Detroit, working in a bodega outside Jacksonville. But then her memory—or her father—flashed her back to that couch and that ugly flower arrangement, and she remembered where her mother was, where she and her father had left her, and she'd swallowed down the lump in her throat like she was doing now. If she was becoming like her mother, was that going to be her fate too? A locked door, a forever view of stupid bushes and a length of grass outside a barred window?

"Lennox," Allison hissed, leaning over. "You okay?"

Lennox swallowed hard, her stomach roiling. She blinked the tears away and put on her practiced smile. "I'm fine," she whispered back. "Just zoning out."

Is this how it starts?

Lennox gritted her teeth and focused hard on the teacher.

"Today, class, we're going to be working in charcoals. Allison, please show Lennox where to gather her materials. I'm not going to give you any particular subject, but I am going to give you this concept: discovery."

Allison leaned into Lennox's shoulder and lowered her voice. "Ms. K is a little woo-woo with her concepts, but she really lets you do whatever you want as long as you draw. Come on, I'll show you where everything is."

Lennox was shaken from her melancholy the second the supply closet opened. Allison handed her an unused pack of charcoals, an apron, and actual artist's paper.

"This is amazing," she murmured to Allison. "At my last school, the 'art department' doubled as the cafeteria, and we used copy paper that smelled like old spaghetti."

Allison laughed. "Well, welcome to a school where art is appreciated!"

Ms. Kincaid picked up her phone, and classical music began playing softly from the speakers.

"I feel like I'm at some kind of spa."

"Relax, da Vinci, it's just art class. What are you going to draw?"

Lennox sat down at her easel and arranged her materials. "I don't know, discovery? What does that even mean?"

Allison cocked her head. "I feel like I discovered you."

"That sounds slightly offensive."

Allison laughed. "I'm kidding! I don't know, what are things you discover?"

Lennox chewed on her bottom lip as the students dropped into silence, concentrating on their pieces. She looked around, doing her best to focus. *What could I discover? What needs discovering?*

She didn't want to think of the girl. She didn't want to think of her mother.

"Discovery," she whispered. "Explorers, the new world, Discovery Channel…"

Lennox shifted on her stool, picked up one of her pencils, and drew an arc. The classical music swelled behind her, but she could still hear the drag of charcoal on paper, could smell the hint of pencil shavings as the group—her team—leaned into their artwork. Lennox felt alive and content, like she had been waiting for this very moment all her life.

Her fingers darkened as she smudged and shaded. She worked fast as the music crescendoed, her heartbeat catching up, her breath lodging in her throat. Other students were dropping their materials, rolling their papers. Lennox kept drawing. She was gone, lost in the strokes and the lines, the gentle swirls and dark arcs.

"Five minutes more, everyone, but as usual, if you're caught in the flow, you'll want to step gently, gently back."

Somehow, the music began to fade. Around her, kids packed up their bags and started to whisper to each other. Lennox could hear the clatter of pencils returning to jars, of bags shifting and cell phones coming out.

"Clean up—wow."

Allison was leaning into Lennox, her eyes wide and focused on Lennox's piece. "That's incredible. You're really, really talented, Lennox. It's scary, but...wow."

Lennox crashed back into the classroom, onto her little stool in front of the easel. The lines and swirls and shades and shadows had a mind of their own, and they had connected, forming a picture Lennox couldn't remember considering.

It was a girl with wide, horrified eyes. Her lips were turned up into a grimace, her palms splayed in front of her as if protecting herself. Her hair fanned out behind her, long and light but in shadow. The locket around her neck sat in the hollow of her collarbones. All around her there was darkness, but there, scrawled at the bottom of the page in script Lennox didn't recognize, were words that she did: FIND ME.

"Did you enjoy your first class?" Lennox hadn't noticed Ms. Kincaid approaching. "Here, I can put away your things for you. It's nice to see a student so engaged."

"Come on, Lennox, we should go." Allison seemed shaken too, gathering her things and pulling Lennox by the arm.

"Is—is it okay if I take this home to work on?" Lennox asked.

"Yes, of course, can I—" Ms. Kincaid leaned over Lennox's easel, and Lennox leaned in, blocking her view.

"It's not done yet."

"But it is awesome," Allison said, eyes wide. "Except—isn't that the locket you found?"

Lennox didn't remember drawing it. She didn't remember placing it in the hollow of the girl's throat, working on the shading it cast.

"What locket?"

Lennox swung around to see Owen strolling into the art room, backpack slung over his shoulder, looking like he was walking onto set for his scene. She swooned—and Lennox wasn't a swooner—forgetting the wide-eyed girl she had just drawn, forgetting the message that had terrified her all morning.

"Hey, Owen."

He grinned. "I thought I'd find you here."

Lennox blinked. "You did? I just got here."

"And she was just packing up and probably needing a walk to her next class, right, Lennox?" Allison said, standing up and handing Lennox her backpack.

"Uh, yeah."

Owen leaned over Lennox's easel, and Lennox could feel heat explode in her cheeks. "It's just—just a doodle," Lennox said, snatching the page down. "I haven't added any detail or any real"—she glanced up at Ms. Kincaid, who was watching her with a serene smile on her face—"anything."

But Owen had seen the drawing, and something flickered in his eyes. Lennox could feel herself pale.

"It's just a—just a drawing." Lennox pushed the drawing into her bag and swung it over her shoulder. "I should—I'm probably late."

"Hey, but I came here for you."

"You did?"

Owen leaned over Lennox's shoulder. "Do you want to walk with us, Allison?"

Allison shook her head. "No, I do not. Bye." She darted out of the classroom like a shot, her brown hair fanning out behind her.

"I think your friend really likes me." Owen followed Lennox out of the art room. "So, that drawing…"

"It was—"

"Really good. But the girl, is that—"

Lennox sucked in a breath and dropped her voice. "That's her. But I don't want you to think I'm creepy."

"Oh, too late for that."

Lennox's eyes went wide and Owen smiled. "But I like creepy."

"What I was going to say is that I don't want you to think I'm creepy or morbid, but that was the girl I saw. I know—I know." Lennox looked at her feet. "You think I was dreaming."

"No, Lennox, please don't think I'm trying to—to brush away what you're feeling. I mean, everything you've described is actually really scary. Thinking you saw someone on the road—"

"I *did* see someone."

"Okay, but thinking you hit them with your car—that has to be really scary. And the girl at the window. It sounds like someone is out to scare you."

Lennox shivered, running her hands over her bare arms. "But who would do that? I barely know anyone at this school, and only you, Allison, and Eva know about what happened that night. There was no one else around, remember? We got out of the car, we looked everywhere."

Owen pulled Lennox down next to him onto a bench in an alcove. "Please don't think I'm trying to patronize you, but I am the police chief's son. I know a little bit about how crimes work."

Lennox leaned away from Owen, feeling her shoulders pressing into the wood slats of the bench. "Did you tell your mom about—"

"No." Owen held his hands up in protest and shook his head. "No, because I don't think there is anything to tell. And even if there was, do you think I'm the kind of guy who would turn in a cute girl?"

Lennox wanted to stay focused, but she swooned. She felt heat bloom in her cheeks, and her heart did a little double-thump. *He thinks I'm cute!* She chewed the inside of her cheek to keep her ear-to-ear grin in check.

"Go on."

Owen nodded. "Just bear with me. You said that there couldn't have been another person there watching or anything because you girls got out of the car and looked around."

Lennox nodded, but she was only half listening, her mind dotting cartoon hearts over the terrifying images of Hicks Road.

"So, if there was no *other* person out there that night, what makes you so certain that the girl was there? Again"— Owen's eyes were wide, pleading—"I'm not trying to say you're crazy or wrong or anything, I'm just saying that there is a possibility, you know?"

The hearts in Lennox's head popped. Owen was right.

"I get that, I do. And frankly, at this point, I want nothing more than to believe that nothing happened and that I'm just cracking up a little bit, which wouldn't be totally out of the norm for me. You go to as many schools as I have, and you develop—"

"A thick skin?" Owen said with a smile.

"I'm not sure if 'thick skin' is the right phrase. I was thinking more like a scrambled brain." She smiled back. "Anyway, I really would like nothing more than to brush this all away and hang out with a guy who thinks I'm cute." She looked at her hands gripped in her lap and tried to bite back that smile. "But things keep happening."

"Like, high school things?"

"No—"

"Like dances and stuff."

"What? No—"

"Lennox." Owen turned to face her, and that double-thump in Lennox's heart started up again. "Now that we're incredibly late for our next class, I should probably come clean."

Lennox's breath caught. "What do you mean?"

"The whole reason I came to your art class was because I wanted to—I want to—I am asking you to the dance."

This time Lennox didn't bite back her grin. "Wait, what?"

"I want to take you to the dorky school dance."

Lennox clapped a hand over her mouth. "Oh, Owen, I would love to go to the dorky school dance with you! But one question: If the dance is so dorky, why do you want to go?"

Owen stood and hiked his backpack over his shoulder. "Maybe it's not so much that I want to dance as that I want to hang out with you." His cheeks and the tips of his ears blushed a fierce pink, and Lennox had to grip the armrest of the bench to keep from throwing herself at him. He looked so sweet and sheepish, a sweet half smile playing on his lips.

"So, what do you say? Are we going or not?"

Lennox nodded hard. "Going. I mean, yeah, I guess I could do that."

TWENTY

Lennox nearly ran to her next class, sliding into her seat in a rush of heartbeats and fluttering papers.

"Nice of you to join us, Ms. Oliver."

It was the last period of the day, and normally Lennox would be mortified for not only being noticed but actually being called out in class. But this was Normal Lennox now, Teenage Girl. She had friends and a crush, and it didn't even matter that her mom went crazy and her dad made them nomads because at this single moment in time, everything was right with the world.

"I have news," she hiss-whispered to Eva.

Eva raised one eyebrow, keeping her other eye focused on Mr. Dawson. When he turned his back to write something on the white board, Eva leaned in. "You have to tell me everything. Now."

"Owen."

Mr. Dawson looked back over his shoulder, his eyes cutting, the set of his mouth hard and annoyed.

"Dance," Lennox breathed when he turned his back again. "Me. He thinks I'm cute!"

Lennox's heart thumped when she saw her friend's mouth drop open. Eva did a little dance in her chair and Lennox joined in. *So this is what normal feels like.*

Lennox's dad was sitting at the kitchen table, staring at his phone and eating a steaming bowl of oatmeal, when Lennox came home from school. He was barefoot, wearing his pajamas, the spoon held absently in the air as a voice message droned on.

"Hey, Dad."

Her father clicked off his phone and smiled at Lennox. "Hey, daughter. How was school?"

Lennox shrugged, even though her sweet secret was gnawing at the edges of her mind. "School. How are you? How's work going?"

Lennox's dad rocked his head back and forth. "It's okay, I guess."

A stripe of heat rushed to her cheeks. "What do you mean, okay? Dad, you're not thinking of moving again, are you?"

"Well, my contract will wrap up at the end of next month. We've never been to Texas, you know. I hear Austin is nice."

Lennox pulled out a chair and sat opposite her dad. "I don't care about Austin, Dad. I want to stay here. I want to stay at my school, with my friends."

"Lennox, you make friends everywhere you go! You've never had a problem with that."

Lennox's nostrils flared. "Are you really that dumb? I'm a

teenager who's been dropped in a dozen freaking schools in my life. Do you actually think I regularly make friends? Think back, Dad. Think about it: When have I ever had a friend over?"

"Well, weren't the girls here—"

"Yes, *here*. Here I have friends. You know I've never been invited to a birthday party that wasn't for one of your friends from work? That I've never gone to a school dance or been on any kind of team?"

Her dad looked taken aback. "I don't know where all this is coming from."

"It's coming from me, your daughter? The one you drag from place to place like carry-on luggage, the one who never has a say in where we end up?"

"Lennox, no, you always have a say. We always pick out our next spot together."

Lennox gritted her teeth. "Yes, together. I'm there with you, sitting at this stupid dining table that we carry from place to place, but it's wherever *you* decide to put in your applications that matters and then who offers you a job. You know what my part is in that? Nodding and smiling, Dad, because what other choice do I have? I never want to hurt your feelings, so I always go along with everything."

Lennox saw her father's face fall, and a hint of guilt shot through her.

"But we've always had so much fun traveling and exploring."

Lennox's shoulders slumped. "It used to be fun, Dad. But

now...I've made friends. I'm in a great art class. I...have a date to the dance."

Her dad crossed his arms in front of his chest. "Is that what this is really about? Some boy? Or some girl—you know I'm totally okay with that." He smiled.

"It's not funny. And there is a boy, but that's not what it's about. It's about you being so totally out of touch that you don't even know if I'm gay or straight."

He frowned. "I was just being—"

"It's not funny anymore, Dad. I just want to stay put. I want to stay here."

"Staying put isn't always for the best, Lennox," he said to her back.

Lennox wanted to run to Allison or Eva. She wanted to sink into their lives, into their normalcy. Even the girl on Hicks Road seemed to have something over Lennox. Real or not, she was rooted, she was whole. Lennox turned to grab the necklace looped around the key rack, but it wasn't there.

"Sometimes it's time to move on."

"What—what happened to the necklace that was here?"

Her father shrugged. "I don't remember seeing any necklace."

She turned. "The chain was broken, but there was a little heart. Like a locket or a bauble. You didn't see it?"

He shook his head, and Lennox fell to her knees. "Maybe it just fell." She patted the heavy-pile carpet, dropping lower until she was on her belly. Her father's toes stopped in front of her.

"Did you find it?"

Lennox sat up onto her knees. "No."

"Was it something important?"

"You're sure you didn't see it? I left it right there, looped around that key-holder thing."

He shook his head and shrugged again. "Are you sure you left it there?"

"Yes."

"I'm sorry, kiddo. I never saw it. I'm going to hop in the shower. Are we good?"

Lennox stood. "No, we're not good. I'm not leaving San Jose."

Her dad pinched the bridge of his nose, then scooped up his cereal bowl. "Can we talk about this later, please? We have a whole month to figure this thing out."

Lennox crossed her arms and stood her ground. "Nothing to figure out. We're staying. Or at least I am."

He dropped his bowl into the sink and began to walk away. "We can talk more about this later, okay, hon? I love you."

Lennox was left staring at her dad's back as he walked away. She was fuming; for the first time, the idea of leaving wasn't just an annoyance, it was a threat. She turned back to the key holder and traced the smooth wood, willing the necklace to drop out of nowhere. It couldn't just disappear.

As dark streaks started to appear in the sky, Lennox tried

to focus on her schoolwork. She read the same problem over three times in her biology book, but each time the words swelled and jumbled in front of her, making no sense. She went for her English book next, but her fingers grazed the rolled-up charcoal drawing from art class. She unfurled the girl from Hicks Road little by little. Her stomach roiled as she saw the terrified eyes, the splayed hands.

I didn't make it up.

The necklace that had disappeared from Lennox's living room was safely locked around the girl's neck.

How could I forget drawing that?

The girl was a phantom, Lennox decided. A gut reaction to too much stress—*not like my mom.* She unfurled the rest of the drawing: the trees clawing at the road, her own white headlights. A little piece of yellow paper flitted out from the rolled-up bottom of the print.

FIND ME.

Lennox balled it up, shoved it in her jeans pocket. She changed into her pajama bottoms next, glancing at the mottled black-and-white cover of her therapy journal in her drawer. She flipped back to the pages before she'd driven out to Hicks Road in the darkness and barely recognized her own writing. It was small and tight at first, then big and slashy toward the end. She considered starting another list when her father's voice broke through her concentration.

"Laundry?" Lennox's dad gave a soft rap on the door, and Lennox pushed it open with her foot.

"Huh?"

He jiggled the laundry basket on his hip. "Laundry train. Anything to wash?"

"Colors or whites?" Lennox asked.

"Ha, you're funny."

Lennox gathered up the discarded clothes on her floor and tossed them into her dad's basket. "Thanks."

"Lennox, about this—"

Lennox's phone buzzed on the floor and her heart thudded. "Can we just talk about this later, maybe?"

Her dad stared at her for half a beat as if trying to read her. Then he bobbed his head and padded down the hall, laundry basket balanced on his hip. Lennox dove for her phone, groaning when she saw it was Allison and not Owen.

ALLISON: Come over!

Lennox looked over her shoulder. "Hey, Dad, can I go to Allison's house?"

"Now? You're in your pajamas."

Her dad looked at his watch.

"Height of fashion. But we're both having problems with our biology class so, you know, great minds, or two minds, or whatever?"

Her dad eyed her, then shrugged. "Two hours, tops."

Lennox nodded and grabbed her backpack, doing her best to look nonchalant while she searched for the necklace.

It couldn't have just disappeared. When Allison buzzed Lennox's phone again three minutes later, Lennox's cheeks flushed and she turned to her dad. "Was just looking for my phone. I'll be back on time."

TWENTY-ONE

Allison was scrolling through her phone, Eva was painting her toenails, and Lennox was trying to play it cool, hanging out with her friends in a very normal situation. They were at Allison's house, and Lennox wanted to revel in the moment, but her mind kept going back to the necklace, her fingers twitching as if they could still feel it. She longed for a pencil and a pad of paper to sketch out the delicate rings of the chain, the grooves of the heart that she couldn't forget.

"Oh!" Eva gasped. "I can't believe I forgot! I've been shopping. I've got our dresses for the dance!" She held up a bulging shopping bag, and Lennox's mouth dropped open as Eva pulled out three sequined dresses, tags still attached.

"You bought all those?"

Eva shrugged. "Mom did. Don't worry, you don't owe me anything."

Lennox raised her eyebrows.

"See? There are some benefits to coming from a broken home." Allison said it flippantly, but Lennox saw the color grow in Eva's cheeks. She tried to catch her eye, but Eva seemed to shake it off just as quickly, handing out the dresses. Lennox wanted to ask Eva what Allison meant but was quickly overwhelmed by the dress Eva held against herself, a flimsy thing with spaghetti straps and a skirt that was dangerously short—the kind that Lennox was used to rolling her eyes at, glad that she would never have to wear one.

"These are awesome!" Allison said, dropping her phone and grabbing the navy blue dress. "I call this one!" She stood and held the dress against her wiry frame. "This is gorgeous!"

Eva handed Lennox the second dress, this one an icy blue that sparkled under the overhead lights.

"Wow, it's really pretty. But I don't think so."

Eva's face fell. "What do you mean?"

Lennox stood next to Allison, holding the dress in front of her. "These will look amazing on both of you, but I am a head taller than you with half as much boob."

"That's why it's going to look incredible on you too. Come on, at least try it. You have to."

Lennox looked at the dress and at her friends and sighed.

"Three Musketeers and all that," Eva said with a nod.

"Did we even decide we were—"

Eva cut Lennox off and batted at the air. "Besides, when Owen sees you in it, he's going to freak." She grinned, and against her better judgment, Lennox felt a little twinge of excitement.

"I guess I can try…" She went to the bathroom and took

off her clothes, carefully stepping into the dress. She felt like a sausage as the fabric clung to her every curve, but when she slid the straps on and looked in the mirror, she didn't hate it.

"Well," she said, opening the door, "what do you guys think?"

Allison howled. Eva whistled. They were both wearing their dresses, and all three of them posed in the mirror, crushing their hips together to see the ombre of the blues darkening, then giggling and dancing around. Lennox flopped on the bed, her cheeks hot with laughter. She rolled over, her eyes settling on a framed picture on Allison's nightstand.

"Aw, this is us!" The picture was of the three of them, arms entwined, smiles wide. "From the party, right?"

Allison nodded. "Yeah, I just loved it. I can make you guys copies."

"Yes, please!"

Lennox squinted at the print. "That's so weird. The lighting or whatever makes the shirt I was wearing look red."

Allison and Eva exchanged glances. "Yes, because it was red."

Lennox shook her head. "No, it's blue."

"No." Eva took the picture and stared at it. "It's red."

"I totally remember because I was going to ask to borrow it to go with my red leather boots," Allison said, smoothing the sequins over her thighs. "Do you think I could wear them with this?"

"No," Lennox said with a forced chuckle. "I've had that shirt forever. It's blue. Almost the color of your dress." She gestured with her chin toward Allison.

Allison slid into the red leather boots. "Maybe you're thinking of a different shirt. Because"—she kicked her legs up—"red boots. What do you think?"

Eva frowned. "I think you look like you're competing in a Little Miss Firecracker pageant. If you can twirl flaming batons, I might give you a prize. Try those shoes." Eva dug through Allison's closet, handing over a pair of strappy sandals.

"You guys, I know my own shirt, and it's blue." Lennox studied the picture harder. She recognized her jeans, her hairstyle, even the necklace that Allison had lent her. "I know it's blue because the reason I borrowed that necklace, Al, was because the stone was blue. Ha!"

Allison popped open her jewelry box. "This necklace?"

Lennox nodded.

"Stone is red."

Lennox felt her face drop. "No, I specifically remember—"

"The stone is red because it's my birthstone. Why are you freaking out about this? It's a stupid red shirt. I mean, it's stupid cute, but it's nothing to get upset over."

Lennox snatched the necklace from Allison and held it a hairsbreadth from her face, then up to the light. The stone shone bloodred, casting a little rainbow on the wall.

"It's red," she murmured.

"Okay, we're wearing these, and everyone should do a neutral shoe."

"Are Converse neutral?" Eva wanted to know.

"Lennox?"

Lennox blinked, almost surprised she was still sitting on Allison's bed in a sequined dress she barely recognized. "I think I'm going crazy."

At home, Lennox went straight for her closet and began tearing through it, flipping clothes aside, looking for the shirt.

"Nice to see you too, hon."

She paused and sat back on her knees. "Oh, hey, Dad."

"Something I can help you with?"

Lennox looked at her father standing there in her doorway. He had dark rings rimming his eyes, and his lips were turned down. For the first time, she could see the deep lines around his mouth, fanning from the edges of his eyes.

"You look tired, Dad."

He nodded. "I am, but if you need me, I'm here to help." He held up his mug and took a sip.

Lennox shook her head. "It's nothing."

Her father stepped into the room, toed the pile of clothing on Lennox's floor. "Doesn't look like nothing."

"It's just me being...could you...do you forget things?"

He smiled, set his coffee mug down on Lennox's nightstand as he sat on the floor next to her. "Never. I just happened to find this coffee mug in the microwave, right where I left it two days ago."

"Ew!" Lennox wrinkled her nose.

"Don't worry, I washed it out. Now, what's going on?"

"It's kind of dumb. I just—I remember that I have this specific blue shirt that I wore to a party I went to. But Allison had a picture of us from that night, and the shirt was red."

"Okay?"

"But I *know* the shirt was blue."

Her father gestured to the pile. "And you're doing some research?"

"I know the shirt was blue, Dad. I know it. But I can't find it."

"Have you checked the laundry?"

Lennox chewed her lip, then pawed through the laundry basket.

"You know, it'd be easier to find things if you—"

"Actually put my clean stuff away. I know, Dad. But I'm kind of in the middle of a—dammit." Lennox turned around, mouth open. "It's red." She held up the shirt, inspecting it from every angle. "The shirt is red."

Lennox's dad shrugged and pushed himself off the floor with a groan. "Red, blue, does it really matter? As long as you're covered..." He took his coffee cup and walked out the door, leaving Lennox alone in her room.

Her hands started to shake.

The shirt was red. She sniffed it, half certain that someone was playing a prank on her, that someone must have climbed into her room and into her laundry basket, and planted the red shirt.

The girl in the window...

Lennox dropped the shirt and grabbed her hair by the handful, pulling until she felt the comforting sting of pain on her scalp. Then she wriggled into the red shirt, certain it would be too big or too small, like it was a bowl of porridge, certain an ill fit would prove that this wasn't her shirt at all. But it fit perfectly, just like she remembered, and she frowned.

"There was no girl, there was no blue shirt." She sat down on her bed and said it again, this time slightly louder, this time willing herself to believe it. "I'm Lennox Marie Oliver, and everything is totally normal. I wore a red shirt to a party and didn't hit a blond girl with my car. Everything is totally normal."

Then why do I feel so damn crazy?

TWENTY-TWO

Lennox balanced her sketchbook on her lap, doing her best to focus, but her mind kept going to her red shirt, and her pencil wasn't moving. She'd spent the day trying to convince herself that everything was okay, but she didn't believe it. Her fingers trailed over the Zoom link on her phone. Her rescheduled therapy session wasn't for another week, but Lennox wasn't sure if she could wait that long. She wanted her therapist to tell her that she was just under stress or that it was pollution or too many Cheetos that had caused the memory lapse, that it was a normal teen thing, but she knew deep down that she would see the frown lines framing Dr. Hartzog's thin lips. She would probably put out a therapist all-points bulletin, telling them to pick Lennox up on her way to school tomorrow because it was clear she was knee-deep in familial schizophrenia.

The ringing of the doorbell popped Lennox out of her head. She listened to her dad walk across the linoleum floor, then heard muffled male voices. After a beat she heard, "Lennox, your date is here."

Heat zinged up Lennox's spine. *My date?* She glanced at her phone, thumbing through the calendar. Nothing was listed, and she couldn't remember making a date.

"Lennox?" her dad asked again.

"One sec." Lennox looked at herself in the mirror, then threw on the closest clean shirt she could find. She dragged a brush through her hair and dabbed at her drooping eyeliner, then padded into the living room with bare feet.

"Owen?"

Owen was sitting on the couch across from Lennox's father. He smiled when he saw her, his dark eyes lighting up. "You look great."

"Tha—do we—I'm sorry." Lennox shook her head and then leaned down to Owen. "Did we have plans for tonight?"

His face fell, and Lennox saw that behind him on the couch was a cellophane-wrapped bouquet of flowers. His cheeks colored a fierce red.

"I know flowers are kind of cheesy, but...do you not want to go out? You said you were free tonight."

Lennox's mind reeled. She couldn't remember making a date with Owen—but she also couldn't remember the color of her own clothes. She took the flowers.

"These are beautiful, and of course we're still going out. I just forgot it was right now, is all."

She glanced over her shoulder at her father, her eyes pleading. He gave a quick nod and looked around her. "Just have her back by nine, okay, Owen? It is a school night."

"Nine, dad? Come on!"

Lennox's father pierced her with a stare.

"Okay, okay, nine it is," she said.

Lennox got into the passenger seat of Owen's car and turned to face him. "I'm sorry that I'm so scattered, things have just been—kind of weird lately."

Owen fed his keys into the ignition and started the car, then looked at Lennox with one of his signature half smiles.

"No worries. We were supposed to grab burgers and watch the game tonight. Is that still okay?"

Lennox paused for a beat, hoping the memory would come flooding back, but her mind remained blank. She gritted her teeth and smiled, just happy to be with Owen. "I'm game for anything."

Owen put his foot on the gas, and Lennox slid back into the seat. "Ow! Your car bit me!" She felt around behind her, pulling a barrette from the folds of the leather seat. It was rose gold with a spray of rhinestones in a circular pattern. "You should keep better track of your hair accessories, Owen."

Owen glanced at the barrette, then back at the road. "So that's where that thing got off to. Can you put it back in my hair, please? It keeps my bangs back…"

Lennox laughed. "Should I be concerned that you have ladies' hair accessories in your car?"

"I told you," Owen said mock sternly. "It's mine!"

Lennox beamed and unclipped the barrette, sliding it into Owen's hair. "Oh yes, very chic."

"It makes me feel pretty."

"So you buy yourself hair accessories."

Owen tugged the barrette out of his hair and tossed it in the back seat. "It belongs to my sister."

She sat back, feeling warm and happy, shrugging the events of the day off when Owen leaned over, their shoulders touching, his hand finding hers. She smiled contentedly and brushed strands of blond hair off her jeans, making a mental note to ask about Owen's sister some other time.

They settled into a booth at Sando's, Owen assuring Lennox that it had the best burgers in town. After they had downed burgers, milkshakes, and fries, he looked across the table at Lennox.

"So, you feel like hanging out?"

Lennox wiped her mouth with her napkin. "I thought we were hanging out."

He shrugged. "Still want to watch the game?"

Lennox continued to draw a complete blank but didn't want Owen to catch on, so she just nodded. "Yeah, let's do it. Are we going to...school?" She racked her brain, trying to think of what game they were going to watch and where. *Why can't I remember?* Her mind flitted through a thousand conversations, but she wasn't sure that she and Owen had ever had any of them; the pictures crashed and melded together, the words thrumming in her head like a hive of angry bees.

Owen chuckled, swiping the remains of both their dinners onto a tray. "You're funny. Let's break into the school and watch the game on one of their tiny TVs. Nah, I thought we'd go to my house. Unless you'd rather watch at your place?"

Lennox was taken aback. "Oh, yeah, right. I was totally joking. No, watching at your place is fine. Totally. My place is—just—we don't—our TV is broken."

He cocked an eyebrow, still grinning. "It was working fine when I came over."

Heat singed from the tips of Lennox's ears up to her hairline. "I meant...sports channels. Broken. Weirdest thing. Anything with a ball and the TV just—can we just go so I can stop talking now?"

Owen was still grinning, staring at Lennox. "I think you're cute when you're anxious."

He linked arms with her, and Lennox's nerves balled in the pit of her stomach, her heart clanging like a fire alarm. She wanted to worry about going to a boy's house, about what her father would say, but all she could think about was Owen's sweet smile and the way he held open her car door and chatted the whole way.

She had never been to a boy's house before and tried to brush it off as normal now, but it wasn't *just* a boy's house: it was Owen's, and she hadn't asked her dad (who definitely would have told her no way), and now Owen was pulling into the driveway. Lennox's breath sped up, her burger and milkshake vibrating in her stomach.

What do I do? What does he want?

Lennox's head spun even as she commanded herself to be normal. *One foot in front of the other, don't sweat to death, don't take off running, don't barf.*

"I'm just a normal girl doing normal things," Lennox murmured through gritted teeth.

"Did you say something?"

"Just talking to myself." Lennox felt like clapping a palm over her face.

For a brief moment, Lennox wished she were back in her own house, or even face-to-face with the girl from the road. Then she could close her eyes and wish the girl away, depend on her muddled mind to throw a thousand false visions in front of her. Now she was with a boy in real life, and she had to be normal and regular and not the girl who saw visions, the girl whose mother was locked up in some dressed-up excuse for a mental hospital, who would be packing her bags and in another zip code before anyone in school even remembered she was there. Now normalcy was right in front of her in jeans and a button-down shirt with a tiny dot of ketchup on the collar, and Lennox wanted to bolt.

"Can I use your restroom?"

"Of course," Owen said, ushering Lennox into the house. "Right there on the left."

Lennox locked herself in the small washroom and turned on the faucet, splashing cold water on her face. "Be normal, be normal, be cool..." She thought of Allison and Eva and how easy they made it look. She could be like them. She *was* like them. They were best friends.

Lennox stepped out, feigning confidence. She wasn't sure what she was expecting, but Owen's house was small and comfortable, the kind of house that meshed stylish and lived-in seamlessly.

"How long have you guys lived here?" she asked, shrugging out of her jacket.

"Since…birth. I guess." Owen smiled and grabbed the remote control. Lennox sat next to him on the couch while he flipped through channels. He snuggled into her when the game was on, stretching an arm across her shoulders.

Lennox had never liked romances—not movies, not books. She always thought the female leads were too swoony, too "love is the most important thing," but here she was, cuddled up with Owen, and all she could hear was the hum of the crowd on TV and the satisfied *thump-thump-thump* of her heart. Somewhere deep in her brain, there were flickers of memories, thoughts, and responsibilities, but here on Owen's couch, there was nothing but him and her, and she sank into the realization that this was how life could be—easy and normal—if she stepped out of her head every once in a while and lived a little. That's what she was thinking when the lock on the front door clicked and an officer in full regalia—uniform, hat, big black gun in a woven leather holster stepped into the house.

Lennox's stomach was in her throat, her heart slamming against her rib cage. She looked from the officer to Owen.

"Hey, Ma."

His mom!

Lennox's knees went rubbery and all the breath left her body. She felt like laughing out loud, then thought better of it, not sure which would be the better first impression: freaking out, or laughing like a madwoman in her new boyfriend's mother's face.

"Ma, this is Lennox. Lennox, my mom, June."

June crossed the living room in two strides, holding a hand out to Lennox. Her face was worn and lined, but she had the same warm smile as Owen, the same cocoa-brown eyes. "Lennox, hi, it's so nice to meet you!"

Lennox waited a half beat for June to start reciting the Miranda rights to her as she cuffed her on the spot. But there was nothing except a firm handshake, a yawn, and an apology.

"Nice to meet you too," Lennox said, hoping her voice wasn't as meek as it sounded in her own ears.

"I'm sorry. It's just been a really long day," June said. "I need to get into something more comfortable. Will you excuse me?"

Lennox nodded and sat while Owen crumpled on the couch. He pulled her hand, and she sat too, although stiffness made her sit bolt upright.

"I forgot that your mom is a cop."

"Is she?" Owen said. "I hadn't noticed."

"Is that...weird?"

Owen glanced at Lennox. "No, why would it be?"

"I don't know, she just, you know, wears a gun and…"

"And am I worried she's going to shoot me if I don't finish the laundry? Negative. She just does her thing and I do my thing."

"What about your dad?"

Owen chewed his bottom lip. "He does his thing with his other family in Oakland." He offered Lennox a smile that had no joy in it. "Can we talk about something else?"

Lennox was taken aback. "Oh, yeah, of course, sure. I didn't mean to pry. It's just my dad and me too. It kind of sucks sometimes, being without my mom."

"I'm sorry."

Lennox nodded, a wave of sadness washing over her. "Thanks. But my dad and I do pretty well. I mean, other than being dragged across the country for his job. It's weird. It always feels like we're running away from something."

Owen swallowed, his Adam's apple bobbing. "I get that."

Lennox licked her lips. "It's like, we never stay anywhere long enough to really do anything, you know? So it makes us kind of depend on each other." For the first time in her life, the realization made Lennox uneasy.

"Wonder what he's running from?"

Lennox nodded slowly, about to speak, when Owen's mom came down the stairs dressed in sweatpants and an oversize T-shirt and sighed. "You guys eat already?"

Lennox nearly jumped off the couch, then smiled

sheepishly. Her hip was resting against her purse, which began to vibrate. She dug for her cell phone.

"You okay, Lennox?" Owen asked.

Lennox looked up. "Jeez, I've missed seven calls from my dad." Her mouth went dry. "I should—do you mind if I—"

June's eyes narrowed. "He knows you're here, right?"

"Oh, yeah." Lennox nodded, although with her clouded mind, she couldn't really be sure. "Excuse me." She went into the hall and dialed her father, her heart thudding.

"Lennox! Finally!"

"Uh, hi, Dad. I just saw that I missed some calls. Sorry about that."

"Some calls?" her father snapped. "I feel like I've been calling you for hours. Where are you?"

Lennox looked over the back of the couch to where Owen was stretched out, his mother sitting in a chair to his left. They were chatting and smiling, and Lennox fell in love with the ease of the scene. It felt like she and her dad were constantly on different wavelengths lately, and she missed the time when they'd been a team rather than opponents.

"I'm with Owen," she whispered.

"And you were coming home by nine so you could get me to my shift, remember?"

Lennox frowned. "What?"

"My car is in the shop. We talked about this earlier, Lennox. Man, something is really off with you lately. Is it drugs? You know what? I don't have time for this right now. Just get over here and pick me up before I'm late for work, okay?"

Lennox nodded as her father hung up the phone and tried to blink away tears. She couldn't remember agreeing to take him. She bit her lip—no, she did remember; she had just forgotten. He would be furious and late for work, but at least it was just a slip of her memory and not a complete wipeout. That had to count for something, right?

"So, I'm super sorry, but—"

"You've got to run?"

Lennox nodded. "I just forgot that I'm supposed to pick up my dad. I can't believe I forgot; I'm not usually so"—she looked at Owen—"distracted. Are you mad?"

Owen shrugged. "Not mad at all." He stood, grabbing his keys. "Cinderella ran out on Prince Charming, and look how that turned out."

Lennox's father didn't say anything the entire ride to the hospital. He either didn't notice or didn't care about the hard set to Lennox's jaw as she gripped the wheel, her spine stick straight as every cell was on high alert. Sweat beaded her brow, and she turned the radio down to barely a murmur as she tried her best to focus on every movement, every flash of light around her.

"We're here," she said carefully, pulling into the hospital drop-off zone. "I'm really sorry—"

"It's okay, Lennox, but just please try to be less forgetful, okay? Write things down or something." He clapped a palm to his head. "Okay, like father, like daughter. I meant to tell you that I found out some information about Thursday night. You asked if anyone came into the hospital, any young girls?"

Lennox nodded, still on high alert. "And?"

"There were two, came in after my shift. A teen, age sixteen, broke her wrist. The second was a young woman or a teenager, but there wasn't much information on her because she was DOA." He gave her a soft kiss on the cheek and waved as he slid out of the car, disappearing behind the glass doors of the emergency department.

Lennox sat frozen in her car, hands on the steering wheel, headlights flooding the darkness in front of her. She was back on Hicks Road last Sunday night. A girl had come into the emergency room, but there wasn't much information on her because she was dead on arrival.

TWENTY-THREE

Lennox pushed her car into park and followed her dad through the glass doors. "Dad, Dad!" But he was half a hall ahead of her, his blue scrubs disappearing in a sea of other nurses and orderlies.

"Ma'am, can I help you?"

Lennox spun. "No, I was just—do you know about the girl?" she asked, dropping her voice to a throaty whisper. "A blond girl who was brought in dead last week?"

The front desk nurse stared at Lennox. "Is this person a family member?"

Lennox shook her head, a sob lodging in her throat. "No, but I just need to know—I need to know what happened to her. Can I see her?"

The nurse gaped. "Ma'am, you need to leave."

"But I—" Lennox stopped, the blood in her veins running cold. *But I could be responsible*, she both wanted and didn't want to say. *If I'm responsible, I'm not going crazy—but I'm also a murderer*, she thought grimly. There was no better or worse.

"Ma'am, if you don't leave the premises right this instant, I'm going to have to call the police." The woman's eyes were hard set, and she had the handset raised, her fingers ready to dial. Everything that Lennox had built—her social network, her stab at normalcy, was ready to crash down to the ground.

She shook her head no and forced her feet to move, taking great care to put one foot in front of the other.

Once home, Lennox let herself back into the house, her whole body shaking, teeth chattering. A girl was dead. A teenage girl—

Or a woman. It could have been a woman, Dad said.

—was dead.

Bile itched at the back of her throat, and she darted for the bathroom, her stomach clenching, tears dripping from her eyes. She fell to her knees, the vomit coming in waves. A girl was dead—because of her? She should have pushed, should have nailed down every tiny detail, but her dad was so mad and had slid out of the car, and of course it was Lennox's fault, it had to have been her fault.

Just like a hundred times before, the scene played out in front of Lennox's eyes: a burst of light like a camera flash; the girl, caught in the beam, eyes huge, hands splayed out; then that stomach-souring, sickening thud.

"No body, no blood," Lennox said, her jaw clenched so tightly it ached. "A coincidence." She sat, the tiles cool against her back. "This is a huge city." She wanted to say that people died every day, that accidents happened every day, and not every one was her fault, that maybe even this one wasn't her fault, but she couldn't. The words sounded wrong, the reasoning faulty.

She thought back to June in her police uniform, her holstered gun and the handcuffs tinkling at her waist.

"I didn't kill anyone," Lennox said, her voice firm. "I didn't kill anyone," she said again. "There would have been a body or blood or missing posters or a big press conference."

There was a body.

No, no, she thought again, sanity pushing through. *There was nobody there that night. Nobody on Hicks Road.*

Lennox had lived in enough big cities to know the protocol.

"Nothing happened," she said again.

I'm just going crazy.

<hr />

Lennox was dragging at school the next day. She wanted to swoon over her date with Owen, but the whole thing seemed like a watercolor memory, the paint running together, leaving nothing but an unrecognizable blob. Every time she tried to call up a good memory—the feel of Owen's fingers on her bare skin, the way they'd sat so close together she could hear his heart beat—her mind threw up something else: her dad's lips slipping over the phrase "DOA," the flash of her headlights on the pavement on Hicks Road.

"Lennox! Lennox!"

Lennox turned when a wad of paper hit her in the back of the head. "What was that?"

"I can ask you the same thing," Allison said, scooting her stool closer to Lennox's easel. "Where are you? You've been staring at that the entire class." She pointed her pencil toward Lennox's easel, and Lennox frowned. At some point, she had drawn an oval in the middle of the paper, then a second one on top of that and a third one. Next to her, Allison had a nearly complete self-portrait, as did the student next to her.

Lennox dropped her pencil and rubbed her eyes. "Sorry, I just—I'm totally zoning out."

"I hope you're mentally replaying your date with Owen and not still fantasizing about your dead Hicks Road deer." She crossed her arms in front of her chest.

Lennox blinked. "You know I went out with Owen last night?" She couldn't remember making the date or telling Allison about it. The reality sank like a stone in her stomach, and Lennox clamped her lips together, certain she was going to throw up. But she'd probably forget about that too.

Ms. Kincaid clapped. "Okay, class! Tonight you will finish up your self-portraits, and tomorrow we will hang them in the gallery."

Lennox sucked in an impressed breath and leaned over to Allison. "This school has a gallery?"

Allison shrugged one shoulder. "Don't get too excited. It's also called the cafeteria. The nice thing is, when you get your work back, it has the delightful smell of mystery-meat hash and those uncooked biscuits." She winked, and Lennox nodded. "Oh my gosh, Lennox! Snap out of it! Was your date awful or something? I thought for sure you'd make your self-portrait of you in a wedding dress."

Lennox sucked in a slow breath. "The date was...nice, but...I honestly don't even remember making the plan with Owen. I've been so wrapped up in the girl on the road."

"Ah." Allison nodded sagely. "The girl who doesn't exist."

"She exists, Ally. I—Owen thinks I dreamed her, but I'm sure she came to my house."

Allison stopped. "Wait, what?"

"I thought it was just a dream too, but there—there was this note. And I suppose it could have been from someone else, but..." She trailed off. "There are all these weird coincidences, and part of me thinks I'm going to be dragged off to jail for a hit-and-run, and the other part of me thinks I'm going to be dragged off to a mental institution because I'm losing my mind. Like the shirt, and the necklace—you saw the necklace, right?"

Allison nodded, picking up her pencil again and focusing on her drawing. "Of course I did."

"Well, it's gone now."

"What do you mean, gone?"

"You were going to take it, but instead, I hung it up on the key rack." Lennox darkened the oval outline on her drawing while she spoke, her eyes darting from the paper to where

Ms. Kincaid was perched, as if she was listening. "When I went back for it, it was gone."

"It was broken, Lennox. It probably just fell."

Lennox shook her head. "I looked everywhere. It's just my dad and me, and when I asked him if he saw it, he said no."

"Maybe...your dad is lying?"

Lennox snorted. "Why would he lie about something like that?"

"I don't know." Allison didn't move her eyes from her drawing. "Maybe your dad knows more about the necklace than he's letting on."

Lennox wrinkled her nose. "That's ridiculous. My dad is...like, a regular dad. Terrible jokes, socks with sandals. The same jeans across seven states. Are you suggesting he's some sort of psycho murderer?"

"Wow. You know you just went from zero to murder in, like, five seconds flat, right? You've said it a dozen times: nothing happened that night, and you even have weird, fuzzy memories. So fuzzy you can't remember what you wore."

"The blue shirt."

"Red, according to photographic evidence. And you have a broken necklace that may be from that night or may be from a druid priestess circle circa 1999. And someone came to your window?"

"The girl I saw that night. And she left a note that said 'find me.'"

"So, you think the real girl came to your window asking for help but then ran away to...?"

Lennox shrugged. "I don't know, freak me out? Make sure I stay quiet?"

"But the girl wasn't like, 'Here's my email, find me.'"

Lennox pinched the bridge of her nose, where pain was starting to thunder like a snare drum. "None of it makes any sense, does it?"

"No, it really doesn't."

"But who would do—"

Allison put her pencil down again, smoothed her hand over the edge of her drawing. "Someone who wants to mess with the new girl."

"I'm not that new."

"Maybe you pissed the wrong person off."

The bell rang, and Allison grabbed her shoulder bag and squeezed Lennox into a quick hug before joining the throng of students melting into the hall.

"Wait!" Lennox said, her voice dissolving in the thunderous hum of the hallway. "Who is the wrong person?"

<hr />

At home, Lennox unrolled the heavy paper and clipped it to her easel. She set up her mirror on her desk and grimaced at her reflection, pulling her ears and making monster faces. How was she supposed to do a self-portrait? She thought of her private sketchbook, the one tucked under the mattress, and the slew of faces she had hastily sketched there: a woman across from her on a subway, a homeless person with a vague resemblance to her mother. She drew faces easily, so why was sketching her own form suddenly so difficult?

Start with the basics.

She drew an oval, using barely there sketch marks to hash out quadrants of her face. She placed blank almonds for the eyes and arches for her brows, a nose vaguely left of center, and too-thin lips pulled down at the corners. She worked quickly, glancing in the mirror and then back at her page, shading her eyes and sketching out her lashes, thickening her lips and trying to get her cheekbones just right, but each time she pulled away, there was something wrong, something off about the portrait. The eyes were blank and wooden-looking. The lips weren't hers, and the set of the brows gave the whole portrait a sense of smug disinterest. Lennox kept working, using long strokes for her hair and going back to her eyes, the arches of the brows, the Cupid's bow of her lip. Her lines got darker, more certain, but the portrait looked less and less like her.

Lennox's lip started to tremble. The hand holding her pencil started to ache.

"Mom."

"Lennox, honey, that is remarkable."

She had no idea when her dad had come in. He was standing in the doorway now, one hand holding his chin, his eyes wide.

"You two look so much alike."

Her father seemed pleased, and Lennox wanted to be, but his words—the recognition—made Lennox's blood run cold. This was supposed to be a self-portrait. *Her* self-portrait.

Only it wasn't.

"That's not what—" she started to say. "That wasn't the assignment."

Her dad stepped over and took a picture before Lennox could throw her hands over the portrait. "Dad, no!"

"Your mother will be so flattered. I'll send it to her." He smiled, and Lennox's heart splintered. Her father was proud—overjoyed, even—and all Lennox could think about was how she didn't want to be like her mother. How she didn't even want to *look* like her mother.

"Okay," she managed to croak. "Sure."

Lennox glanced back at the picture. It did look startlingly like her mother, but like Lennox too—Lennox mixed with someone—or something else, something as yet undefined. Now, with deeper lines and more shading, the eyes didn't look so blank, so lost.

They just looked haunted.

TWENTY-FOUR

Lennox rubbed her eyes. She had tried the search at least a dozen times, from every angle: *dead teen in San Jose emergency room; fatal accidents San Jose; Hicks Road teen murderer; accidental deaths San Jose.* There was a two-line article about that missing girl in Santa Cruz, but nothing else, and by the time her father had taken the bus home from work, she was already asleep.

When she pulled up in front of the school the next morning, her eyes widened. The horseshoe-shaped administrators' parking lot was crammed with police cars, and uniformed officers huddled in a group right outside the school office. Owen was there too, looking off into the distance. He was shoulder to shoulder with his mother, who looked sharp and professional in her uniform. Lennox's heart started to do a nervous little patter, but then everything inside her froze.

Lennox drove into the back lot on autopilot, her sweaty palms nearly slipping on the wheel. *Did Owen say something to his mom? Is that why there is a team of police at the school—to arrest me?*

Lennox's legs were Jell-O as she stepped out of the car, eyes darting like there were cops or spies or phantom blonds everywhere. *Owen wouldn't do that to me,* Lennox told herself. *And besides, I didn't do anything wrong.*

Except hit-and-run.

That little voice in the back of her head niggled at Lennox, and she did her best to tamp it down, to turn it off, but it kept playing like a drumbeat with every step she took. She stopped in the street before stepping onto campus. She felt like a prisoner walking to her death. Were they waiting for her? If she stepped into the school, would they arrest her? There were half a dozen officers and one of those large paddy wagons. *Do they think I'm that dangerous?*

Lennox's mouth was paper dry, her feet planted on the asphalt. *Go,* she told herself.

She jumped when a student in a Pontiac the size of a boat laid on the horn. "Get out of the street!" he yelled.

Lennox stumbled backward, away from the school and into the lot. She was walking, and then she was running, her backpack slamming against her spine. She knew what she had to do. She had to find her.

Lennox wasn't sure how long she drove around San Jose. She wasn't sure how many calls she missed from Owen, Allison, and Eva. She felt like a criminal now, like a woman on the run, but she wasn't even sure what from. If the police couldn't find Lennox at school, wouldn't they just go to her house? Would her dad give her up?

But her dad was ready to move.

Lennox chewed her bottom lip. She would go with him. She would run. They had done it before, moving from place to place. Why not now?

But in those days, her father was going from job to job, not running from a crime. The realization made Lennox's blood go cold, and she pulled over, killing the engine and resting her head against the steering wheel.

What is going on?

The tears started to fall fast and hard, and soon Lennox's shoulders were shaking with the sobs.

Evidence. She sobbed. *I have evidence.* She thought of the necklace and then remembered that it was gone. But the note... Lennox dug into her jeans pockets, first one and then the other, then checked her back pockets, where her fingers came upon the soft, washed remnants of the paper.

The laundry.

She pulled out what was left of the note and tried to smooth it against the steering wheel. Most of it disintegrated underneath her palm.

"No, no, no!"

The penciled letters were smeared and faded. Lennox frowned, then crumpled the note and threw the remnants in her glove box, giving in to a fresh wave of tears. The blaring of her phone stopped her, and she glanced at the screen: Owen.

She imagined Owen in the school office on one of those giant phones with a microphone attached, the entire police force standing by and saying things like, "Get her to keep talking so we can triangulate her position." When she could stand it no longer—being a fugitive on the run or the main suspect in a crime that may or may not have happened— Lennox steeled herself and thumbed the phone.

"Hello?"

"Hey, it's Owen, are you okay?"

Lennox nodded, then cleared her throat. "Yeah, sorry."

"Are you sick? I'm sorry to bug you, but I sent a thousand text messages and you didn't respond, so I thought..."

"I'm at Fischer and King, if you want to tell your mom."

There was a short pause, then, "If I want to tell my mom what?"

"Where to come get me. Or should I go there?"

"To my house?"

Lennox bit her bottom lip, her voice a tight whisper. "To the police station."

"Um, okay. But also no. Lennox, what is going on?"

"Look, Owen, I came to school this morning. I saw all the cop cars and you with your mom. I know you told her."

"About the dance? Yeah, I told her I'm taking you—"

"Not about the dance! About what I told you. About that

night on Hicks Road and the girl coming to my window. I had a note. It said, 'find me.'"

"You *had* it?"

Lennox swung her head miserably, knowing Owen couldn't see her. "My dad washed it. It was in the pocket of my jeans, and my dad did laundry."

"Okay, but what are you talking about with my mom and wanting to come to the police station?"

"I know that you told your mom I hit someone and that's why the police are at the school, to arrest me. I'm turning myself in, sort of. I mean, I want to call my dad first to say goodbye, but I'm not going to obstruct justice. I'm going to do the right thing."

Owen didn't answer, and Lennox pressed the phone harder against her ear, trying to hear him murmur to the police that he'd gotten a confession.

"Owen, are you laughing?"

He heaved a breath into the phone and broke into another round of laughter so strong it made him cough.

"This is funny to you? I'm on my way to jail, and you think this is funny. I thought you were a great guy, but you're an asshole. Do you and your mom plan these things so you can nab criminals?"

"Lennox, wait." He breathed heavily and cleared his throat. "Please, stop. I am so sorry, and I promise I'm not laughing at you. It's just—I'm sorry, but my mom and her crew are here for an assembly, not to arrest anyone, least of all you. And I didn't tell my mom about Hicks Road because there's nothing to tell. I told her I'm taking you to the dance, and believe me, my mom's a little overprotective, but not to the point that she'd arrest my date. At least I don't think."

Lennox's shoulders slumped. "Oh my God."

"Lennox, you didn't do anything wrong. There was no crime—"

"But the note and the girl!"

"You may have seen someone on the road, but you didn't hurt them, at least not enough to make it a crime. And I think someone saw you guys that night—that's the only explanation. There were at least twenty people at that party, which meant about twenty cars headed down that road. Someone is playing a prank on you. It's a really, really crappy one, but you're no criminal."

Lennox sucked in a breath, suddenly feeling weak and overtired. "I feel kind of dumb now."

Owen didn't say anything, and Lennox rambled on.

"Do you still want to go to the dance with me?"

"Are you kidding? A criminal on the run who clearly has a heart of gold? That's every boy's dream date."

"You suck, Owen."

"Come back to school."

"How do I know this whole thing isn't a scam? That your mom isn't there coaching you through this entire conversation?"

"Take the risk, Al Capone. There could be free pizza in it for you."

"I do like pizza."

"See you in ten minutes?"

"Okay."

Lennox clicked off her phone and glanced in the rearview mirror. Her cheeks were red and blotchy, her mascara in tiny black chips around her lashes. She looked a little worse for wear, but she wasn't a criminal. She wasn't.

She slammed her palm against her forehead and rolled her eyes. "I just tried to turn myself in to my crush's mother. Great, Lennox, you're fitting right in."

Lennox turned over the ignition, put the car in gear, and pulled away from the curb.

TWENTY-FIVE

The Senior Hall was buzzing when Lennox walked into school on Friday. Though it wasn't ever quiet in the halls, today's din had a weird, sinister slant to it, and she couldn't help but feel a sense of dread with each step.

"Lennox, there you are!" Eva's eyes were wide as she laced her arm through Lennox's and pulled her aside.

"Yeah, I'm here. What's going on?"

Eva blinked. "You don't know?"

Lennox turned and noticed the kids around her were moving at a snail's pace, slowing even more when they got to her and Eva, all eyeing her with sad gazes.

"Eva, what the heck is going on?"

Eva swallowed hard. "I don't want you to be mad. Or freaked out or scared. I'm sure it's just some stu—"

"Let me guess: some stupid prank?" Lennox shook her head, butterflies zooming through her gut. "Just tell me what happened."

Eva sucked in a breath. "I'd rather show you." She laced

her fingers through Lennox's and led her down the hall toward the "gallery." "I'm really sorry," she said.

Lennox stepped into the cafeteria-slash-gallery, where students were leaning on benches and sitting at tables, chatting and eating. A few kids walked slowly past the bank of self-portraits from Lennox and Allison's art class, but about a dozen were clustered around one portrait: hers. Lennox's lips quirked up. *Do they like it? Is it really that good?*

She took a step toward the group, and it was like everyone in the cafeteria collectively took a breath and held it. The silence was overwhelming, and all Lennox could hear was the wild *pound-pound-pound* of her heart. She took another step, and the group parted, giving her a wide berth, their eyes never leaving Lennox.

Lennox looked at her portrait on the wall and gasped.

The eyes that she had worked so hard to get right were gashed out, the white from the wall showing through. Someone had used thick black ink to doodle a zigzag pattern across her lips, making it look like they were sewn shut. The words *I'll never tell* were carved into her cheek, and a heavy red line circled her throat.

Lennox's fingers went to her own neck, and she gulped, feeling bile itch at the back of her throat. The hands in her drawing were mutilated with tears and something resembling stab marks, two bloodred rings braceleting each wrist with blood bubbling down her arms.

"Oh my God," Lennox murmured.

"Lennox." Eva slid her arm around Lennox, and she slumped against her best friend. "It's just someone's idea of a sick joke," she said in a soothing tone.

"No." Lennox's voice was a choked whisper. She stumbled backward, Eva still holding her up.

"Who did this?" Eva snapped at the crowd. "Did you?" She was pointing randomly, and Lennox swung forward, bending her knees and pushing her head between them.

"I think I'm going to be sick," she choked, crossing her arms in front of her stomach. "Eva…"

Eva pulled Lennox up and threaded her arms around her. "Lean on me," she whispered. "Come on." Eva led Lennox toward the door, then stopped, whirled around, and snarled, "If any one of you is responsible for this, I hope you go to hell!"

There was some laughter from the crowd, but Lennox couldn't stay to watch. She sprinted down the hall and into the ladies' room, crumbling in front of a toilet before she threw up. Behind her, she heard Eva enter the bathroom and run water over a paper towel. Once Lennox was done vomiting, Eva let herself into the stall and pressed the wet paper towel to Lennox's forehead, letting Lennox lean against her.

"I'm so sorry, Lennox," she said. "Kids suck. They can be really jealous of awesome work."

Lennox wished she could believe that. "I don't think it was a prank, Eva."

"What do you think it was?" Eva wanted to know.

Lennox drew a shallow breath and stared at Eva. "I think it was a warning."

Lennox was called into Mr. Apex's office after the first bell. She bit her lip when she saw the look of consternation on his face, those stubby paws of his laced and resting on the desk. He gestured for her to take a seat.

"It's nice to see you, Lennox."

Lennox nodded but frowned. She didn't want to see him even on good terms; today was even worse. She kept her mouth shut and shook her head when he offered her one of those fat little waters from his mini fridge in the corner.

"Do you know why you're here?"

Lennox did, but she shrugged anyway.

Mr. Apex pressed his lips into a sad little smile, then pulled Lennox's self-portrait out from behind his desk.

"You're here because of this."

She winced and looked away. It was just lines on paper, charcoal and ink, but the gashes and stab marks felt violent and physical, and Lennox's stomach roiled. Her saliva was sour, but she licked her lips and tried her best to keep her head up.

"That's awful," she managed.

Mr. Apex looked weirdly surprised. "So you agree?"

Lennox nodded. "Can you put that down, please?"

He waited a beat, then lowered the picture, and Lennox felt pricks of relief cool her skin.

"So you're saying you don't want to look at your own artwork?"

Lennox frowned. "I don't want to look at my artwork that someone vandalized. I mean, look what they did to me. It's hideous. It's"—she shuddered—"scary, almost."

"Vandalized? Lennox, are you sure you didn't do this yourself?"

Lennox's eyes widened. Her mouth dropped open. "You think I did that? Why would I do that to my own work? It took me almost three whole hours to finish that. Why would I ruin it by making myself look like some kind of freaky goth princess?"

"Okay, okay, calm down. No one is blaming you."

Lennox gaped. "You are. You just asked me why I would do something like this! I'm asking you, why would someone else do that to my portrait?"

Mr. Apex was back in school counselor mode, aggravatingly calm, lacing his fingers again. "Kids have reasons that we don't always understand, Lennox. Haven't you ever done something and then, perhaps, not known exactly why?" He pinned her with a stare, and Lennox felt her blood go cold. *Is he talking about that night? Does he know? Does he know I left?*

Lennox shook her head. "W-w-what are you saying?"

Mr. Apex shrugged. "I'm saying maybe it was a meaningless prank."

"A prank? What is it with this school? I think your student body might be a little bit off if this is the kind of thing that passes as a prank. Someone drew me covered in blood. With my throat slashed. That's not—don't you think that's some kind of threat? Because I do."

"Lennox…"

Lennox was on her feet, pacing. "Please don't try to tell me to brush it off, Mr. Apex, because something is going on. I—I—I keep forgetting things, and things are going missing, and I think I saw—" She looked up to see Mr. Apex leaning forward in his seat, eyebrows furrowed, lips in that thin little line that told her he was listening. She stopped. "I just don't…" Lennox slumped back into the chair, pressing her fingertips against her temples and making little circles, hoping for the drumbeat of a brand-new headache to cease. "Maybe I'm just going crazy."

Maybe that was the buzzword Mr. Apex was looking for. He cleared his throat and jumped into action, opening and closing drawers and clicking pens. "There is nothing wrong or abnormal about the way you are feeling, Lennox, I want you to know that."

She arched an annoyed eyebrow.

"As I mentioned, I am always here, my door is always open, but if you'd like someone to talk to—you know, a professional in the field—"

Lennox hung her head. "You think I'm crazy too."

"No! No, and, just as a matter of practice, we don't say

'crazy.' You're not crazy. Your feelings might feel a little bit—"

She pinned him with a stare. "Someone came to my window, Mr. Apex. I didn't make her up. And the stuff with my self-portrait, that wasn't me." Lennox looked at her hands, feeling defeated. "I should just go."

She stood, and so did Mr. Apex, reaching out a hand. "Sit, Lennox, please. Look, I know from your transcript—"

Lennox gritted her teeth, her jaw aching. "That was a long time ago."

"Mental health issues—"

Tears stung behind Lennox's eyes. "I'm not crazy," she said, her voice barely above a whisper.

"When a parent leaves a child..."

Lennox closed her eyes, willing the earth to open up and swallow her. She wanted to disappear into the walls, slip into one of Mr. Apex's stupid posters about well-being and forming a community. She had tried to be well. She had tried to be part of the campus community. *And now I can't even walk down the hall without being gawked at.* Lennox swallowed hard and reached out for the little piece of paper Mr. Apex scribbled on.

"These are two of the best therapists in town. They specialize in—"

Lennox offered a smile with no mirth. "Not crazy teenagers?"

Again, Mr. Apex's eyes darkened. "Lennox—"

She put her hand on the doorknob. "Kidding. Thanks."

Just before the door snapped shut behind her, Lennox saw Mr. Apex still standing at his desk, arms threaded in front of his chest. There was something in his eyes that Lennox didn't recognize, but it set her on edge. She crumpled the piece of paper he'd handed her and dumped it in the first trash can she could find.

TWENTY-SIX

Lennox opened her locker and frowned, thumbing through the books packed in there.

"That's so weird," she mumbled to herself.

She unzipped her backpack, then went back to her locker, methodically pulling out each book and examining it before pushing it back in.

"Where. Is. That. Stupid. Book?"

"Something I can help you with?"

Owen cut through the sea of students—actually, they seemed to part for him like he was some sort of pharaoh— and grinned, handing Lennox a Coffee Spot cup.

"What's this?" she asked.

"Thought you could use a little coffee."

Lennox warmed through, a near sob catching in her chest. "You knew I needed this! Is that because of your mom? Is the graffiti all over the police blotter?"

Owen shrugged. "Graffiti?"

Lennox looked back in the direction of her ruined art, her

stomach roiling with the sip of coffee. "Never mind. It's just been a—weird day. Again, thank you for this."

"Don't thank me. Perk of being my mom's son."

"You don't have, like, your own set of coffee-fetching security guards or something, do you?" She poked him in the shoulder. "Goons who do your bidding or something?"

"First of all, I love that you talk like a nineteen-thirties gangster, and second of all, I have a desk drawer full of San Jose Police Department pens and stickers, but not a single goon." Owen pushed out his lower lip, and Lennox had every urge to kiss it.

"Poor you."

"Indeed. So I had to leave campus to get coffee."

"How does being the chief's son help with that?"

"It doesn't, I was just trying to impress you. What do you have next?"

"History," Lennox said with a frown. "And I am one hundred percent certain that I put my history book in my locker, and now I can't find it."

"Did you check your—"

"Backpack? Of course. But I remember putting it in here. Like, total muscle memory. I looked at the cover, I slid it in between these two books"—Lennox gestured—"and now it's not here. Call your mom. A crime has been committed."

Owen chuckled and eased Lennox's backpack from her shoulder, sliding out all the books. "Okay, biology." He handed it to her. "Spanish workbook. *California Laws and*

Regulations." He raised his eyebrows, and Lennox felt her cheeks redden.

"It's for...some class."

"And your history book."

"What? No, no way. I looked in my backpack forty times." She took a slug of her coffee. "It wasn't there."

Owen held up the book. "Sorry, but it is now."

Lennox narrowed her eyes at Owen, then squinted at her coffee cup. "I think this stuff is magic. Either that or I really am going crazy. Hey, can you get Alzheimer's when you're seventeen?"

"Maybe you should ask your dad about that."

Lennox raised her eyebrows. "My dad? Why?" She immediately flashed back to her mother, the blank stare she gave Lennox when she said hello. "What do you mean?"

"Isn't your dad a doctor or something?"

Lennox nodded, relieved. "Yeah, he's a nurse."

"He might know why the brain—or the backpack—acts so mysteriously." Owen wiggled his fingers and stepped into the flock of students pouring through the hall.

"You're super weird, you know."

"Just trying to keep it interesting" was his reply.

Lennox chuckled and tried to think of Owen, but the history book in her hand was puzzling her. It hadn't been there before he'd shown up—she was sure of it. She remembered putting it in her locker, remembered sliding it in between...didn't she?

She turned the book over and over in her hands, flipping

through the pages as if, miraculously, some explanation would be there, but there was nothing. She sighed and slid the book into her bag, slamming her locker door shut.

"No big deal," she said to herself through gritted teeth. "Just a dumb mistake."

Lennox turned to enter the sea of students, but suddenly, she couldn't remember where she was going. She blinked, the Senior Hall wobbling in and out, the students' faces gaunt, then long, stretched out, grotesque. Everyone was looking at her. She knew it. She could feel it. And they were talking to her too, but she couldn't make out the words. Their voices were deep and slow, then clipped and ultra high-pitched. Lennox pressed her palms against her ears, trying to drown out the sound, the buzz like a thousand wasps in her ears.

Someone was touching her. She could see the arm, the hand on her shoulder, but she couldn't feel it, couldn't move under the weight. Her eyes flashed, and she tried to scream at the eyeless face in front of her. Lennox felt her mouth open, felt the ache of her lungs expanding, but there was no sound, not a word coming out.

"Lennox." It was a man, and he was holding her more tightly now. The rush and buzz of students came to a stand-still as they surrounded her, stared at her, reached for her.

"No." She was able to push the word past her teeth, was able to make an audible sound. "No!" she said again, this time louder, and suddenly she was able to move her feet—and then she felt herself falling backward into a black abyss.

She saw lights move across the ceiling and Mr. Apex's wide eyes. Somewhere behind her, she heard Allison call her name and Eva squeal. Lennox tried to reach out, but her body wouldn't work, her mind caught in an endless loop of lights flashing, hands reaching. Her heartbeat was a panicked frenzy, and Lennox struggled to breathe, feeling her windpipe shrink smaller and smaller.

"Everyone give her room!"

She vaguely recognized Mr. Apex's voice, deep and authoritative.

"Get back!"

Lennox wanted to tell him to stop. She wanted everyone to leave, to get on with their day and leave her alone. She wanted to walk away, but Mr. Apex was cradling her head, and she was lying on the ground, too exhausted to be mortified as she watched sneakers and heels move past her.

"I'm okay," Lennox said.

"We're getting the nurse."

"No." Lennox tried to shake her head. "I can get up."

But she couldn't.

"I just tripped," she said. *That's what happened, right?*

Mr. Apex was fanning her, and the nurse was rushing forward, cradling Lennox's head under her arm.

Allison was kneeling on the floor, shoving Lennox's book into her bag. "I can call her dad."

Lennox's whole body was moving in molasses-slow motion. It was as if she had to tell herself to breathe, had to tell her heart to beat. She could feel each cell in her body moving independently, could feel her blood plodding along in her veins, could feel the tiny pricks and pulls of her hair growing from her scalp. She wanted to talk, to brush it all off and run away, but gravity held on, held her down, even as Mr. Apex and the nurse began to help her up, Allison alongside them.

"Don't forget your bag," she was saying.

Lennox shook her head with monumental effort. "I'm fine," she said, but it sounded labored, and Allison's eyes widened as she handed the bag to the nurse.

"I swear I'm okay."

But Lennox felt weak and confused when they sat her on the cushy plastic gurney, the nurse attaching a blood pressure cuff and taking her temperature.

"Thank you for your help, Mr. Apex, you can go."

Lennox hadn't even realized that Mr. Apex was still there, still had his hand on her shoulder, and she recoiled, though she didn't mean to, her body moving with a will of its own.

She watched Mr. Apex slide her backpack off his shoulder and rest it on a chair. The movement felt too intimate, too familiar, and Lennox's mind wandered back to the missing book that had reappeared. She closed her eyes, trying to get the image out of her head, and the nurse squeezed her hand.

"Your temperature is fine, but I'd like you to stay here for a while. I'll have the office call your dad."

"No," Lennox said, shaking her head. "There is no reason to do that. I just—I tripped or something…"

The nurse pulled up a chair, and Lennox could feel her jaw set hard. She knew that expression, the one that said they were going to have a little "talk," something about Lennox's mother or fitting in or mental health.

"Lennox, do you know what a panic attack is?"

She sucked in a breath. "Of course I do."

"So you've had one before."

Lennox looked away, not wanting to engage this woman, not wanting to relay her whole mental health history to yet another stranger who pretended to care, who would see that Lennox's mother had been committed and believe that Lennox was on her way there too.

"I move around a lot. It's no big deal. I've had a couple of panic attacks in the past. This was not that."

The nurse pressed her lips together in a patronizing smile, and Lennox wanted to stand up, to knock this lady out of her chair and run out of the office. This lady didn't know. Were school nurses even actual nurses?

"I just—"

"It's totally normal and nothing to be ashamed about. The best thing to do is—"

Lennox narrowed her eyes, flared her nostrils. "I know, deep breathing, count to ten, et cetera, et cetera."

"That's very helpful in the moment, yes, and to diffuse situations before they get to the physical point. But I see in your file—"

Lennox's stomach dropped. The file.

TWENTY-SEVEN

That damn file followed her everywhere, a testament to every mistake she'd ever made, everything her mother had ever done publicly that school "specialists" across the country had pulled out as Lennox's future milestones.

"Can I get a glass of water, please?"

The nurse nodded curtly and stood up, leaving the file on her seat. Lennox snatched it up the second she heard the click of the door, scanning the pages, the logos of Schools of Lennox's Past. There were photocopies of scribbled notes about attendance and absences and one page entitled "Mental Health Evaluation." She did her best to scan it, but one thing flooded her vision. One thing she couldn't block out: her parents' signatures. Both of them, from when Lennox was in third grade.

Something about an "episode."

Something about Lennox losing consciousness.

Something about another student.

Lennox racked her brain but couldn't remember third

grade. She couldn't even remember what state she had been in at that time, and the crest of the school—Leaf Valley— offered no clues.

Suddenly, Lennox was pulled back to that night on Hicks Road, the girl in the headlights. Had she blacked out?

No, the headlights clicked off.

Had she lost consciousness?

No. Lennox gritted her teeth. *The girl was real.*

You're seeing things... a voice taunted at the back of her head. *You're going crazy like your mom.*

The nurse stepped back inside, and Lennox threw her file on the woman's chair. Her eyes followed Lennox, and she offered that same patronizing smile. "It's your file. You're entitled to look through it."

Lennox reached for the water the nurse handed her. "No thanks. Can I go back to class now?"

The nurse shook her head. "Your dad should be here any minute. We agreed that you taking the rest of the day off to relax is the best plan of action. We value mental health highly around here. It's nothing to be ashamed of."

"I'm here for Lennox Oliver."

Lennox let out a sigh of relief when she saw her father winding through the office to get to her. He was dressed in his scrubs and was still wearing his Crocs and surgical hat, his credentials clipped at his waist. She immediately felt bad for pulling him out of work when she was obviously just—*what*? Her own brain couldn't even compute what had happened.

I lost a book.

I drank some coffee.

I got confused.

Lennox's mouth started to water, her saliva bitter. *The coffee! Was there something in it? Did Owen...* No. She shook her head again. Of course not.

Owen was her boyfriend. What good would poisoning her in the middle of the Senior Hall do?

"Hey, Dad, sorry for all this. Can we just go home?"

Her dad broke into a smile when he saw her. He threw his arms around her and pulled her into a deep hug.

"Just lost yourself a little, huh, muffin?"

"Please don't ever call me that, and no, I just"—Lennox's eyes cut from her father's to the nurse—"I just need a breather is all. I have my car, though."

"You're not driving. I'll run you home, set you up, and we can get your car later."

Lennox just wanted out of the nurse's office, where the walls were closing in and she was sure that everyone everywhere was listening.

"Sure, whatever."

Lennox sat in the passenger seat of her dad's car, running her thumbnail along the upholstery as he pulled out into the flow of traffic.

"I'll just have to drop you off, as I'm only on lunch. But if you need me, I can stay. I'm sure I can get someone to cover, it just might not be right away."

Lennox shrugged. "I can stay home alone, I'm a big girl."

He glanced over at her, and Lennox saw that his eyes were glossy, his eyebrows downturned with concern. "So, what happened?"

Lennox swallowed. "The nurse thinks I had a panic attack."

There was a beat of silence. "What do you think?"

Lennox yawned, suddenly exhausted. "I think I'm tired and want to go back to bed."

Her dad smiled. "Can't argue with that."

"Do *you* think I had a panic attack?"

He slowed the car to a stop at a red light and looked at Lennox. "Is there something you want to talk about?"

Lennox sighed, her stomach doing a double flutter. "Did I have mental problems as a kid?"

Her dad frowned, then pushed the car into gear when the light changed. "Not more than any other kid."

"I saw my file. It said there was an incident. You and Mom signed it." Lennox studied him for any sort of tell, but he just shrugged.

"Not anything I can remember. You had an imaginary friend for a bit, but I don't think that would be something they'd write up."

"I had an imaginary friend? I don't remember that."

"Oh yeah, big-time. She was always popping up. Blond girl."

Lennox's eyes widened, her throat constricting. "I had a blond imaginary friend?"

"Long blond hair—you always said she was brushing it. And then you'd brush yours too. Really cute."

"Did she have blue eyes?"

"Probably."

Lennox's mouth went dry, her stomach turning over. She thought of her mother in those last days, her mouth frantically moving but no sound coming out as she positioned herself in the corner and spoke to someone Lennox couldn't see. The conversation had been wild and animated but silent, and Lennox had felt even more like an outsider to this woman who had overtaken her mom. "There are always people around," her mother had told her. "People watching and listening."

Bile itched at the back of Lennox's throat, and tears pricked at the edges of her eyes. Her mother wasn't crazy, she was sick. But she had truly believed she saw all those people.

Just like Lennox truly believed she'd seen the girl on the road.

The girl with the long blond hair.

"How long did this friend stay around?" she asked, her voice tentative and small.

"I don't really know," her father said, guiding the car into the driveway. "Another movie came along, and then that princess was your imaginary friend."

"You're talking about a Disney princess?" Lennox snapped, her hand pressed against her pounding heart.

"Well, yeah. According to you, you were best friends."

Imaginary friends were normal.

But seeing the girl on the road is not.

"You don't have to get out, Dad. I can get myself settled."

Lennox slammed the car door behind her before he had a chance to speak.

Back in her room, Lennox started to pace. She tried to trace what had happened—the hallway, the book, Owen—but there was a blank slash through her memory. Even though it had happened hours ago, her heart still ramped up each time she thought of herself going down, and fear rippled through her once again.

I'm going crazy.

She sat down gently on her bed and chewed the inside of her cheek, her teeth breaking through and unleashing a metallic wash of blood in her mouth. She started to cry.

Is this how it happens?

Lennox pulled out her notebook and began to write:

1. *Hicks Road*
2. *The broken necklace / necklace disappears*
3. *The girl in the window / blood*
4. *Portrait gets graffitied*
5. *Panic attack at school (?)*

And then, slowly, she wrote,

6. *Couldn't remember the color of my shirt*

She stared at her list, her neat writing starting to swirl. She used the back of her hand to wipe away tears before drawing the black-gray lead of her pencil across number one: *Hicks Road.*

"No one saw it but me," she whispered. Her pencil hovered over number two before she drew a line through that entry too.

"The necklace could have been from anywhere and"— here Lennox sucked in a breath that seemed to constrict her lungs—"it disappeared into thin air."

She paused at three, *the girl in the window.*

"I *saw* her," Lennox said aloud, her voice firm. "I know I did." Her pencil hovered.

But no one else did! that little voice taunted from the back of her head.

The note!

The note was real. It was solid, tangible proof that someone had been there.

And you washed it to pieces.

Lennox went on to number four, putting a check mark beside it and trying not to flash back to the panic attack, to the wide eyes staring at her as if she was crazy.

"I'm not crazy," she whispered, putting a check mark next to number four, *portrait gets graffitied.* "That happened."

She stopped again at her final entry, looking away from the notepad and finally dumping it on the bed.

"So I forgot the color of a shirt…"

A shirt you've had for years.

"No. Big. Deal," she spat pointedly.

You wore it a week ago. You wore it to the party. It was red.

"It was blue."

Red, that little voice countered. *You know it was red.*

Lennox shook her head.

Red as blood.

TWENTY-EIGHT

Lennox was curled in her bed when her father came home.

"You okay, kid?"

She turned away from him, unwilling to meet his eye. "Yeah, just tired, I guess."

Lennox felt her father's weight as he sat gingerly beside her on the bed. "You're okay, you know."

She shrugged. "I know. Panic attacks happen to everyone."

"You have a lot going on. I mean, the moves, a new school, your mom…"

Lennox gritted her teeth, her tongue going heavy in her mouth. "What about Mom?"

"Just that she's not here. I know…being a girl"—he cleared his throat—"a woman, sorry—young woman—that it can be hard to tell things to your dad or—"

Lennox sat up and glared at her father. "You think this is a period thing?"

His eyebrows shot up, and he shook his head. "No, no—I'm just saying, sometimes…"

She sucked in a sharp breath and pinched the bridge of her nose, hoping the pain would ward off the drumbeat headache she could feel coming on.

"I think I'm going crazy. Things are happening. I'm seeing—hearing—I can't remember. Something is going on, Dad, and I feel like…" Lennox didn't want to cry, but the tears were there again, falling in a steady rain down her cheek, plopping onto her bedspread and staining it dark. She sucked in another breath, feeling the tremor of bat wings in her stomach.

"Is it possible…is it…could I have what Mom has?"

Her father's eyes went wide. He raked a hand through his thinning hair and stood up. "Oh, Lennox. Oh, hon, no. That's not—what Mom has… I mean, it can run in families, but it's not…and usually—" He sighed and sat down again, gathering Lennox in a hug that pinched her rib cage, but she wasn't ready to be let go.

"What happened, honey?"

Lennox swallowed. "I was driving on Hicks Road. I hit someone."

She felt her father stiffen, and he held her at arm's length. "You what?"

"I *think* I hit someone with the car. A girl, but there was no one there. Allison and Eva were in the car too, but they swore they never saw anyone. They swore that if I hit anything, it was an animal or something. And I couldn't go to the police because it was illegal for me to be driving because it was after ten, and Dad, neither of them saw her, but I am sure that I did."

"Okay," her father said slowly.

"I stopped, of course, and we got out of the car. We looked everywhere to try to find...her. But we couldn't find anything." Lennox's voice was small. "Or anyone."

"And that's why you asked me about our intake that night?"

Lennox nodded, eyes wide. "I had to be sure. And then you said there was a girl who came in DOA."

"A twenty-six-year-old woman whose family came in to claim her late yesterday. She passed from a drug overdose, not a car crash."

Lennox shook her head. "I don't know if I want her to exist or not, Dad. I don't know what would make it better. I even went to the place where I thought I'd hit her, and there was nothing—well, not nothing, there was some tramped-down bushes and the necklace—"

"The broken necklace?"

Lennox nodded.

"It could have been there for ages, though, Lennox. I mean, do you know? Did you see it on someone, or on this girl that you think you hit?"

She shook her head miserably. "No—I mean, yes. I mean, I made a drawing of her, and I drew it on her. Only it was like my body took over, because I don't exactly remember drawing it, so maybe my mind knew it was there?"

"Or maybe you tucked it in absently because you wanted to make some sense of the situation."

Lennox felt her chest tightening. "I just don't know. The girls say there was no one, but then this girl, *the* girl, she came to my window—" Lennox was holding on to her Dad's shirt now, the fabric crushed in her sweaty palms as she tugged, begging him to validate her or assure her that everything was in her imagination but that it was normal and she wasn't crazy and—

"Lennox." Her father pulled her in closer, and Lennox let him, his big arms wrapping around her small frame. She felt ten years old again, when she could relax into her father with one big hug and everything would melt away. They'd pack up and go somewhere else, somewhere fresh, somewhere where nothing could get to them.

"Let's go, Dad. Let's leave here." She tried to stamp out images of Owen and his kisses and her new best friends and their smiles and everything she loved about this life when it was normal, when she was normal, which now seemed too long ago but also just slightly out of her reach.

"We can go somewhere else. You have offers, right?"

She'll follow you.

"No." Lennox said it out loud. "No, she won't. She can't. She can't...go."

"Lennox?"

The hum in Lennox's head was louder now, voices and images crashing through her mind like shards of broken glass, but she kept her eyes on her father, focused on the idea that they could leave, a shiny beacon of safety. Her voice rose as she tried to drown out the thrum of doubt, the accusation, the girl on Hicks Road.

"How about Oregon? Or Texas? We should go now—we can go now and you'll find a job right away, you always do. And maybe I could go on independent learning or something instead of regular school? I can even sell my car."

Owen, Allison, Eva.

She pressed her palms against her ears. "No!"

"Lennox, honey, you're scaring me. Just relax, okay? Slow down."

Lennox pushed back her covers and jumped out of her bed. She strode to the closet and began pulling things off hangers, yanking out a bruised box and stuffing things in.

"Lennox!" Her father was behind her, hands on her shoulders, trying his best to turn her around. "Lennox, stop. We can figure this out. You can talk to someone—"

She turned, tears streaming down her cheeks, heat searing the tips of her ears. "I don't want to talk to anyone! Talking can't help me! We need to go. Please, Dad, we need to go now. Please?" Her voice was small now, childish, and that made the tears fall harder. "We left when you—and when Mom... Now I need to not be here."

Another crushing hug, Lennox's small body wracking against her father's. He was crying too, and Lennox was vaulted back to the one and only other time she'd seen him cry. He'd been holding her then too, in another house, in another time, after they had closed the door on Lennox's mother. They had walked away, and she wouldn't even look at them, Lennox's once-beautiful mom in a bathrobe that was too big, that swallowed her gentle hands as she was led away.

"You're not crazy, Lennox. You're not going crazy, you're not sick, and even if you were, I'd take care of you. I'll take care of you no matter what happens, but baby, Lennox, you'll be okay." He took the box from Lennox's hands and slid it back into the closet. "We're not going anywhere, not right now. You're going to get back in bed and take a nap. We'll have dinner when you wake up, and in the morning, we'll schedule an extra appointment with Dr. Hartzog—"

"I don't need a doctor."

He shook his head, taking Lennox's cheeks in his warm palms. "Just to talk. Just to get some tips on what we can do. If you are sick, love, we'll take care of you. We'll make it better."

Lennox nodded, a thousand-pound weight settling on her shoulders, her eyelids growing heavy. Her dad helped her to her bed, and she lay down, letting him tuck the covers around her like he did when she was young, loving the feeling of being safe and cozy and protected by her father and the comforter, and by the time he kissed her forehead and clicked the lights off, Lennox was already asleep.

Lennox woke up to a swath of blue-gray fog choking out the morning sun, an ache roaring deep and low in her belly. It

was half past eleven. She had tossed most of the night, thinking of the girl from the road and a tangle of other things, guilt
settling on her hard.

She knew she wasn't crazy. She knew she wasn't seeing
things. She knew she needed help. She dressed carefully and
tiptoed down the hall with her shoes in hand. She could see
her father asleep in his bed, stayed for a beat to watch the
gentle rise and fall of his chest.

Lennox drove the seven and a half miles to the police
station, chewing her bottom lip as she pushed open the building's double doors.

If the girl from the road really was out there, Lennox
needed to help her—even if it meant risking herself.

⚬⚬⚬

"So, Lennox, what can I help you with?"

Officer Hart was way too jovial and comfortable to be
wearing a holster with a gun and Taser, and Lennox shifted
her weight from foot to foot. "I hope I'm not wasting your
time, and thank you for letting me—for talking to me."

Hart bobbed her blond head. "No problem. Can I get
you something to drink? Glass of water, Coke?"

Lennox's mind veered back to every crime show she had
ever watched where officers tricked unsuspecting murderers by
offering beverages and then lifting prints and DNA to seal their
twenty-five-to-life fate. She shook her head. "No thanks."

"Okay, how about we talk in here?"

Lennox sucked in a breath when Officer Hart opened the door with a shiny INTERROGATION placard nailed to the front. She paused, her toes on the threshold, her heart thudding in her throat.

"Is this—should I—"

Officer Hart laughed and batted at the air. "This isn't an interrogation, if that's what you're worried about." She narrowed her eyes playfully. "Unless you're here to admit to something."

Lennox's stomach clenched, and her bladder squeezed. "No." Her voice was barely a whisper, and she prayed that Officer Hart couldn't see the sweat beading on her forehead. "No."

"It's just a quiet place to talk. Come on." She ushered Lennox into the small room and pulled a chair out. Two desks were pushed together to make a square table, and Officer Hart sat across from Lennox. Her smile was broad and kind, but it did little to put Lennox's mind at ease.

"So, you wanted to tell me about something that happened quite a few nights ago?"

Lennox nodded, her entire body feeling leaden. Her brain was scrambled, sending mixed signals: *Run! Stay where you are! Throw yourself at her mercy! Lie!* Lennox licked her dry lips, wishing she had a glass of water after all, fingerprints or no. Hart seemed to read her mind, because she filled a tiny disposable cup with water from the cooler and slid it over to Lennox.

"You look like you could use this."

Lennox drank gratefully, then cleared her throat. She looked at Officer Hart, at her wide open face and slight smile, and let out a breath. "I went to a party on the other side of Hicks Road."

Lennox expected Officer Hart to click on a recorder or pull out a notebook and start writing, but she did neither. She just leaned back in her chair, bobbed her head, and kept smiling. "I used to go to a lot of parties up there when I was in high school. Hicks Road has always attracted kids."

Lennox nodded. "Yeah, I heard that."

"So, were there drugs at this party? Drinking?"

She felt her eyes widen. "Oh. No—I mean, yes? But that's not really what I'm here about." Lennox cleared her throat again, knitted her fingers in her lap as nerves thundered through her gut. "We were driving back down Hicks, my friends and I, and…" She looked at Officer Hart, whose smile had faded. "There was a car in front of us. It, uh, slammed on its brakes and…and it hit someone."

She glanced up. Officer Hart was sitting forward in her chair now, eyebrows raised.

"I'm pretty sure the other car hit someone."

"And then what happened?"

"Um, that other car, it drove away, and so we stopped because, you know, good citizens, and we looked for the girl—uh, the person they hit. But we couldn't find anyone."

Officer Hart nodded slowly. "What can you tell me about

this other car? Do you know who was in it? Driver, passenger? Or what kind of car it was?"

Lennox's mind spun. "I don't know who was in it."

"What color was the car?"

"Uh, red?"

Suddenly Officer Hart's gaze was steady and unyielding, and Lennox felt trapped.

"Do you remember the make?"

"Prius? It may have been a Prius. But it was dark, so I don't really know, exactly."

"So, what happened directly after you stopped your car?"

Lennox chewed her cheek, wondering if Hart would call in backup if she tried to run out of the interrogation room. Would they catch her before she got into her car?

"Uh, my friends and I got out. We looked for—for a body or something, but we couldn't find anyone. We looked really hard. I mean, it was dark, but my headlights were on." Lennox winced, remembering the click of her headlights going off, the flood of darkness in the cab just before she'd heard that sickening thud. "We walked around the car and looked down the embankment and everything, but there was no one there."

Officer Hart rested her elbows on the table and leaned forward. "So, what is it that you want me to know, Lennox?"

"I just—well, the girl—is she okay? I just want to make sure she's okay because, you know, a hit-and-run..."

"A hit-and-run is a serious crime."

"Yeah." Lennox nodded. "Yeah, I know that. But if the girl is okay—if she—do you know?"

"Are you asking if anyone has reported anything like that?"

Lennox paused for a beat, then slowly nodded. "Did anyone?"

"I can do a little checking, okay? What night was this?"

Lennox filled Officer Hart in and pressed her hands against her chest when the officer told her to sit tight, then snapped the door shut behind her. She sat, rapping her fingernails on the table and craning her neck to see out of the one window, that looked over the floor of the police station. She saw Officer Hart's blond head leaned over a desk, chatting to another officer who was typing on a computer. Both officers glanced in Lennox's direction; her eyes widened, and she stared at her hands in her lap, certain the whole force could see through her lies and would come arrest her at any minute.

What am I doing here? Her mind fumbled while her heart pounded. *I'm basically turning myself in.* She could feel sweat on her palms and rubbed them against her jeans, forcing herself to breathe deeply. *Oh, God, this is the stupidest thing I've ever done!*

Lennox stood and started pacing, but, realizing it might make her look guilty, she sat quickly and began biting her thumbnail. Officer Hart was still heads bent with the other officer, and Lennox tried to look cool and nonchalant, but she was sure her thundering heartbeat was being broadcast through the entire police station. The only thing that could make this worse was—

"Owen?"

He was on the other side of the glass, zigzagging through the station and waving at everyone, his smile wide and friendly like he was the mayor of Police Town.

What is he doing here?

Lennox ducked when he looked in her direction. She wasn't sure why; if pacing made her look guilty, kneeling on the floor would be worse. She took a deep breath and poked her head up, watching Owen pull open an office door and disappear inside.

"His Mom, duh," Lennox muttered, slapping her forehead.

Lennox was back in her chair and scrolling on her phone when Officer Hart came back. Her face was different somehow; the way she looked at Lennox wasn't the same, and Lennox tensed up all over again.

TWENTY-NINE

"Is—is something wrong?"

Hart took her seat and offered Lennox a small smile. She had a sheaf of papers in front of her tucked into a manila folder, and Lennox's stomach folded over itself. *Is that a police report? Had the blond girl filed a police report?* She felt a weird mix of relief and absolute dread. If the girl had filed a report, Lennox was going to jail for hit-and-run. But at least she'd know she wasn't going crazy.

"No, no. But Lennox, I couldn't exactly find any reports matching the incident you described."

She nodded mutely.

"But you knew that already, didn't you?"

"Wait—what? Why would I already know that? I mean, I wasn't *there* there, but I saw it. I swear I did."

"You saw a hit-and-run on a dark road, but there was no body, and this red car, did it actually ever stop?"

"No?" Lennox whispered.

"Lennox, you know that making a false statement to the police is a crime, don't you?"

She nodded slowly.

"Especially since this isn't the first time you've done it."

Lennox's mouth fell open. She felt tears prick the back of her eyes and turned around in her chair, looking out the window to where her father was frantically gesturing to the woman at the front desk, wearing his scrubs and hospital badge. The betrayal crashed over her. He was supposed to be home asleep. He was supposed to be supporting her. Something broke inside Lennox, and she gritted her teeth until she could feel the ache in her jaw.

"I didn't make a false report."

"Back in Virginia. You reported that your mother had gone missing."

The room swirled in front of Lennox's eyes. "She had."

Lennox was in another town in front of another squat building that looked like every other brick building. She wheeled her bicycle to the rack and strode through the double doors, the blasting air conditioning creating icy trails on her cheeks, which were still wet from her tears. The officer behind the front desk was the neatest woman Lennox had ever seen, with clear blue eyes and hair pulled back, straight white teeth and a uniform that was pressed into sharp lines.

"Can I help you, dear?" Her soft voice didn't match the sharpness of her facade.

"My—my—my mom," Lennox stuttered. "It's my mom. She's gone. She's...missing."

"You reported that the house had been ransacked and it looked like there had been a struggle."

The officer's eyes went wide, and she came around the desk, hunched down to Lennox's level. "Are you sure, sweetie?" She reached out and touched Lennox's hand, and it was like the world stopped, shattered. This woman with her hard uniform and severe hair had soft eyes, and she saw *Lennox, and touched her, and cared, and suddenly Lennox was heaving and crying that her mother was* gone, gone, gone, *and had been for more time than she wished to think about.*

"I was nine. I was a kid."

"You insisted—"

Anger flicked in Lennox's gut. "I was just a kid. I made a mistake."

"Lennox, you knew your mother was leaving."

Lennox watched a teardrop fall on her jeans, turning the denim extra dark. She wouldn't look up. She couldn't look up.

"I didn't understand."

Lennox heard murmuring behind her and looked up to see her father ushered into the room. He knelt in front of Lennox, and she recoiled, pushing herself back in her chair until her shoulders ached.

"You told them?"

Her father shook his head, but his eyes were full of betrayal. "No, Lennox, it wasn't like that."

She looked from her father to Officer Hart, each of their faces drawn with something like sympathy. "Then what was it like?" she spat. "Do you think I'm crazy too? I saw something that night; I'm not making it up!"

Lennox stood up so fast the chair clattered to the ground behind her, and the entire world seemed to hold its breath. The silence was smothering, and Lennox fought to move, to press herself forward, shuffling one foot in front of the other. She stepped out of the interrogation room, and everyone seemed to avert their eyes, to get immersed in the papers or screens in front of them.

Lennox's dad led her out of the police station, his hand at the small of her back. Once they were out the door—and out of earshot—Lennox shrugged her dad's hand off and glared at him.

"It's not like what happened is in some kind of permanent file, is it?"

Her dad shook his head slowly. "No, Lennox—"

"So you told her?"

Lennox's father's lips turned down in a deep frown, but his eyes were sharp. "When a police officer calls and says your daughter is at the station—"

"Yes, I was at the police station because—I saw—a hit-and-run."

"Lennox—"

"I told you and you didn't believe me."

"When Officer Hart called, I was worried about you. She wanted to know if I knew anything about what you were saying, and to tell her the truth, hon, I was totally confused."

"You weren't in the dark, you weren't listening. You didn't listen, so I had to come here!"

Her father went on as if she hadn't spoken. "I've been in the dark with you for days, I feel."

"Whose fault is that?" Lennox spat. "You choose the weirdest hours to work! It's almost like you do it just to avoid me. Most single dads do everything they can to have time with their kids, but not you, no, not my dad. You make sure to be asleep or gone when I'm home, right up until you drag me to another stupid town."

"Where is all this coming from?"

"We're standing in front of a police station, Dad. You told people that I made a false police report—"

"Lennox, I was just trying to help."

"Help?" Lennox bit off the word. "Back then, you acted like I was crazy."

"Lennox, I knew you were just confused. But you have to admit you knew what was going on with your mother and me."

Lennox bit down hard on her bottom lip, willing herself not to cry, but the lump in her throat was too much. She could feel the tears building behind her lashes; she blinked hard to try to stop them from falling. "I'm not making this up. I wish you could just support me for once."

Lennox's dad unlocked the passenger-side door and opened it, gesturing for Lennox to get in. She shook her head and sniffed. "I have to get my car."

"We'll get it later. Get in."

For a half beat, Lennox thought about refusing, but in the graying light of the afternoon, she could see that her dad's face was deeply lined, that the bags under his eyes were heavy and dark. A light drizzle started, and Lennox pulled her hood over her head and nodded once, then got in her father's car. She snapped the door shut behind her and dropped her head into her hands.

"I'm on your team, Lennox, remember?"

Suddenly, Lennox hated the way her name sounded in her father's mouth. There was something so pitying about the way he said it now, and she wasn't sure if she was feeling white-hot anger or drowning sadness.

"I'm not lying, Dad. I saw something on that road."

Without answering, her dad reached out a hand and patted Lennox's thigh. "Let's just put all this behind us, okay? We'll go home, grab some dinner. We can curl up and watch a movie, right? Worry about all this tomorrow?"

Lennox glanced at her father in profile. His lips were set so hard the muscle along his jawline jumped. He was gripping the wheel like the spitting drops of rain were a monsoon about to flood the road. The last time she had left a police station, her father had said the same thing: they would tackle it tomorrow, talk about it tomorrow. They had curled up with burgers or pizza or ramen, watched a movie, and he had never brought up the subject again. He rarely brought up the subject of Lennox's mom again, but to Lennox, it never went away. Just like the girl in the road: she wasn't going to go away.

THIRTY

Lennox and her father rode in silence the rest of the way home. Lennox kept her eyes focused on the road in front of them, the black asphalt growing slick and shiny with rain. Her father clicked on the headlights about a block before they reached the house, and Lennox felt her heartbeat speed up, felt dread pool in her stomach that made it hard to breathe.

They pulled into the garage, but Lennox was still on high alert; everything seemed too loud, too bright, and she pinched the bridge of her nose, wondering when the throbbing headache had started or if it had just never gone away. Her father seemed lighter, that hard set to his jaw gone as he whipped out his phone and started scrolling.

"How about we grab a late lunch. Burgers, pizza?"

"What happened to you hauling me to the shrink?"

"I'm not hauling you anywhere, and our appointment is tomorrow at nine."

Lennox nodded, but inside she was numb. She had been here before, had been in this story before when she was nine years old and terrified and confused and her father had offered her fast food to quell the ache in her heart. She thought she should say something to break the cycle, to get her dad to talk, but at seventeen, she was still scared, still confused, still a nine-year-old girl walking into a house that felt empty and cold, that she barely recognized.

"Either one," she said, her lips feeling thick and swollen. "Pizza it is."

Lennox followed her father into the house and peeled off to her bedroom, where she dumped off her backpack and took off her clothes, turning on the shower to red-hot. She stood under the water and cried, letting the fresh water wash away her salty tears. She had never felt quite so alone in all her life. *And Owen!* she thought, a fresh round of tears dropping. Did he know? Would Officer Hart tell his mom that Lennox was a liar, just some kid with an overzealous imagination and a penchant for filing false police reports?

She gritted her teeth.

"I know what I saw," Lennox murmured under the spout of water. She saw flashes of that night, of the slick asphalt and the girl—that damn girl with the blond hair and the wide, terrified eyes.

FIND ME.

Lennox knotted the tie on her bathrobe and turbaned a towel around her head. Her phone was lying on her bed, vibrating like crazy. She picked it up and sighed: Owen. Seven missed calls. Plus two from Allison and one from Eva.

Lennox's heart was in her throat. Did Owen know? Did he tell everyone? She wasn't ready to find out. She plugged in her phone and padded down the hall. Her father was in the living room, pacing in front of the big picture window.

"Our pizza is finding its way here as we speak." He craned his neck. "If the driver can find our house. And don't worry, I added green peppers, so…healthy." He smiled, and Lennox tried to smile back, but she felt like she was walking through molasses. She felt dread in every cell, a sense of loneliness like none she had ever felt. Her father was talking to her. Owen, Allison, and Eva had left messages and texts on her phone. But Lennox felt alone. *No,* she shook her head, *not alone, exactly. Like public enemy number one.*

Someone was playing a prank on her. They'd taken her parking permit. Someone had vandalized her portrait. She specifically remembered a shirt being one color when everyone else remembered it as another. She'd forgotten dates and to drop her father at work. A phantom girl had appeared in front of her windshield and at her bedroom window. The note.

She flopped on the couch, pulling her knees up to her chest and stretching the fabric of her bathrobe to her ankles.

She should feel crazy. She should feel wrong and lost and

needy and meek, but she didn't. She wasn't crazy—everyone else was. *I know what I saw,* Lennox thought. *I know it.* But the only proof she had was a phantom memory and a note destroyed in the wash. The necklace was gone. It was her word against everyone else's.

FIND ME.

The words flashed again in her mind's eye, and Lennox was transported. In front of her, her father chatted up the pizza delivery guy, but Lennox was a million miles away. She was on Hicks Road. She could feel the gravel underneath her sneakers. She could see the steam rising from the hood of her car, could sense Allison and Eva to her left and right.

What did you see?

The girl. Bright, vivid.

The dent. Small but apparent.

The footprint.

Lennox blinked, crashing back to her living room sofa, to her father clicking shut the front door and singing loudly about the moon hitting your eye.

Lennox had seen a footprint, she was sure of it. A sneaker print. She had thought it must be Allison's or Eva's, but they had both been wearing sandals.

FIND ME.

Lennox licked her lips. "I will," she said in a low whisper.

That night, Lennox couldn't sleep. Finally, she kicked off her covers, clicked on her light, and grabbed a notebook, scrawling *What I Know* on the top of the first page.

She listed the things she knew she remembered from that
night: where the party was located, what time they came
and left. She paused, her pen tip hovering just above the
paper as she thought about what she'd been wearing. Her
eyes traveled to the hamper, where the red shirt was thrown
aside, and did her best to ignore it. She moved on to writing about Hicks Road, about the legends Allison and Eva
had told her about, about how the road hugged and curved
around the side of the mountain, one side dense forest,
the other side a fairly steep drop-off. She wrote about the
trees and bushes she remembered seeing, about how she
had seen a burnt-out tire on the side of the road and how
Eva had splashed half a can of La Croix all over herself in
the back seat.

"My memory isn't bad," she murmured.

Just past that blown-out tire, Eva had mentioned the
legend. Lennox closed her eyes and saw Allison's slender arm
reaching over, her perfectly manicured nails moving to the
gearshift and clicking off Lennox's lights. And Lennox could
see the girl.

Clear as day.

She had run out from Lennox's left, from the forest. *But
there was something else...* Lennox squeezed her eyes shut,
trying to enlarge the picture. There had been another reason
Lennox had looked to her left. What was it?

"Pizza time!" Her dad snapped her out of her reverie, and
Lennox's heart thudded against her rib cage.

There was something else. Something she was missing. *But what was it?*

Lennox piled two slices on a paper plate and turned to head toward her room when her dad grabbed her by the arm.

"That's it?"

"Um, thanks for the pizza?"

"You're welcome, but I thought we would, you know, sit down and have dinner like regular people. At the table." He gestured to the hand-me-down carried-everywhere table like it was some kind of prize, and Lennox sighed.

"I just have a lot of homework and—"

"I think we should talk about the police station and what you think you saw on the road." Lennox's dad took a bite of his pizza and chewed while keeping his gaze on Lennox.

"It's not what I *think* I saw. I saw her." She pulled out a chair and slid into it, setting the pizza on the table. Suddenly, her fingers weren't functioning. The blood in her veins had turned cold.

"Tell me about her. The girl from the hit-and-run. Or the girl with the necklace? Or was there only one girl?"

Lennox looked to the blank spot on the key rack where the necklace had hung. "Yeah. About that..."

He took another bite, studying her as he chewed.

Lennox shook her head slowly. "Are you going to listen this time?"

"Lennox, I'm trying. Can you try too?"

"I'll try, but..." Lennox felt the familiar ache of a sob straining in her throat. "I don't know anything anymore."

Her dad nodded as if expecting more, and Lennox couldn't tell if he was being fatherly or attempting to grill her. After a beat, he gestured to her plate.

"You should eat your pizza now. The grease will turn it into one solid mass if you wait." He smiled, flecks of red sauce at the edges of his mouth, and her mind immediately went to blood.

No! Lennox commanded herself. *This is your father, not some murderer!*

"I swear, I really must be cracking up. I even thought... maybe you..."

He raised his eyebrows. "Maybe me what?"

Lennox poked at a piece of pepperoni. "Maybe you know more than you're letting on?"

"About the girl or the necklace?"

Lennox cocked her head. "About the girl *and* the necklace." She forced a smile, but her father's expression remained unchanged. There was a hint of something dark there, but Lennox couldn't pinpoint it.

"Are you mad, Dad?"

He slowly wiped his hands on a napkin, his gaze still steady on Lennox. "No, no, Lennox, I'm not mad. I'm frustrated. And don't I have a right to be? You basically kept all this from me until now, and then I found you at the police station!"

Lennox pressed the pads of her fingers against her eyes. "There probably is no girl, or if there is, she's fine and nothing—and I'm just—" The tears starting rolling down her cheeks. "I'm just so confused and scared of all of these memories and feelings. I know it sounds dumb, but Dad, what if I'm just like Mom? What if the girls are right and I'm...but I know it's not in my head. There are all these clues, but they don't add up."

He reached out and grabbed Lennox's hand. "You're safe, Lennox. There is no one, nothing out to get you. You are not your mother. And you've got these really nice friends who come by to check on you. So many people care about you. Everything is going to be okay, I promise."

Lennox half knew that her father was using the safety words Dr. Hartzog had taught them—things like "you're safe" and how people "cared" about her—and she was desperate to believe him. She nodded, sniffling.

THIRTY-ONE

Lennox wasn't sure what woke her up—or if she was really awake at all. It was that groggy twilight between sleep and waking when shapes morphed in the darkness, real life and dreams melding together. She rolled over onto her side and glanced at the clock on her nightstand: 2:42. Her father was at work, and the house was painfully still—except it wasn't.

Lennox sniffed and pushed her covers back, sliding her bare feet onto the carpet. She yawned and blinked, trying to get her eyes to adjust to the darkness as she padded down the hall, coughing at the choking smoke in the house.

There was smoke in the house.

It was wafting in huge clouds that stung her eyes and scratched at her throat, and then the crackling rage of the fire was there in front of her, yellow-red flames licking at the doorway.

"Oh my God!" she screamed. "Oh my God! Dad?" She knew he wasn't home, but the call was instinctual. Her knees buckled, and she sat down hard on the carpet, tears and smoke stinging her eyes and burning her cheeks. The door was in front of her. The flames, reaching and streaking, were surging up the walls, leaving shadowy plumes of smoke. If she crawled forward, she would enter a ring of fire; if she moved backward, she was trapped.

"Dad," Lennox cried again.

The fire licked the ceiling in front of her and caught, the hanging light fixture engulfed in flames so hot that Lennox could feel heat on her head, could feel sweat bead around her eyebrows.

"I have to get out of here!"

Lennox gripped the carpet and crawled to her bedroom, slamming the door shut behind her. Her mind was vaulting, spinning, trying to remember every "be safe" lecture she'd had in a dozen schools where firefighters showed up and told everyone what to do in case of a fire.

She couldn't think of anything.

She started to shake, the roar of the fire shut out behind her flimsy bedroom door, tendrils of smoke coming under the one-inch gap. Lennox started, her teeth chattering, stepping away from the door until her shoulder blades were pushed against the cold glass of her bedroom window. She turned and scratched at it, then pounded with closed fists as the flame caught the edge of her door and snaked its way into the room, reflected in the glass.

Lennox kept pounding.

"Help me!" she screamed. "Somebody help me!"

She didn't know if anyone could hear her. She didn't know if she was making any sound. The glass was cold on her fists, but the heat was at her back, that solid, serpentine tongue of flame licking in and out.

"I'm going to die in here," Lennox wailed, the skin on her fingertips tearing open as she scrambled for the window lock, the blood smearing across the glass.

She coughed, feeling the smoke fill her throat, flood her lungs.

"Lennox!"

Lennox's eyelids were heavy. "Who?"

She saw the blond hair, the wide eyes. Palms flat, outstretched against the window. Lennox matched hers to the girl's, and that was the last thing she remembered.

The beeping wouldn't stop. It was loud and incessant, a constant howl in Lennox's brain.

"Lennox, Lennox…"

Someone was chanting her name now, and Lennox couldn't decide if it was a cheer or a taunt. She tried to open her eyes, but they were glued shut, just like every inch of her body was glued to—wait, where was she?

"I think she's waking up."

Lennox coughed and the pain was unimaginable: a blaze tearing down her throat, singeing her insides. She winced hard.

"Poor thing."

Finally, the glue must have worn off, and Lennox managed to lift her eyelids, trying her best to focus her poor dry eyes on the scene around her: impossibly white. Couldn't tell ceiling from floor. That beeping.

"Where am I?"

There was a soft palm on her arm, and though the touch should have been comforting, it was excruciating. She wanted to flinch, to shrink back, but she was glued down, her body a thousand pounds.

"That hurts," she whispered.

"Oh, goodness."

She recognized that voice. Her father.

"Dad?"

"Lennox!"

She blinked repeatedly, willing the room to come into focus. The walls *were* white, and the ceiling and floor as well, but there were blobs of color now too, and they were walking forward: her dad, a nurse she didn't recognize.

"Owen?"

He was hanging back, shifting his weight from foot to foot, his eyes the size of saucers. They softened when Lennox was able to focus on him, and a sad smile formed on his lips.

"Hey," he whispered.

"What happened to me?"

"Do you remember anything?" Lennox's father asked,

stepping forward and gently—ever so gently—taking her limp hand in his. "Anything at all?"

Lennox nodded, though it took effort. "She was there," she said finally.

"The nurse? No, Lennox, this is Nurse Turner, she's been taking good care of you—"

"There was a fire. It was so hot. And I was stuck. But she—the girl from that night—she was there. She...she got me out?" It came out as a question, although Lennox was sure it was true. "Isn't that what happened?" She looked from Owen to the nurse to her father; they all had pained expressions on their faces.

"You put something on the stove and must have gone to bed. A fire broke out—"

Lennox shook her head. "No, that's not right. The fire was already...it was already there."

"You were probably asleep, hon. The fire alarm must have woken you. And thank God it did."

Lennox sank back into her pillows. Her memory of anything before she opened her eyes was a big blank hole, but nothing her father was saying sounded right. She remembered the fire, the flames, the heat on her—she gingerly pressed a bandaged hand against her head. Her hair felt like hay, and she frowned.

"Am I okay?"

Nurse Turner took a step forward, removing the folder from the foot of Lennox's bed. She flipped through it, and when she looked up, her smile was warm and friendly, her eyes round and soft. "You're going to be fine. Just in here as a precaution, really. You sucked in some smoke and sustained a few minor burns, abrasions, and lacerations."

Lennox looked at her gauze-wrapped hands. "Lacerations?"

"Cuts, hon. From when you went through the window. Thank God for that."

Lennox thought back to her palms matching the girl's and remembered—

"She said something to me," she mumbled. "Her mouth was moving, she was talking—telling me...how to get out?" She closed her eyes hard, willed the memory to come back, but all she could see were plumes of black smoke, those licking flames.

Behind you, the girl had mouthed.

Behind you.

Lennox coughed again, her body remembering when the glass had broken, when the fresh night air had coiled in and she had breathed—

"You were there," she said to Owen. "And you were there." She pointed to her father.

Owen looked at his feet and then up again, a red flush on his cheeks that went up to his ears. "I heard the call on my mom's scanner. I recognized the address."

"They called me at the hospital."

Lennox shook her head, confused. "That's not right. None of this is right."

"Lennox, honey, you've been through a lot," her father started.

"I wasn't cooking anything," she said.

"All right, we can talk about all this later, hm? Let's let the patient rest while I start her discharge papers." Nurse Turner began to shuffle Lennox's father and Owen out the door, but Lennox was still shaking her head, the cobwebs and black smoke gone.

"That's not how it happened," she said again, trying to push the words out through her Sahara-dry mouth. "That's not what happened."

But Owen and her father were gone. The door snapped shut behind them, and Lennox was alone in the white room, the *beep-beep-beep*ing of the monitors incessant and annoying, her pain and confusion replaced by an overwhelming sense of dread.

"The girl in the window..." she murmured. "She was trying to..."

Lennox's eyes traveled to the little window in the door, through which she could see Nurse Turner talking to Owen and her father. They looked over their shoulders back into Lennox's room, and she did her best to disappear into the pillows, to make herself appear as meek and frail as possible.

"She was trying to save me," Lennox whispered to herself.

THIRTY-TWO

Lennox picked at the hospital tag around her wrist while her father pulled up to their house. Despite the licking flames and smoke damage, the fire had been contained and the house was still livable, but Lennox felt uneasy.

"Are you okay?" her father asked.

Lennox shook her head. "I'm not sure I'll ever be okay."

He squeezed her hand. "Lenn..."

She pulled away and forced a small chuckle. "No, I'm fine. It's just the—you know, all the stuff. Hospital, fire."

"You'll feel better after a good sleep in your own bed."

Lennox nodded, but the rental house didn't feel like home anymore.

"Yeah, I'll try."

Lennox slept fitfully, and when she woke up, the sun was shining through her window, bright-yellow slits dotted by drops of rain. She could hear the whir of the fan in the kitchen, pushing out the faint smell of smoke. She sat up and squinted, pushing the curtains back, then grabbed her phone.

11:51.

Lennox had left the hospital after the doctors checked her, observed her, then dragged their feet with her discharge papers. She had gone to bed when the sun was setting and woke up groggy and disheveled almost fifteen hours later on Monday morning. A subtle panic rushed through her. "Dad? Dad?"

Her father came padding into the room holding a coffee mug and smiling softly. "Hey, sleepyhead."

"Dad, it's almost noon."

"You were tired."

"I am three hours late for school."

"You're staying home today. The doctors kept you an extra day and now I am." He smiled thinly. "Observation."

Lennox kicked her covers back and planted her bare feet on the soft pile carpet. "Dad, I'm not—"

Charlie sat on the edge of the bed. "You're not anything, hon. You had a traumatic day yesterday. It's fine to take a mental health day and get yourself back up to speed. Think of it as a three-day weekend."

Memories crashed into Lennox's brain with such ferocity that she winced. "I have a paper due, and there's the dance this weekend—" She went to stand, but her dad put his coffee mug down and gingerly took her arm.

"Lennox, Lennox. Take a breath. Hang out on the couch or in bed. The paper will get turned in, and if you're feeling better tomorrow, you can go to that dance. But right now, I'm worried about you."

Lennox was torn between wanting to sink into her father's concern and wanting to scream that she wasn't crazy. She wasn't her mother, she wasn't losing her mind—

FIND ME.

The words and the girl flashed in her mind's eye. Lennox's shoulders slumped, all the fight except the tiniest flicker extinguishing in her belly. She sat back on her bed and slid her feet under the covers.

"Okay, Dad. I guess you're right. I guess I am still a little tired. But what about the fire? The kitchen, is it…"

"We're not going to get our security deposit back, if that's what you're asking." He stroked the hair from Lennox's forehead. "But that's a small price to pay. You could have been really hurt."

Lennox's jaw tightened. She wanted to argue. She wanted to tell her father that it wasn't confusion or forgetfulness, that she may not remember everything, but she knew she hadn't started the fire or fallen asleep cooking. Instead, she just nodded.

"Everything is going to be fine if you just get a little more rest, I'm sure of it," her father said, pulling the blanket up to Lennox's chin. "A little exhaustion. We all get that way, and we all need to listen more to our bodies."

He smiled, and something in Lennox hardened. His eyes searched hers, and Lennox was certain he was looking for something, for some crack in her psyche, maybe for the same something he'd seen in her mother all that time ago.

Lennox pasted on what she hoped was a convincing smile. "You're right, Dad. Are you going to stay home today?"

His smile faltered, and that vein of concrete inside her kept hardening. "For a bit, but I have a shift that I can't get out of."

Lennox nodded. "Sure, of course."

"But if you absolutely need me—"

"No, I'll be fine. Just need some sleep, remember?"

Lennox's dad patted her shoulder and picked up his coffee mug as Lennox settled against her pillow, pinching her eyes shut. She heard him pad out of the room, shutting the door softly behind him. She listened to him turn on the TV and rattle around in the kitchen.

At two o'clock, Lennox's phone chimed.

YOU GOOD? Allison wanted to know.

Lennox sat up and began typing. YA, MENTAL HEALTH DAY, HOUSE ALMOST BURNED DOWN. She was about to hit send, then deleted and retyped: FINE. JUST TIRED.

She watched the text bubble pop up, and then Allison's message came through: LUCKY. I HAVE 2B BLEEDING FRM THE EYES TO STAY HOME. CAN YOU STAY AT YOUR HOUSE AFTER THE FIRE?

Lennox blew out a sigh. YEAH. KITCHEN IS TOAST THO.

Allison texted back: WANT COMPANY? OR FOOD :D

Lennox peeked down the hall to where her father was. She saw him dressed in his scrubs, shrugging into a thick jacket and dangling his car keys.

LATR? NEED TO TAKE CARE OF SOMETHING.

It was 3:40 by the time Lennox's father made it out the door, and soon afterward, Lennox was showered, dressed, and sitting in her car, rolling her key chain in her palm. The sky was eight o'clock dark, choked with rain clouds that occasionally spit just enough moisture to dirty up her windshield.

"Now or never," she said, sinking her key into the ignition and turning over the engine.

Some sunlight was piercing through the clouds by the time Lennox reached the turnoff to Hicks Road. Her resolve was starting to falter; she swore two cars were following her and that a third was an undercover cop car, tailing her and getting ready to call in backup.

"You're a nut," she breathed through gritted teeth.

She turned onto Hicks, and the temperature—and visibility—dropped as the city faded away and the trees and ferns grew bigger and denser at the edges of the road.

"I'm going to figure this out once and for all."

Lennox zoomed past the reservoir but slowed when she hit the winding part of the road, where the trees started to choke out the mottled sunlight and the edges of the foliage reached out and whipped at her car doors. Her heart started an anxious little patter, somewhere between excitement and pure dread, and she chewed the insides of her lips, trying to pull herself back to that night.

She was at her house in a bath towel, frowning at the contents of her closet. Part of her screamed to pull on her usual armor, dark-colored hoodie and equally dark-washed jeans, but something else niggled at her, something that told her she should put something else on and maybe play at being normal, noticeable. It was only for a few hours, after all, and she had these two new friends, Allison and Eva. Allison was a brunette goddess in whatever she wore with her California-tanned skin and her miles-deep dark eyes, and Eva was a fashion icon who walked the Pioneer halls as if she were stomping down the runways in Milan. Lennox fingered a blue blouse she had dragged from place to place, never daring to wear it. The fabric was a blaring royal blue and the neckline was plunging. It was out of her comfort zone, but she loved it still, her stylish security blanket. She slipped it on now, feeling the fabric drape and settle over her frame. She looked at herself in the mirror and smiled, her lips immediately seeming brighter and plumper, the blue giving her cheeks a swath of bright color. She looked like a normal girl who had a normal life, not like the nomad Lennox usually identified with, the seventeen-year-old who had never once been invited to a party.

But today she had.

When Allison stepped out of her house, Lennox smiled at her friend's sky-high skirt, chunky sandals, and oversize sweatshirt. Allison was effortlessly chic, and she plopped into the passenger seat with a wide grin and a waft of something tropical.

Eva was next, in tulle and faux fur, the most outrageous strappy heels, and a streak of hot pink in her hair that looked completely natural on her.

This is it, *Lennox thought*, this is being a normal teenager.

They drove up a dark road lined with enormous redwoods,

spying mile-long driveways and mansions that seemed to explode out of nowhere. The party house was just as grand, with a rounded driveway and a cluster of cars.

Now or never, *Lennox told herself as Eva and Allison linked arms with her.*

The music was thumping inside the house, the sickly sweet smell of something herbal winding through the living room. Kids were scattered everywhere, maybe dancing, maybe talking, drinking from red Solo cups and cans, and Lennox thought the whole thing looked so wonderfully, pathetically normal. It wasn't a scene out of a movie; there were no low lights, no stereotypical jocks building beer can towers. Just kids hanging out, having fun. Lennox grinned, felt her anxiety melt away, her shoulders loosen.

She wasn't sure how many hours passed, but her cheeks hurt from laughing, and she couldn't remember how many ridiculous conversations she'd had or how many people she'd said hello to, but she was warm inside and genuinely, purely happy. Being normal was bliss. Being a high school girl at a high school party was fun, and she didn't have a single care in the world, like making sure the house was all packed or Tetris-ing boxes into the back of the car. She wasn't her dad's navigator, wasn't having another first day at another new school. She was normal, and everything was great.

"Turn here!" Allison urged when they were back in the car. "Do it!"

Echoes of laughter reverberated in Lennox's head.

Her palms started to sweat, her heart thudding against her rib cage and pulling her out of her reverie.

Lennox clicked off her headlights, the scene outside her windshield burning on her eyelids. This was it. This was where it happened.

Lennox slowed her car to a stop. It was well after six, and the darkness was all-encompassing, menacing and deep. She heard her sneakers crunch on the gravel as she slammed her car door and stepped to the forest to her left. The foliage was still tamped down, leaving a trail. She could see the pounded earth and stepped onto the moist trail, pine needles stealing the sound of her footsteps.

Someone came through here.

Lennox stopped, the darkness heavy with something that she couldn't place. A smell, a memory.

"Hello?"

She heard a twig snap, the rustling of branches. As her eyes worked to adjust to the darkness, she saw the tips of two mud-covered tactical boots right in front of her.

THIRTY-THREE

Lennox gasped and stumbled backward, her jeans catching on a branch.

"Lennox, let me—" Mr. Apex leaned closer to her, his hands clawing at the air just in front of her, and Lennox went down. "Be careful, there's—"

Lennox tried to free herself, twisting around to snap the branch that had hold of her. Only it wasn't a branch. Her hands closed around a stiff, cold hand, its fingers mud-caked and clawing, the index finger neatly snagging Lennox's cuff.

Lennox screamed, kicking, skittering backward on her butt until her hands entwined in blond hair splayed on the soft forest ground.

The hand was attached to a body. A teen girl with long blond hair that was now looped with leaves and dirt and wrapped around Lennox's fingers, tiny cuffs tightening around her scrabbling hands.

"Oh, God. You—" Her eyes cut to Mr. Apex, still looming over her.

"Lennox—"

"You dumped her—" White-hot fear poured over Lennox. She tried to force her legs to move, her hands to free themselves from the lengths of hair, but everything, including her body, seemed to slow to an aching pace, sealing her in this moment off Hicks Road with a dead girl.

"Lennox, this is a crime scene."

His voice sank through her like ice water, and every muscle in Lennox's body stiffened, every synapse held taut.

"Don't you know it's not safe for you out here?"

Lennox's teeth started to chatter. She heard twigs break as he stepped closer to her, was certain he could hear the blood that rushed through her ears.

"I know how it looks, but you have to let me explain."

Lennox was on her feet in a flash, stance wide, arms up.

"I'm not here to fight with you."

Lennox felt a muscle flicker in her jaw. "Don't come any closer."

"Lennox, it's just me, I just—"

"I should have known it was you!"

"Lennox, what are you saying? What was me?"

"You did it, didn't you? I didn't kill her, you did!"

Mr. Apex put his hands up, and Lennox felt a wash of relief and then another douse of terror. She was in the woods. The sky was moving from moody gray to pitch black. Mr. Apex was dressed for hiding a body in the woods: hiking boots, tactical pants, dark blue shirt with a bright orange patch spelling out RESCUE.

"Lennox, I—"

Whump!

"Lennox, run!"

Lennox whirled as Mr. Apex's eyes went wide, then rolled back in his head. He fell to his knees, then fell face first on the ground in front of Lennox and the girl's body. Lennox's teeth chattered, every bone in her body going gelatinous.

"Oh, thank God I found you." Owen dropped to his knees in front of Lennox as the terror of what had happened—and who Mr. Apex was—roiled through her.

"What are you doing here, Owen?"

His eyes were earnest. "Hopefully saving you. I was so worried—I knew Mr. Apex—"

His voice trailed off, and Lennox glanced at Apex's prone body and then back at Owen, who had a baseball bat in his hand. "You knew Mr. Apex what?"

"He was weirdly into you, into teen girls." His brown eyes went over the body crumpled next to Lennox's. "He must have done this to her and then dumped her body here. That monster."

Lennox was trying to connect the dots, to realize that she was safe and that rather than committing a crime that night on the road, she had instead witnessed one.

"Is that blood on your face?"

Owen smeared the drop across his cheek, and Lennox's

heart thundered in her ears. She couldn't get her mind to stop the endless loop: *Mr. Apex, the girl, Owen.*

"We have to call the police, call your mom. I think he was after the girl. I think she—" Lennox pinched her eyes shut, her fisted hand knocking against her head as if she could force some sense, some understanding into it, but all she could hear was an insistent humming, a wasps' nest of buzzing.

Mr. Apex had the word RESCUE sewn onto his shirt.

"Lennox," Owen said, brushing his palm up and down Lennox's arm. "Relax."

"I don't know what's going on, Owen, but I know we have to get out of here." She tried to push herself up, but something jabbed her palm. Lennox glanced down.

A barrette, clipped around blond strands of hair. Hair of a dead girl.

Lennox's saliva soured.

The barrette matched the one Lennox had found in Owen's car.

Something flickered in Owen's eyes, and a kind of calm descended over him. He cocked his head and locked eyes with her.

"You don't have a sister."

He stared for a moment, searching for the right words, then seemed to decide something. He smiled, did jazz hands. "Surprise."

Lennox took a step back, her heels brushing against Mr. Apex's feet. She heard him groan, and Owen's lips curled down into something between a grimace and a frown. Lennox watched Owen's his arms go up, sinewy and muscled, the baseball bat gripped in his palms.

"Owen, no!"

But Lennox heard the sickening thud of metal bat against flesh and Mr. Apex's low groan, then dead silence.

She started to stumble, unable to take her eyes off Owen, even when a fine spray of red—bloodred—shot across his face, droplets clinging to the hair she had brushed back from his forehead just the other day.

Lennox was on her feet, her pulse thundering as she tried to make out the trail back to the road. A memory came crashing back.

The flood of yellow headlights. The blond, running. She darted out of the forest because someone was behind her, pushing her...

The forest was holding its breath. Lennox's whole body went leaden. She could hear Owen, the boy she had a crush on, behind her, and she looked, his sweet face a twisted mask of evil and fury.

Lennox vaulted forward, but Owen was faster, his free hand clamping around her elbow, the bloodied baseball bat in his other hand.

"Don't you dare run away from me!"

"You were there that night. And Mr. Apex wasn't stalking the girl, he was trying to find her."

Owen grinned. "You don't know what you're talking

about. You seem a little confused...well, you've always seemed a little confused lately, haven't you?"

Lennox could hear the din from the party. She could smell Eva's Gatorade, hear Allison's high-pitched laugh. She saw Owen across the room, following a blond girl out the sliding glass doors.

"You were with her."

Owen chuckled. "I think you're a little hysterical."

Lennox gritted her teeth. "I saw you with her. You were fighting."

"So then you probably remember that I tried to stop her from running out into the road. But it was too late."

Lennox's mouth was Sahara-dry. "Because I hit her."

THIRTY-FOUR

Owen shook his head, his eyes soft. "I was just trying to protect you."

"From who? Why?"

Owen snaked an arm around Lennox's shoulders and pulled her close. His usual smell of soap and cut grass was drowned out by the smell of fresh dirt, the metallic scent of blood, and Lennox's stomach lurched. "From everyone, Lenn. You were new in school. Your mom is crazy, and her daughter"—he used the tip of the bat to gently touch her chin—"is a murderer."

The body flashed in front of Lennox's eyes. She could feel the blond hair wrapped around her fingers, the barrette burning in her palm.

"She tried to warn me," Lennox whispered.

"She was dead, Lennox. You killed her. Not paying attention, driving with your headlights off, and maybe, just maybe, sliding into the same psychosis that got your mom—"

"How do you know about that?"

Owen smiled again. His teeth were glowing white in the dimness, the blood on his lips and cheeks giving him a demonic look. "I've got friends in high places. So, what do you say? We'll check in with my mom, come clean. I'm sure you'll get a reduced sentence due to... you know." He circled his index finger around his ear and *cuckooed* like a clock.

Anger ignited in Lennox.

"I didn't kill anyone. And I'm not crazy."

He scratched his chin. "Sure, Lennox. Honestly, you just made it easier for me. I didn't want to do it, but she kept running her mouth." He looked around. "It's so much quieter around here now, don't you think?"

"You killed someone because she talked too much?"

Owen set his jaw, and his eyes flashed from sweet and contemplative to hard and dark. "She said I was abusive." He snorted. "Me! When she was such a bitch, always on my case. She got under my skin—it wasn't my fault I snapped a little. One time I grabbed her arm and she twisted—once! And maybe I got in her face after she yelled at me. What was I supposed to do?"

Lennox stiffened. "You could have just left her alone."

"I loved her sometimes. But she could be such a nag. She was so crazy and loud and—"

Lennox flashed back to her mother and father in the kitchen, her mother's voice screechy, loud and high-pitched, her arms flailing like windmills. And her father wrapping his arms around her, even as she pelted him with her fists. He had just held her.

"So you hit her."

"Okay, you got me there. But she hit me first. I mean, girls want to be treated like equals, right? An eye for an eye. She deserved it. She was asking for it. And then she broke her arm and blamed it on me."

"*She* broke her arm?"

Owen took a step away, his breath becoming more jagged. "She said she was going to tell people I was beating her! Get me arrested on gross assault charges. Didn't care that it would have ruined my life."

Lennox licked her lips, a weird sense of calm settling over her. "But you were guilty."

"We were both mad!" Owen stomped his foot. "She hit me too. We just had one of those relationships."

"If she was hurting you too, why were you so worried about her talking? You could have told your side of the story."

Rage lit fires behind Owen's eyes. "She was going to ruin my life! No one was going to believe me! She was a liar! If she had just shut the fuck up—"

"You chased her into the woods."

Owen shrugged. "And you were driving recklessly."

"You pushed her in front of my car."

He gritted his teeth. "You couldn't even finish the job. While you were losing your mind, I snuck out to check. When I saw she was still alive, I had to shut her up for good. You slowed her down so I could. I guess I should thank you for that."

Bile itched at the back of Lennox's throat. "It was an accident. I didn't mean to hit her."

"An accident? Was it? Maybe you just wanted to help." He grinned, a tiny fleck of blood marring his tooth. "Who even knows what really happened? Crazy girl running in the road gets hit by a crazy girl driving erratically with her lights off, who then goes off her rocker. Two crazy girls..." He grinned sweetly. "I guess you could say I have a type."

Lennox gripped the barrette and, in one fell swoop, dug the pointed end into the fleshy part of Owen's cheek.

"Bitch!"

She heard his word echo as she cut through the forest, her chest opening when she saw a thread of yellow light.

"The road!" Lennox whispered, pushing herself forward.

Her heart started to pound, a quick rhythm matching the one starting in her forehead as her sneakers hit pavement.

The headlights coming around the bend illuminated her, and Lennox waved her arms, a sob escaping as the car came to a stop, pulling over just a few feet away. She started to step backward, gathering speed until she fell, her palms gripping at the asphalt.

"Owen's car."

The car door opened, and Lennox pushed hair out of her eyes, squinting at the yellow lights.

"Allison! Eva! You guys have got to save me! It's Owen,

he's psychotic. He killed a girl, he pushed her in front of my car, and—" Lennox was hiccuping now, crying so hard the sobs hurt her chest. "I don't know what to do. Who do we even call?"

Allison and Eva were standing next to the car, making no move toward Lennox.

"Owen didn't kill anyone."

"No, Allison, I saw—"

"She's *dramatic*," Allison said, drawing out the word.

"What are you talking about?"

Eva reached out, resting her arm on Allison's, but Allison shook it off, beelining toward Lennox.

"She's a liar. She tried to tell people that Owen hit her! Can you imagine? Thank God she went back to Santa Cruz and shut up. If people had actually listened to that psycho, Owen could have lost his scholarship. Just because she lied about him beating her up."

Lennox felt like ice water had been poured over her. "You think she's in Santa Cruz? Allison, she's not. She's dead. I just saw her body."

Allison's voice was soft. "She deserved it."

Lennox's stomach turned. "You knew?"

"We *had* to keep it a secret. And it wasn't Owen." Allison pointed a finger. "It was you. You killed her. You went out to Hicks Road—"

"Because you told me to!" Lennox gaped at Allison and then at Eva. "Were you in on this? Was this—am I just—wait, you needed me to be on that road. You wanted me to hit her."

"No." Eva shook her head. "It wasn't my idea. It was—"

Allison cut Eva off. "And you couldn't even do that right, Lennox! You clipped her! And then you wanted to *find* her. She was a menace. You did what you had to do."

"It was an accident on my part," Lennox said, her voice even. "You wanted me to do Owen's dirty work."

Allison was seething. "It wasn't Owen's fault! She got what she deserved. He had to catch up with her somehow, he had to finish what *she* started."

"Owen killed a girl, Allison. Don't you understand? And Eva, you went along with all this?"

Eva's eyes went wide, downtrodden. "I didn't want...I wanted to stop it."

"At first we just wanted you to forget all about her. When Owen had to kill her, we thought it would be better if she disappeared. But you wouldn't let it go! You were like a dog with a bone. So we tried to flip your crazy switch. A crazy girl kills another crazy girl. When her body was found, you'd be the prime suspect. It was perfect, what with your history."

"My history?"

Eva's eyes filled with tears. "I'm so sorry, Lennox. I didn't want to. I tried to warn—"

"Find me," Lennox said. "That was you?"

"I didn't think it would go this far," Eva said, her voice weak. "I thought maybe if you looked a little harder, you could figure—"

"SHUT UP! Shut up, shut up, shut up!" Allison screamed,

giving Eva a hard shove. "This isn't about you. It's about Owen and me. He's *my* boyfriend."

Lennox started to tremble. "Allison, you and Owen?"

"Don't be so naive, Lennox. It's always been Owen and me. It'll always be Owen and me. Sure, he has his flaws, but whatever, we're in high school." She bared her teeth in a slick white smile.

"He's not just a high school boy, he's a murderer. You helped him orchestrate a murder. Why did he pretend to be with me?"

"He wasn't dating you, he was *watching* you! You were just too dumb to realize it. And it didn't take much to switch your cycle from normal to nuts so no one would believe a thing you said."

"How could you do that to me?"

"My shirt! It's blue, it's red!" Allison feigned in a high-pitched voice. "Your parking pass." She snorted. "I really thought it was going to take some work."

Lennox looked at Eva, who immediately looked away.

"Who do you think photocopied your file? The shopping princess here even bought you a nice new red shirt. And your daddy let her right into the house."

"Eva?"

Eva glanced up, something like an apology in her eyes.

"Well, look what we have here!"

Lennox spun, and Owen was behind her, close enough to touch. She jumped back.

"Are you proud of yourself? You've got your harem here. Or are you going to kill us too?"

Owen tapped the baseball bat against his shoulder. "That's rich, coming from the girl who drove over an innocent teenager."

Allison snorted with laughter, but her eyes were flat. Lennox didn't even recognize her friend, and she felt a deep but fleeting sadness. Allison wasn't who she pretended to be. Allison had never been her friend.

"You are crazy," Lennox breathed.

"Ha! Coming from the chick whose mom was dumped in the loony bin."

Something hummed along Lennox's spine, something like guilt or anger or the sheer need to defend her own.

"Fuck off." She swung around to face Eva. "And you too!"

Eva looked away, rubbing her arm. "I'm so sorry. They didn't tell me they were going to kill her! I thought we were just going to scare her on haunted Hicks Road. I didn't—I didn't want to. Lennox, I really do like you, but—but—"

"But her dad's a drunk." Owen stepped closer to Allison, a crooked smile on his face that looked grotesque with the dried spatters of Mr. Apex's blood. He had the bat over his shoulder and tipped an imaginary hat, like strolling through a dark forest in the night was the most natural thing in the world.

"If my mom found out about his latest DUI, she was

going to sign the divorce papers. And once we told her Olivia was dead…well, then she was the one involved in a crime."

Lennox gaped. "You can't do that. He can't hide a DUI." She gestured to Owen. "He doesn't have that kind of power!"

Eva looked away.

Lennox finally caught her breath. "So, I don't understand any of this, but I think the cops can sort it out." She pulled her cell phone out of her back pocket, but no one moved. No one looked alarmed.

Owen smiled. "I am the cops."

An unexpected surge of superhuman strength roiled through Lennox. She covered the distance to her car before she could let out the breath she was holding. She grabbed the door handle, then let out an inhuman screech when she realized the car was locked and she didn't have the keys.

Suddenly, Owen was behind her, his lips at her ear. "Looking for these?" he asked, dangling the keys next to her ear.

Lennox trembled as Owen giggled, jogging back to his own car. Allison had already slipped into the driver's seat and turned the key in the ignition, the engine rumbling to life. She clicked on the headlights, bathing Lennox in their glow as she tapped the gas.

Lennox stayed rooted. "Are you going to hit me?" she asked, staring Allison down. "Go ahead. Hit me."

"Lennox, no!"shouted Eva.

"Hit me!" Lennox's voice was loud now, reverberating

through the forest, and Allison gunned the engine, tires squealing. For a brief second, Lennox saw fear in Owen's eyes, but she saw nothing but hate in Allison's as the car vaulted toward her.

She heard the thump.

Lennox was off her feet, the forest around her blurring into streaks of dark green. Someone screamed. Her head hit first, shoulder second, and rainwater slapped against her cheek. She closed her eyes.

THIRTY-FIVE

Sirens broke through the pleasant sound of rainfall, and somewhere in the distance, Lennox could see lights.

"You killed her!"

"I'm not—I'm okay," Lennox said, and surprisingly, she was. Nothing hurt outrageously; a fern on the side of the road had cushioned her fall. When she sat up, she could see slats of rain through the yellow of Owen's headlights and a single sneaker in the road. She looked questioningly at her own feet, at both her sneakers, and frowned. Lennox was on the side of the road, but there was someone in the road.

Someone had pushed her.

Someone had *saved* her.

Lennox turned slowly, her stomach sinking. It was Eva.

She was crumpled on the ground just behind Owen's car. He was still in the passenger seat, facing forward, and Allison was in the street, on her knees, the raindrops blanketing her as she screamed at Eva to get up.

But Eva didn't move.

She didn't move when the rain got steadier. She didn't move when the cops bookended Owen's car and put handcuffs on him and Allison.

But then, when the paramedics were loading Eva onto a gurney, Lennox saw her friend's eyes flutter open, the rise and fall of her chest.

"She pushed me out of the way. She saved me."

Lennox felt intense relief that Eva was alive. Maybe the two of them could find a way forward together after all this.

Lennox's father came around the ambulance, scrubs hidden under a black jacket slick with rain.

"Dad? How did you even know we were here? How did the police?"

"Mr. Apex called once he got back to his car. He was pretty banged up. The police were dispatched immediately. They found Olivia's body. Are you okay?"

"I will be."

ACKNOWLEDGMENTS

Once upon a time, we were lying on the floor in Michele's darkened living room. The usual gang was there: Jen, Robyn, BJ, Lejon, Kevin, Michele, and me. We had probably just come from getting pizza or bugging Matt at Sizzler or who knows, maybe even driving down Hicks Road in Kevin's white Thunderbird while belting out Prince's new album. Lejon was telling us about the time Trent got out of the car at the top of the road and they drove away laughing, slamming on the brakes and then hitting the gas every time Trent tried to get back in the car. They started to drive, and Trent started to run, laughing at first, then looking behind him, his face a mask of terror. Something was chasing him. No, it was keeping up with him, keeping up with the car, and Trent was punching the car door, his fingernails scratching at Kevin's paint job. Lejon said the brakes squealed and then Trent was somehow in the car, white as a sheet and cold as ice.

"He wouldn't say what he saw, but when we looked behind us, we could see it. No face or anything, just this black blob standing in the moonlight, watching."

There was a thump on the front door, and we all screamed. It was Robyn's mother, Sue, and when she asked what we were doing, we sheepishly admitted we were talking about the things that happened on Hicks Road. Sue smiled and sat down.

"You think you know stories about Hicks Road?" She chuckled. "Let me tell you what happened on Hicks Road when I was a kid..."

Thank you to Kevin Kwan and our Scooby Gang, and to Sue Parker and everyone else who keeps passing down the Hicks Road legends that make San Jose, California seem like less of a sprawling city and more of a small town where things still go bump in the night (or screech on the road).

ABOUT THE AUTHOR

Hannah Jayne decided to be an author in the second grade. Back then, she wrote terrible stories about penguins, ice floes, and beachcombers, because that was a word she had recently learned. After years of writing, growing, and learning even more new words, Jayne has realized her dream, and she hasn't looked back. Jayne lives in the San Francisco Bay Area with her husband, daughter, and cat and proudly teaches amazing young writers at the Teen Writers Institute through the San Jose Area Writing Project. Reach her at hannah_jayne.com

FIREreads

🔥 #getbooklit

Your hub for the hottest young adult books!

Visit us online and sign up for our
newsletter at FIREreads.com

 @sourcebooksfire

 sourcebooksfire

 firereads.tumblr.com